Arturo Pérez-Reverte

The Fencing Master

Translated from the Spanish
by Margaret Jull Costa

THE HARVILL PRESS
LONDON

First published with the title *El maestro de esgrima*, by Alfaguara, Madrid, 1988

First published in Great Britain in 1999
by The Harvill Press
2 Aztec Row, Berners Road, London N1 0PW

www.harvill-press.com

3 5 7 9 8 6 4 2

A CIP catalogue record for this book
is available from the British Library

ISBN 1 86046 454 8 (hbk)
ISBN 1 86046 455 6 (pbk)

Designed and typeset in Galliard at
Libanus Press, Marlborough, Wiltshire

Printed and bound in Great Britain by Butler & Tanner Ltd
at Selwood Printing, Burgess Hill

For Carlota. And for the Knight of the Yellow Doublet.

I am the most courteous man in the world. I pride myself on never having once been rude, in this land full of the most unutterable scoundrels, who will come and sit down next to you and tell you their woes and even declaim their poetry to you.

Heinrich Heine, *Reisebilder*

Contents

The plump brandy glasses reflected the candles burning in the silver candelabra. Between puffs on the solid cigar – from Vuelta Abajo in Cuba – which he was engaged in lighting, the Minister studied the other man surreptitiously. He was in no doubt that the man was a scoundrel, yet he had seen him arrive at Lhardy's in a superb carriage drawn by two magnificent English mares, and the man wore a valuable diamond set in gold on one of the slender, manicured fingers now slipping the band off a cigar. That, plus the man's elegant self-assurance and the detailed report that had been drawn up about him, automatically placed him in the category of distinguished scoundrels. And for the Minister, who was far from considering himself a radical on questions of ethics, not all scoundrels were equal; their degree of social acceptability stood in direct relation to each individual's fortune and distinction – especially if, in exchange for that minor moral violation on the Minister's part, large material benefits were to be obtained.

"I need proof," said the Minister, but these were empty words, for it was clear he was already convinced: he, after all, was paying for supper. The other man merely smiled in the manner of one hearing exactly what he expects to hear. Still smiling, he tugged at his immaculate, white shirt cuffs, revealing a striking pair of diamond cufflinks, then slipped his hand into his inside jacket pocket.

"Of course you do," he murmured in a tone of gentle irony.

The sealed but unstamped envelope lay on the linen cloth at the edge of the table, within reach of the Minister's hands. He did not touch it, though, as if he were afraid of some contagion; he merely looked at the other man.

"I'm listening," he said. The other man shrugged and gestured vaguely in the direction of the envelope; it was as if its contents had ceased to interest him the moment it left his hands.

"Oh, I don't know," he said, as if it were a matter of no importance. "Names, addresses . . . a rather interesting report, interesting at least to you. Something to keep your agents busy for quite a while."

"Are all those involved named?"

"Let's just say that all those who should be there are there. I have to manage my capital prudently."

With those last words the smile reappeared. This time it was blatantly insolent, and the Minister felt irritated.

"Sir, I have the impression that you are taking this whole matter rather lightly. Your situation . . . "

He left the phrase hanging in the air like a threat. The man seemed surprised, then made a face.

"Surely", he said, after thinking for a moment, "you don't expect me to come and collect my thirty pieces of silver, like Judas, furtive and sorrowing. After all, you leave me no option."

The Minister placed one hand on the envelope.

"You could refuse to collaborate," he said, clenching his cigar between his teeth. "That would be positively heroic."

"I could," said the gentleman, finishing his brandy, then getting to his feet and picking up his walking stick and top hat from a nearby chair. "Heroes, however, have a habit of ending up either dead or bankrupt, and, as you know better than anyone, I have too much to lose. At my age and in my profession, prudence is more than just a virtue, it's an instinct. So I have decided to absolve myself."

There was no handshake, no word of farewell, just a few footsteps on the stairs and the noise below of a carriage setting off in the rain. When the Minister was alone, he broke the seal on the envelope, put on his glasses and moved closer to the light. A couple of times he paused to take a sip of brandy while he considered the contents. When he had finished reading, he remained seated for a little, amidst the smoke curling up from his cigar. He gave a melancholy glance at the brazier heating the small private room, then got up slowly and went over to the window.

He had several hours' work ahead of him and he swore under his breath at the thought. Madrid, on that December night in 1866, with her Catholic Majesty, Queen Isabel II, still on the Spanish throne, was being drenched by a cold rain driving in from the icy peaks of the Guadarrama mountains.

I

The Fencing Bout

"A fencing bout between men of honour, under the direction of
a teacher inspired by the same feelings, is a diversion proper
to good taste and fine breeding."

Much later, when Jaime Astarloa wanted to piece together the scattered fragments of the tragedy and tried to remember how it all began, the first image that came to his mind was of the Marquis and of the gallery in the Palace overlooking the Retiro Gardens, with the first heat of summer streaming in through the windows, accompanied by such brilliant sunlight that they had to screw up their eyes against the dazzle on the polished guards of their foils.

The Marquis was not on form; he was wheezing like a broken bellows, and beneath his plastron his shirt was drenched in sweat. He was doubtless paying for the excesses of the previous night, but, as was his custom, Jaime Astarloa refrained from making any uncalled-for remarks. His client's private life was none of his business. He merely parried in tierce a feeble thrust, which would have made even an apprentice blush, then lunged. The flexible Italian steel bent as the button struck his opponent's chest hard.

"Touché, Excellency."

Luis de Ayala-Velate y Vallespín, the Marqués de los Alumbres, swore under his breath as he angrily removed the mask protecting his face. He was flushed with the heat and the exertion. Large drops of sweat trickled down from his hairline into his eyebrows and moustache.

"Devil take it, Don Jaime," he said, with just a touch of humiliation in his voice, "how do you do it? That's the third time you've hit me in less than a quarter of an hour."

Jaime Astarloa gave a suitably modest shrug. When he took off his mask, there was the hint of a smile beneath his grizzled moustache.

"You're not at your best today, Excellency."

Luis de Ayala laughed jovially and strode off down the gallery, which was adorned with valuable Flemish tapestries and collections of antique swords, foils and sabres. He had a mane of thick, curly hair and he radiated exuberance and vitality. Strong and well built, he had a loud, deep voice and was much given to grand gestures, grand passions and easy camaraderie. At forty, single, good-looking and – so people said – possessed of a large fortune, as well as being an inveterate gambler and womanizer, the Marqués de los Alumbres was the very model of the kind of rakish aristocrat in whom nineteenth-century Spain abounded. He had never read a book in his life, but he could recite from memory the pedigree of any celebrated horse at the racetracks in London, Paris or Vienna. As for women, the scandals with which he favoured Madrid society from time to time were the talk of the salons, which were always avid for novelty and gossip. He bore his forty years extremely well, and the mere mention of his name in female company was enough to provoke quarrels and arouse stormy passions.

The truth is that the Marqués de los Alumbres was something of a legend in Her Catholic Majesty's pious court. It was said, amidst much fluttering of fans, that during one particular drunken spree he had been involved in a knife fight in a cheap tavern in Cuatro Caminos – which, however, was entirely false – and that on his estate in Málaga, he had taken in the son of a famous bandit, after the bandit was executed – which was absolutely true. There was little gossip about his brief political career, but his love affairs were the talk of the city, for it was rumoured that certain eminent husbands had ample reason to demand satisfaction from him; whether they did or not was another matter. Four or five had sent him their seconds, more because of what people might say than for any other reason, and that gesture had not only cost them the obligatory meeting at dawn but had also found them greeting the new day with their life's blood draining away into the grass of some meadow on the outskirts of Madrid. Certain malicious tongues claimed that amongst those who might have demanded redress was the royal consort himself. Everyone knew, though, that the last thing one would expect of Don Francisco de Asís was for him to feel jealous of his august wife. However, whether Isabel II had succumbed to the undoubted personal charms of the Marqués de los Alumbres was a secret known only to the alleged interested parties and to the Queen's confessor. As for Luis de Ayala, he did not have a confessor nor, in his own words, did he damn well need one.

In his shirtsleeves, having removed the protective plastron, the Marquis put his foil down on a small table, where a silent servant had placed a silver tray bearing a bottle.

"That's enough for today, Don Jaime. I seem incapable of doing anything right, so I'd better just haul down the flag. How about a sherry?"

That drink of sherry, after their daily hour of fencing, had become a ritual. With his mask and foil under his arm, Jaime Astarloa went over to his host and took the proffered glass, in which the wine gleamed like liquid gold. The Marquis breathed in the bouquet.

"You have to admit, Maestro, that they certainly bottle things well in Andalusia," he said, taking a sip and giving a satisfied click of his tongue. "Look at it against the light: pure gold, Spanish sun. We have no reason to envy the insipid stuff they drink abroad."

Don Jaime nodded, pleased. He liked Luis de Ayala and he liked the fact that he called him "Maestro", although the Marquis was not exactly one of his pupils. In fact, he was one of the best swordsmen in Madrid and it was many years since he had needed to take lessons from anyone. His relationship with Jaime Astarloa was of a different kind. The Marquis loved fencing with the same passion with which he devoted himself to gambling, women and horses. He spent an hour a day engaged in the healthy exercise of fencing with a foil, an activity which, given his character and interests, was also extremely useful to him when it came to settling debts of honour. Five years earlier, in order to find an opponent as good as himself, Luis de Ayala had gone to the best fencing master in Madrid, for that was Don Jaime's reputation, although the more fashionable fencers considered Don Jaime's style to be too classical and antiquated. And so, at ten o'clock each morning, excepting Saturdays and Sundays, the fencing master would arrive punctually at the Palacio de Villaflores, the Marquis's home. There, in the large fencing gallery, designed and equipped according to the most demanding standards of the art, the Marquis brought a fierce determination to their fencing bouts, although, generally speaking, his teacher's ability and talent won through. Despite being a hardened gambler, Luis de Ayala was also a good loser and he admired the old fencer's remarkable skill.

The Marquis prodded his own chest with a pained look on his face and, sighing, said, "You certainly gave me a pasting today, Maestro. I'm going to need a good rub-down with alcohol after this."

Jaime Astarloa smiled humbly.

"As I said, Excellency, you were not at your best today."

"You're right. It's just as well that these foils have buttons on their tips, though; if not, I'd be six feet under by now. I'm afraid I've been a less than worthy opponent."

"That's the price you pay for these late nights."

"Don't I know it. At my age too. I'm no spring chicken, dammit, but what can I do, Don Jaime . . . You will never guess what's happened to me."

"I imagine that Your Excellency has fallen in love."

"Exactly," sighed the Marquis, pouring himself another sherry. "I have fallen in love like some young dandy. Head over heels."

The fencing master cleared his throat and smoothed his moustaches.

"If I'm not mistaken," he said, "that is the third time this month."

"So? The important thing is that whenever I do fall in love, I really do fall in love. Do you understand?"

"Perfectly. Even allowing for poetic licence, Excellency."

"It's odd, but with the passing years I seem to fall in love more and more frequently. There's nothing I can do about it. My arm is strong, but my heart is weak, as the great writers of old might have put it. If I were to tell you . . . "

At that point, the Marqués de los Alumbres launched into a

description, laden with hints and eloquent innuendos, of the wild passion that had left him drained and exhausted as dawn was breaking. She was a lady, of course. And her husband was none the wiser.

"In short," and here the Marquis gave a cynical smile, "I have only my sins to blame for the state I'm in today."

Don Jaime shook his head ironically.

"Fencing is like holy communion," he said with a smile. "You must come to it in a fit state of body and soul. If you break that supreme law, then punishment is bound to follow."

"Dammit, Maestro, I must write that down."

Jaime Astarloa raised his glass to his lips. His appearance was in marked contrast to the vigorous physicality of his client. The fencing master was well over fifty. He was of medium height, and his extreme thinness lent him a deceptive fragility, contradicted by the firmness of his limbs, which were as hard and knotty as vine stems. The slightly aquiline nose, the smooth, noble brow, his white but still abundant hair, his fine, well-manicured hands, gave him an air of serene dignity only accentuated by the grave expression in his grey eyes, eyes that became friendly and alive when the innumerable tiny lines surrounding them crinkled into a smile. He had a neatly trimmed moustache, in the old style, but that was not the only anachronistic feature about him. His modest resources meant that he could dress no more than reasonably well, but he did so with a kind of faded elegance that ignored the dictates of fashion; even the most recent of his suits were cut according to patterns dating back twenty years, and were, in fact, at his age, in excellent taste. The overall effect was of someone frozen in time, indifferent to the new fashions of the agitated age he was living through. The truth is that he himself took pleasure in this, for obscure reasons which perhaps even he could not have explained.

The servants brought them towels and a basin of water so that both teacher and pupil could wash. Luis de Ayala took off his shirt; his powerful torso, still gleaming with sweat, was covered with the red marks left by the foil.

"Good grief, Maestro, these look like the welts of a penitent. And to think that I pay you for this, too."

Jaime Astarloa dried his face and looked benevolently at the Marquis. Luis de Ayala was splashing his chest with water, puffing and blowing.

"Of course," he added, "politics is even more bruising. Did I tell you that Luis González Bravo has suggested I take up my seat again? With a view to a new post, he says. He must be in deep trouble if he has to stoop to asking a libertine like me."

The fencing master adopted a look of friendly interest. In fact, he did not care about politics in the slightest.

"And what will you do, Excellency?"

The Marquis shrugged disdainfully.

"Do? Absolutely nothing. I have told my illustrious namesake that he can stick his post, not in those exact words, of course. My forte is dissipation, a table at a casino and a pair of beautiful eyes close by. I've had enough of politics."

Luis de Ayala had been a deputy in Congress and had briefly occupied an important post in the Ministry of the Interior in one of Narváez's last Cabinets. His dismissal, after three months in the post, coincided with the death of the Minister, his maternal uncle Vallespín Andreu. Shortly afterwards, Ayala resigned, this time voluntarily, from his seat in Congress and abandoned the ranks of the Moderate Party, to which he had only ever given lukewarm support anyway. The phrase, "I've had enough", uttered by the Marquis at a gathering at the Athenaeum, had caught on and passed into political vocabulary to be used by anyone wishing to express his profound disenchantment with the hopeless state the nation was in. From then on, the Marqués de los Alumbres had remained on the sidelines of public life, refusing to participate in the deals between civilians and the military that went on under various Cabinets, merely observing, with the smile of a dilettante, the unfolding of the present political turmoil. He lived life at a hectic pace and lost huge sums at the card table without batting an eyelid. According to the gossipmongers, he was permanently on the brink of ruin, but Luis de Ayala always managed to recover his fortune, which, it seemed, was bottomless.

"How's your search for the Holy Grail going, Don Jaime?"

The fencing master paused in buttoning up his shirt and gave his companion a sad look.

"Not too well. Indeed, I think 'badly' would be the right word. I often wonder if perhaps the task isn't beyond my abilities. To be honest, there are moments when I would gladly give it up."

Luis de Ayala finished his ablutions, dried his chest with the towel and picked up the sherry glass, which he had left on the table. Flicking the glass with one of his fingers, he then held it to his ear with a look of satisfaction, listening to the ringing.

"Nonsense, Maestro, nonsense. You are more than capable of such an ambitious enterprise."

A melancholy smile flickered across the fencing master's lips.

"I wish I shared your faith, Excellency, but at my age so many things begin to break down, even inside. I'm beginning to suspect that my Holy Grail doesn't even exist."

"Rubbish."

For years now, Jaime Astarloa had been working on a *Treatise on the Art of Fencing* which, according to those who knew his extraordinary gifts and his experience, would constitute one of the major works on the subject when it was finally published, comparable only to the studies written by great teachers like Gomard, Grisier and Lafaugère. Lately, though, he had begun to have serious doubts about his ability to set down on paper the discipline to which he had dedicated his whole life. There was another factor, too, which only added to his unease. If the work was to be the *ne plus ultra* on the subject he hoped it would be, it was essential that it deliver a master stroke, the perfect, unstoppable thrust, the purest creation of human talent, a model of inspiration and efficacy. Don Jaime had devoted himself to the search from the first day he crossed foils with an opponent. His pursuit of the Grail, as he himself called it, had so far proved fruitless, and now, on the slippery slope of physical and intellectual decline, the old teacher felt the vigour of his still strong arms beginning to ebb away, and the talent that had inspired each movement starting to disappear beneath the weight of years. Almost daily, in the solitude of his modest studio and hunched beneath the light of an oil lamp over pages that time had already yellowed, Jaime Astarloa tried vainly to excavate from the crannies of his brain that key move which a stubborn intuition told him was hidden somewhere, even though it refused to reveal itself. He spent many nights like that, awake until dawn. On other nights, dragged from sleep by some sudden inspiration, he would rise in his nightshirt in order to snatch up one of his foils, with a violence bordering on desperation, and stand in front of the mirrors lining the walls of his small fencing gallery. There, trying to make real what only minutes before had been a lucid flash in his sleeping brain, he would immerse himself in that painful, pointless pursuit, measuring his movements and intelligence in a silent duel with his own image, whose reflection seemed to smile sarcastically back at him from the shadows.

Jaime Astarloa went out into the street with the case containing his foils under his arm. It was a very hot day. Madrid languished beneath an unforgiving sun. When people met, they spoke only of the heat or of politics. They would begin by talking about the unusually high temperatures and then begin enumerating, one by one, the current conspiracies, many of which were public knowledge. In that summer of 1868, everyone was plotting. Old Narváez had died in March, but González Bravo believed himself strong enough to govern with a firm hand. In the Palacio de Oriente, the Queen cast ardent glances at the young officers in her guard and fervently said the rosary, already preparing for her next summer holiday in the north. Others had no option but to spend their summer away; most of the really important figures, like Prim, Serrano, Sagasta and Ruiz Zorrilla were in exile abroad, either confined or under discreet surveillance, while they put all their efforts into the great clandestine movement known as Spain with Honour. They all agreed that Isabel II's days were numbered, and, whilst the more moderate sector speculated about the Queen abdicating in favour of her son, Alfonso, the radicals openly nurtured the republican dream. It was said that Don Juan Prim could arrive from London at any moment, but the legendary hero of the Battle of Castillejos had already done so on a couple of previous occasions, only to be forced to take to his heels. As a popular song of the time put it, the fig was not yet ripe. Others felt that the fig, after so long hanging on the branch, was beginning to rot. It was all a matter of opinion.

Jaime Astarloa's modest income did not allow him any real luxuries, so he shook his head when a coachman offered him the services of a dilapidated carriage. He walked down the Paseo del Prado amongst other idle passers-by seeking shade beneath the trees. From time to time, he would see a familiar face and he would, according to his custom, courteously doff his grey top hat. There were small groups of uniformed nannies sitting on the wooden benches, chatting and keeping a distant eye on the sailor-suited children playing near the fountains. Some ladies rode by in open carriages, holding lace-edged parasols to protect them from the sun.

Although he was wearing a light summer jacket, Don Jaime was sweltering. He had another two students that morning, in their respective homes. They were young men of good families, whose parents considered fencing a healthy form of exercise, one of the few that a gentleman could indulge in without doing any great harm to the family dignity. With the fee he earned from them and from the other three or four clients who visited him in his gallery in the afternoons, the fencing master got by reasonably well. After all, his personal expenses were minimal: the rent for his apartment in Calle Bordadores, lunch and supper at a nearby inn, coffee and toast at the Café Progreso. It was the cheque signed by the Marqués de los Alumbres, punctually received on the first of each month, that enabled him to enjoy a few extra comforts as well as to save a small sum, the interest from which meant he would not have to end his days in a convent-run home for the aged when he was too old to continue working. This, he often reflected sadly, would not be too long in coming.

The Conde de Sueca, a deputy in Parliament, whose eldest son was one of Don Jaime's few remaining students, came riding by; he was wearing a magnificent pair of English riding boots.

"Good morning, Maestro." The Count had been one of his pupils six or seven years before. He had become involved in some matter of honour and had been obliged to enlist Jaime Astarloa's services in order to perfect his style in the days immediately before the duel. The result had been satisfactory; his opponent ended up with an inch of steel in him and ever since then Jaime Astarloa had had a cordial relationship with the Count which now extended to the Count's son.

"I see you have the tools of your trade under your arm. You're on your usual morning route, I imagine."

Don Jaime smiled and patted the case containing his foils. The Count had greeted him by touching his hat, in friendly fashion, but without dismounting. Don Jaime thought again that, apart from rare exceptions like Luis de Ayala, the way his clients treated him was always the same: they were polite, but careful to keep a proper distance. After all, they were paying him for his services. The fencing master, though, was old enough not to feel mortified by this.

"As you see, Don Manuel, in fact, you find me in the midst of my morning rounds, a prisoner in this suffocating Madrid of ours. But work is work."

The Conde de Sueca, who had never done a day's work in his life, nodded understandingly, whilst he checked a sudden impatient movement from his horse, a splendid mare. He looked distractedly about him, smoothing his beard with his little finger and watching some ladies who were strolling near the railings by the Botanical Gardens.

"How's Manolito getting on? Making progress, I hope."

"He is, he is. The boy has talent. He's still a bit of a hothead, but at seventeen that can be considered a virtue. Time and discipline will temper him."

"Well, I leave that in your hands, Maestro."

"I'm most honoured, Excellency."

"Have a pleasant day."

"The same to you. And give my respects to the Countess."

"I will."

The Count continued on his way and Don Jaime on his. He walked up Calle de las Huertas, stopping for a few moments outside a bookshop. Buying books was one of his passions, but it was also a luxury which he could allow himself only rarely. He looked lovingly at the gold lettering on the leather binding and gave a melancholy sigh, remembering better days when he did not have to worry constantly about his precarious domestic finances. Resolving to bring himself firmly back to the present, he took his watch out of his jacket pocket, a watch on a long gold chain, dating from more prosperous times. He had fifteen minutes before he was due at the house of Don Matías Soldevilla – of Soldevilla & Co., Purveyors to the Royal Household and to the Troops Overseas – where he would spend an hour trying to drum some notion of fencing into young Salvador's stupid head.

"Parry, engage, break, come to close quarters . . . One, two, Salvador, one, two, distance, feint, good, avoid flourishes, withdraw, that's it, parry, bad, very bad, dreadful, again, covering yourself, one, two, parry, engage, break, come to close quarters . . . The lad's making progress, Don Matías, real progress. He's still inexperienced, but he's got a feel for it, he's got talent. Time and discipline, that's all he needs." For sixty reales a month, everything included.

The sun was beating down, making the figures walking over the cobbles shimmer. A waterseller came down the street, crying his wares. Next to a basket of fruit and vegetables, a woman sat panting in the shade, mechanically brushing away the swarm of flies buzzing about her. Don Jaime removed his hat to wipe away the sweat with an old handkerchief he drew from his sleeve. He looked briefly at the coat of arms embroidered on the worn silk in blue thread – faded now by time and frequent washings – and then continued on up the road, his shoulders bent beneath the implacable sun. His shadow was just a small dark stain beneath his feet.

The Progreso was less a café than an antonym: half-a-dozen chipped, marble-topped tables, ancient chairs, a creaking wooden floor, dusty curtains and dim lighting. The old manager, Fausto, was dozing by the kitchen door, from behind which came the agreeable aroma of coffee boiling in a pot. A scrawny, rheumy-eyed cat slunk sulkily beneath the tables, hunting for hypothetical mice. In winter, the place smelled constantly of damp and there were large yellow stains on the wallpaper. In this atmosphere, the customers almost always kept their coats on, a manifest reproach to the decrepit iron stove glowing feebly in one corner.

In the summer it was different. The Café Progreso was an oasis of shade and coolness in the Madrid heat, as if it preserved within its walls and behind the thick curtains the sovereign cold that lodged there during winter days. That was why Jaime Astarloa's modest discussion group installed itself there each afternoon, as soon as the summer rigours began.

"You're twisting my words, Don Lucas – as usual."

Agapito Cárceles looked like the defrocked priest that in fact he was. When he argued, he would point his index finger skywards, as if calling on heaven as his witness, a habit acquired during the brief period when – by some act of inexplicable negligence which the Bishop and his diocese still regretted – the ecclesiastical authorities had given Cárceles permission to harangue the faithful from the pulpit. He scraped an existence by sponging off acquaintances or writing fiery, radical articles in newspapers with small circulations, under the pseudonym "The Masked Patriot", which made him the frequent butt of his colleagues' jokes. He proclaimed himself a republican and a federalist, he recited anti-monarchical poems penned by himself and full of the most dreadful rhymes; he would announce to all and sundry that Narváez had been a tyrant, Espartero a coward, and that he didn't quite trust Serrano and Prim; he would quote in Latin for no apparent reason, and was always mentioning Rousseau, whom he had never actually read. His two *bêtes noires* were the clergy and the monarchy, and his ardent belief was that the two most important contributions to the history of humanity had been the printing press and the guillotine.

Don Lucas Rioseco was drumming his fingers on the table; he was visibly irritated. He kept fiddling with his moustache and saying, "Hm, hm", staring at the stains on the ceiling, as if hoping to find in them sufficient patience to continue listening to his colleague's excesses.

"It's all quite clear," Cárceles was declaring. "Rousseau answered the question about whether man is naturally good or evil. And his reasoning, gentlemen, is overwhelming. Overwhelming, Don Lucas, and it's time you admitted it. All men are good, therefore they should be free. All men are free, therefore they should be equal. And here's the best part: all men are equal, *ergo* they are sovereign. Yes, that's right. Out of the natural goodness of man comes freedom, equality and national sovereignty. Everything else", he brought his fist down hard on the table, "is nonsense."

"But, my dear friend, there are evil men too," said Don Lucas mischievously, as if he had just caught Cárceles in his own trap.

The journalist gave a disdainful, Olympian smile.

"Of course. Who can doubt it? One has only to think of Narváez, who must be rotting in hell at this very moment, of González Bravo and his gang, of the Court . . . of any of the traditional obstacles. Fine. To take care of them, the French Revolution came up with a most ingenious device: a knife that goes up and down. That's how you get rid of obstacles, traditional and otherwise. And for the free, equal, sovereign people there is the light of reason and progress."

Don Lucas was indignant. He was a gentleman, getting on for sixty, from a good family that had fallen on hard times, a bit of a snob with a reputation for misanthropy, and a widower, with no children and no fortune. Everyone knew that he had not seen any real money since the reign of the late Fernando VII and that he lived on a tiny income and thanks largely to the charity of some kind neighbours. He was, nevertheless, very careful about keeping up appearances. His few suits of clothes were always meticulously ironed and no one amongst his acquaintances could but admire the elegance with which he tied his one tie and kept his tortoiseshell monocle firmly lodged in his left eye. He held reactionary views, defining himself as a monarchist, a Catholic and, above all, a man of honour. He was always at daggers drawn with Agapito Cárceles.

Besides Jaime Astarloa, the other people present were Marcelino Romero, a piano teacher in a school for young ladies, and Antonio Carreño, a civil servant. Romero was an insignificant creature, tubercular, sensitive and melancholy. His hopes of making a name for himself in music had long since been reduced to teaching twenty or so young ladies from good society how to hammer out a reasonable tune on the piano. As for Carreño, he was a man of few words, a scrawny individual with red hair, a very neat copper-coloured beard and a rather austere expression. He pretended to be both a conspirator and a Mason, although he was neither.

Don Lucas was tweaking his moustache, yellow with nicotine, and giving Cárceles a withering look.

"You have, for the nth time," he said scathingly, "made your usual destructive analysis of the state of the nation. No one asked you for it, but we've had to put up with it. Fine. Doubtless tomorrow we will see it published in one of those libellous revolutionary rags that give your views houseroom in their propagandizing pages. Well, listen, my friend Cárceles. I, also for the nth time, say no. I refuse to go on listening to your arguments. Your solution to everything is a massacre. You'd make a fine Minister of the Interior. Remember what your beloved populace did in 1834. Eighty monks murdered by the rabble, stirred up by conscienceless demagogues."

"Eighty, you say?" Cárceles enjoyed baiting Don Lucas, as he did every day. "That seems rather on the low side to me. And I know what I'm talking about. Indeed I do. I know what the priesthood is like from the inside, you bet I do. What with the clergy and the Bourbons, there's not an honest man can stand this country of ours."

"You, of course, would apply your usual solutions."

"I only have one: for priests and Bourbons, gunpowder and the gun. Fausto, bring us some more toast. Don Lucas is paying."

"Oh no, you don't." The worthy old man leaned back in his seat, his thumbs in his waistcoat pockets, his monocle proudly fixed in position. "I only ever buy toast for my friends and only when I'm in funds, which is not the case today. But I refuse to buy anything for a treacherous fanatic like yourself."

"I would rather be a treacherous fanatic, as you call me, than spend my life shouting 'Long Live Oppression'."

The other members of the group felt it was time to mediate. Jaime Astarloa called for calm, gentlemen, while he stirred his coffee with his spoon. Marcelino Romero, the pianist, dragged himself away from his melancholy daydreams to plead for moderation and tried, without success, to bring the conversation round to music.

"Don't change the subject," said Cárceles.

"I'm not," protested Romero. "Music has a social content too, you know. It creates equality in the sphere of the arts, it breaks down frontiers, it brings people together . . . "

"The only music this gentleman enjoys is the battle hymn of the Liberals."

"Now don't start, Don Lucas."

The cat thought it had spotted a mouse and lunged past their legs after it. Antonio Carreño had dipped his finger in the water in his glass and was drawing a mysterious sign on the worn marble table top.

"So-and-so's in Valencia and you-know-who is in Valladolid. They say that Topete in Cádiz has received emissaries, but who knows? And Prim will be here any day now. This time there's really going to be trouble."

And, keeping any details to an enigmatic minimum, he started describing the plot of the moment which – he had it on good authority, gentlemen – was being hatched, he was reliably informed, thanks to certain confidences vouchsafed to him by the relevant people in his lodge, whose names he preferred not to reveal. The fact that the plot he mentioned was, like a half-dozen others, public knowledge, did not diminish his enthusiasm one iota. In a low voice, looking furtively about him, using hints and taking other vital precautions, Carreño set out the details of the enterprise in which (I trust in your discretion, gentlemen) he was pretty much up to his neck. The lodges – he used to refer to the lodges with the same familiarity with which others spoke of their relatives – were on the move. You could forget Carlos VII; besides, without old Cabrera, Montemolín's nephew would never measure up. Alfonso was dismissed out of hand – no more Bourbons. Perhaps a foreign Prince, a constitutional monarchy and all that, although they said Prim preferred the Queen's brother-in-law, Montpensier. And if not that, then there was our friend Cárceles's great hope, the glorious republic.

"The glorious, federal republic," added the journalist, giving Don Lucas a baleful look. "Just so that the toadies around here know what's what."

Don Lucas flared at the gibe. He was an extremely easy target.

"That's right, that's right," he exclaimed with a dismayed snort. "Federal, democratic, anti-clerical, free-thinking, plebeian and swinish. Everyone equal and a guillotine in the Puerta del Sol, with Don Agapito working the machinery. No Congress, absolutely not. Popular assemblies in Cuatro Caminos, in Ventas, in Vallecas, in Carabanchel . . . That's what Señor Cárceles's cohorts want. We are the Africa of Europe."

Fausto arrived with the toast. Jaime Astarloa dunked his thoughtfully in his coffee. The interminable polemics in which his colleagues engaged bored him enormously, but their company was no better or worse than any other. The couple of hours that he spent there each afternoon helped him salve his loneliness a little. For all their defects, their grumbling and their bad-tempered ranting about every other living being, at least they gave one another a chance to vent their respective frustrations. Within that limited circle, each member found in the others the tacit consolation of knowing that his own failure was not an isolated fact, but a thing shared in greater or lesser measure by them all. That, above all, was what bound them together, keeping them faithful to their daily meetings. Despite their frequent disputes, their political differences, their disparate moods, the five members of the group felt a convoluted solidarity, which, had it ever been expressed openly, would have been hotly denied by all of them, but which might be likened to the huddling together for warmth of solitary creatures.

Don Jaime looked around him and met the grave, gentle eyes of the music teacher. Marcelino Romero was nearly forty and had spent the last couple of years tormented by an impossible love for the honest woman to whose daughter he had taught the rudiments of music. The teacher–pupil relationship had ended months ago, but the poor man still walked each day beneath a certain balcony in Calle Hortaleza, stoically nursing a hopeless, unrequited love.

The fencing master smiled at Romero sympathetically, and the music teacher responded distractedly, doubtless absorbed in his own inner torments. It seemed to Don Jaime that you could find in the memory of every man the bittersweet shadow of a woman. He had just such a shadow in his own memory, but that was all a long time ago.

The post office clock struck seven. The cat had still not found a mouse to eat and Agapito Cárceles was reciting an anonymous poem dedicated to the late Narváez. His attempts to appropriate authorship to himself were greeted with mocking scepticism by his fellows.

> If perchance you are travelling the road to old Loja
> and a hat Andalusian you happen to find . . .

Don Lucas was yawning ostentatiously, more to annoy his friend than for any other reason. Two good-looking women passed in the street outside and glanced in without stopping. All the men present bowed courteously, apart from Cárceles who was too busy declaiming:

> may you pause on your way, Oh gentle pilgrim,
> for be sure that – thank heavens – there lies in this earth
> a bald-headed hero with luxurious tastes
> who for years governed Spain in Algerian style.

A street vendor was walking by, selling lollipops from Havana; he kept turning round every now and then to scare off a pair of shirtless little boys who were trailing him, greedily eyeing his merchandise. A group of students came into the café for a drink. They were carrying newspapers and animatedly discussing the Civil Guard's latest exploits; they referred to them jokingly as the Uncivil Guard. Some stopped, amused, to listen to Cárceles reciting his funeral elegy to Narváez:

> A soldier he was, though no battles he fought,
> but he never retreated from making his fortune
> and he made of his lechery a goddess divine,
> thus 'twixt greed and foul lust he at last found his death.
> If you want to do something to remember him by,
> pick up the said hat and spit in it hard,
> say a prayer for the dead and then shit on his grave.

The young men cheered Cárceles and he bowed, moved by his impromptu audience's favourable reaction. There were a few shouts of

"Long live democracy" and the journalist was invited to a round of drinks. Don Lucas twiddled his moustaches, fuming with righteous indignation. The cat curled about his feet, sleepy and pathetic, as if wanting to bring him some paltry consolation.

The clash of foils echoed through the gallery.

"Watch that distance. That's it, good. In quarte. Good. In tierce. Good. Prime. Good. Now two in prime, that's it. Keep calm. Go back covering, that's it. Be careful now. Over the sword arm. To me. Don't worry, do it again. To me. Force me to parry in prime twice. That's it. Steady! Avoid. That's it. Now on your outside line. Lunge. Good. Touché. Excellent, Don Álvaro."

Jaime Astarloa put the foil under his left arm, took off his mask and paused to catch his breath. Álvaro Salanova was rubbing his wrists; his cracked, adolescent voice emerged from behind the metal mesh covering his face.

"How did I do, Maestro?"

Astarloa smiled approvingly.

"Pretty good, sir, pretty good," he said. He indicated the foil that the young man was holding in his right hand. "But you're still too ready to let your opponent get control of the foible. If you find yourself in that position again, don't hesitate to break the distance and take a step back."

"Yes, Maestro."

They turned to the other pupils, who, already equipped and with their masks under their arms, had witnessed the bout: "If you let your opponent control your foible, then you're at his mercy. Are we all agreed?"

Four young voices chorused a "yes". They were all between fourteen and seventeen years old. The Cazorla brothers, both of them blond and extraordinarily alike, were the sons of a soldier. The third was a young man whose skin was reddened by an infinite number of small spots, which gave him a disagreeable appearance. His name was Manuel de Soto, the son of the Conde de Sueca, and Jaime had long since given up hope of turning him into a reasonable fencer; he was of too nervous a temperament, and had only to cross foils with someone three or four times to get in a complete tangle. Young Salanova, a dark, good-looking lad from an excellent family, was clearly the best. In another age, with the necessary preparation and discipline, he would have shone in *salles d'armes* as a star fencer; but the way things were going now, thought Don Jaime bitterly, the young man's talents would soon be rendered worthless by the world they lived in, a world in which young people were eager for other things: travelling, riding, hunting and any number of other frivolous pursuits. The modern world, alas, offered young people far too many temptations and their minds lacked the necessary discipline to find full satisfaction in an art like fencing.

He placed his left hand on the buttoned tip of his foil and bent the blade slightly.

"Now, gentlemen, I would like one of you to do a little practice with Don Álvaro on that parry in seconde that's driving you all to distraction." He decided to be kind to the spotty young man and chose the younger of the Cazorla brothers instead.

"Yes you, Don Francisco."

The young man stepped forward and put on his mask. Like his companions, he was dressed from head to toe in white.

"In line."

Both young men adjusted their gloves and stood facing each other.

"On guard."

They saluted each other by raising their foils, before adopting the classical combat position, the right leg forward, both legs slightly bent, the left arm back and forming a right angle, with the hand loose and facing forwards.

"Remember the old principle. You must hold the grip as if you had a bird in your hand: gently enough not to crush it, but firmly enough not to let it escape. That applies especially to you, Don Francisco, since you have an irritating tendency to allow yourself to be disarmed. Do you understand?"

"Yes, Maestro."

"Right, let's not waste any more time. To your work, gentlemen."

There was a light clash of steel. The younger of the Cazorla brothers started the bout with grace and good fortune; he had quick feet and hands and moved as lightly as a feather. For his part, Álvaro Salanova covered himself with considerable ease, merely retreating one step instead of leaping back in moments of danger, parrying impeccably whenever his opponent gave him the chance. After a while, they changed roles and it was Salanova's turn to lunge repeatedly, leaving his companion to resolve the problem with his foil in seconde. They continued like that, lunging and parrying, until Cazorla made a mistake that forced him to drop his guard too much after an ineffectual thrust. With a cry of triumph, carried away by the excitement of the bout, his opponent threw caution to the wind and thrust hard twice at his chest.

Don Jaime frowned and brought the bout to an end, interposing his sword between the two young men.

"A word, gentlemen," he said severely. "Fencing is, it is true, an art, but, above all, it is a useful science. When you take up a foil or a sabre, even though it may have a button on the tip or a blunt edge, you must never treat fencing like a game. If you want to play, go back to the hoop, the spinning top or your lead soldiers. Do I make myself clear, Señor Salanova?"

Salanova nodded, his face still covered by the mask. The fencing master looked at him hard.

"I'm afraid I did not quite hear your reply, Señor Salanova," he said, his voice still severe. "I am not accustomed to speaking with someone whose face I cannot see."

The young man stammered an apology and removed his mask. He had flushed scarlet and was staring shamefacedly at the toes of his shoes.

"I asked if I have made myself clear."

"Yes."

"I'm sorry, what was that?"

"Yes, Maestro."

Jaime Astarloa looked at the rest of his pupils. The young faces were all looking at him, grave and expectant.

"All the art, all the science I'm trying to inculcate in you can be summed up in one word: efficiency."

Álvaro Salanova looked up and gave the young Cazorla a look of ill-concealed dislike. Don Jaime was talking, resting the tip of his foil on the floor, his two hands on the pommel of the hilt: "Our objective", he went on, "is not to dazzle our opponent with a graceful flourish, nor to carry out questionable moves like the one performed just now by Don Álvaro, a move that could have cost him dear in a bout fought with bare blades. Our aim is to beat our opponent in a clean, quick and efficient manner, with as little risk as possible to ourselves. Never make two thrusts where one will do; the second thrust might bring a dangerous response. Never adopt gallant or exaggeratedly elegant poses. They distract your attention from your supreme purpose: to avoid being killed, and, if it proves inevitable, to kill your opponent. Fencing is, above all, a practical exercise."

"My father says that fencing is good because it's healthy," said the elder of the Cazorla brothers in mild protest. "What the English call 'sport'."

Don Jaime looked at his pupil as if he had just uttered a heresy.

"I don't doubt that your father has his reasons for saying so, but I assure you that fencing is much more than that. It is an exact, mathematical science, where the sum of certain factors leads invariably to the same result: triumph or disaster, life or death. I am not teaching you to practise a sport, I am teaching you a highly refined technique that could prove useful to you one day, when called on by your country or by some matter of honour. I don't care whether you are strong or weak, elegant or clumsy, tubercular or brimming with health. What matters is that, with a foil or a sabre in your hand, you can feel equal or superior to any man in the world."

"What about firearms, though, Maestro?" said Manuel de Soto timidly. "The pistol, for example. That seems much more efficient than a foil, and it makes everyone equal." He scratched his nose. "Like democracy."

Jaime Astarloa frowned. His grey eyes fixed on the young man with unusual coldness.

"The pistol is not a weapon, it is an impertinence. If two men are to kill each other, they should do so face to face, not from a distance, like vile highwaymen. Unlike other weapons, the sword has its own ethics and, if you press me, I would almost say it has its own mysticism too. Yes, fencing is a mysticism for gentlemen. Even more so in this age we live in now."

Francisco Cazorla raised a hand doubtfully.

"Maestro, last week I read an article about fencing in *La Ilustración*. It said more or less said that modern weapons are making it redundant and the conclusion was that sabres and foils would end up being museum pieces."

Don Jaime shook his head slowly, as if tired of hearing the same old song. He looked at himself in one of the large mirrors lining the gallery: the old teacher surrounded by his last remaining pupils, still faithful, waiting by his side. But for how long?

"Yet another reason to remain loyal," he replied sadly, leaving it unclear as to whether he was referring to fencing or to himself.

With his mask under his arm and his foil resting on his right foot, Álvaro Salanova made a sceptical face: "Perhaps, one day, there won't be any fencing masters," he said.

There was a long silence. Jaime Astarloa was gazing abstractedly into the distance, as if he were observing the world beyond the gallery walls.

"Perhaps," he murmured, absorbed in the contemplation of things that only he could see. "But let me say just one thing. The day that the last fencing master dies will be the day when all that is noble and honourable about the ancient battle between man and man goes down with him into the tomb. After that, there will only be room for the blunderbuss and the knife, for the ambush and the stab in the back."

The four boys were listening to him, too young to understand. Don Jaime looked from one to the other, stopping at Álvaro Salanova.

"In fact," he said, and the lines surrounding his smiling, bitter, mocking eyes grew more pronounced, "I certainly don't envy you the wars that you will live through in the next twenty or thirty years."

At that moment, someone knocked at the door, and nothing would ever again be the same in the fencing master's life.

II

Compound Attack with Two Feints

"Compound attacks with two feints are used to deceive the opponent.
They begin with the feint of a simple attack."

He went up the stairs, fingering the note he had in the pocket of his grey frock coat. The note was hardly illuminating:

Doña Adela de Otero requests the presence of the fencing master Don Jaime Astarloa at her house at no. 14 Calle Riaño, tomorrow evening at seven o'clock.

> *Respectfully,*
> *A. de O.*

Before leaving home, he had dressed with great care, determined to make a good impression on this woman, doubtless the mother of some future student. When he reached the apartment, he straightened his tie, then knocked at the door, using the heavy bronze knocker suspended from the jaws of an aggressive lion's head. He removed his watch from his waistcoat pocket and checked the time: one minute to seven. He waited, satisfied, while he listened to the sound of a woman's footsteps approaching down a long corridor. After a rapid drawing of bolts, the attractive face of a maid smiled up at him from beneath a white cap. While the young woman bustled off with his visiting card, Don Jaime was left in a small, elegantly furnished entrance hall. The shutters were down, but through the open windows he could hear the noise of carriages in the street, two floors below. There were flowerpots with exotic plants in them, a couple of good paintings on the walls and armchairs richly upholstered in silky scarlet velvet. He was, he thought, about to meet a good client and that made him feel optimistic. There was no harm in that, given the times they were living in.

The maid soon returned and, after taking his gloves, walking stick and top hat, asked him to go into the living room. He followed her down the dark corridor. The room was empty and so, with his hands behind his back, he undertook a brief reconnoitre. The last of the sun's rays slipping in between the half-drawn curtains cast a dying light on the discreet pale-blue flowers of the wallpaper. All the furniture was in exquisitely good taste. Over a sofa hung a signed oil painting depicting an eighteenth-century scene: a young woman in a lace dress was sitting on a swing in the garden, looking expectantly over her shoulder, as if awaiting the imminent arrival of the object of her desire. There was also a piano with the lid up and some sheet music on the music stand. He went over to see what it was: the Polonaise in F sharp minor by Frédéric Chopin. The owner of the piano was doubtless a woman of considerable energy.

He had left until last the decoration above the large marble fireplace: a collection of duelling pistols and foils. He went over to them, studying the swords with an expert eye. They were both excellent pieces; the grip of one was French, the other Italian, both with damascene guards. They were in good condition, with not a trace of rust on the metal, although small notches on the blades indicated that they had been much used.

He heard footsteps behind him and turned slowly round, a courteous greeting on his lips. Adela de Otero was very different from how he had imagined her.

"Good evening, Señor Astarloa. I must thank you for taking the trouble to keep an appointment with a complete stranger."

Her voice had a pleasant, slightly hoarse quality to it, with an almost imperceptible foreign accent, impossible to identify. The fencing master bent over the hand she offered him and brushed it with his lips. It was a slim hand, with the little finger curved gracefully inwards; her skin was agreeably cool and dark. Her fingernails were kept very short, almost like those of a man, and were not polished. Her hand was adorned only with a slender silver ring.

He raised his head and looked into her eyes. They were large eyes, violet in colour, with small, golden flecks that seemed iridescent when they caught the light. She had thick, black hair, caught up at the back with a slide in the form of an eagle's head. She was quite tall for a woman, only a couple of inches shorter than Don Jaime, but of average build, perhaps somewhat slimmer than most women of the day, with a waist that required no help from a corset in order to appear slender and elegant. She was wearing a plain black skirt and a raw-silk blouse with a lace front. There was something slightly masculine about her, accentuated perhaps by a tiny scar at the right-hand corner of her mouth, which seemed to impress on the mouth a permanent, enigmatic smile. She was at that age between twenty and thirty when it is hard to judge exactly how old a woman is. The fencing master thought that, in his now distant youth, such a beautiful face would doubtless have driven him to commit certain foolish acts.

Adela de Otero asked him to take a seat and they both sat down face to face, by a low table opposite the large balcony.

"Coffee, Señor Astarloa?"

He nodded, pleased. The maid entered silent and unbidden, bearing a silver tray, on which a delicate porcelain coffee set chinked and rattled. Doña Adela picked up the coffee pot and filled two cups, handing one to Don Jaime. She waited for him to take a first sip, apparently studying her visitor. Then she got straight down to business.

"I want to learn the two hundred escudo thrust."

The fencing master sat holding his cup and saucer, playing distract-edly with his spoon. He thought he must have misheard.

"I'm sorry?"

She took a sip of coffee and then looked at him impassively.

"I have made all the necessary enquiries," she said calmly, "and I was told that you are the best fencing master in Madrid. The last of the old school, they say. I was also told that you are the inventor of a famous, secret thrust, which you are willing to teach to interested pupils for the sum of one thousand, two hundred reales. It's a lot of money, I know, but I can afford it. I wish to hire your services."

Not yet recovered from his astonishment, Jaime Astarloa protested weakly: "Forgive me, madam, but this . . . It is a little unusual. I am the inventor of a secret thrust and I do teach it for the sum you have just mentioned, but, please understand, I would never teach fencing to a woman. I mean . . . "

The violet eyes looked him up and down. The scar emphasized the enigmatic smile.

"I know what you mean," said Adela de Otero, slowly putting her empty cup down on the table and pressing her fingertips together as if she were about to pray, "but I don't think the fact that I'm a woman should have anything to do with it. To put your mind at rest about my abilities, if that's what you're worrying about, I can assure you that I do have a reasonable knowledge of the art that you practise."

"That isn't the point," he said, shifting uncomfortably in his seat, running a finger beneath his shirt collar. He was beginning to feel very hot. "What I'm trying to explain is that taking on a woman as a fencing student . . . forgive me, but it is rather unusual."

"Are you trying to tell me it would be considered improper?"

He stared at her, still holding his cup, the coffee barely touched. That permanent smile was making him feel distinctly uneasy.

"Forgive me, madam, but that is one of the reasons. I would find it impossible and I can only repeat my apologies. I have never before found myself in such a situation."

"Do you fear for your reputation, Maestro?"

There was a mocking, provocative note behind the question. Don Jaime placed his cup carefully on the table.

"It is not the done thing, madam. It is not the custom. Perhaps it is abroad, but not here. Not with me at least. Perhaps you should try someone more . . . flexible."

"I want to learn the secret of that particular thrust. Besides, you are the best there is."

Don Jaime acknowledged this flattery.

"Yes, I may be the best, as you do me the honour of saying, but I am also too old to change my habits. I am fifty-six and I have been practising my trade for over thirty years. The clients who have passed through my galleries have always been, exclusively, male."

"Times change, sir."

The fencing master sighed sadly.

"That is very true. And do you know something? They may be changing too fast for my taste. Allow me, then, to remain faithful to my old habits. Believe me, they are the only assets I have."

She looked at him in silence, nodding slightly as if weighing his arguments. Then she got up and went over to the display of weapons above the fireplace.

"They say that this secret thrust of yours is impossible to parry."

Don Jaime gave a modest smile.

"They exaggerate, madam. Once you know it, parrying it is the simplest thing in the world. I have yet to discover the unstoppable thrust."

"And your fee is two hundred escudos?"

He sighed again. This lady's singular caprice was placing him in an awkward position.

"I beg you not to insist, madam."

She turned her back on him, stroking the guard of one of the foils.

"I would like to know what you charge for your ordinary services."

Don Jaime got slowly to his feet.

"Between sixty and a hundred reales per month per student, which includes four lessons a week. And now, if you'll forgive me . . . "

"If you teach me the secret thrust, I will pay you two thousand four hundred reales."

He blinked, stunned. That was more than four hundred escudos, double what he earned for teaching that particular thrust on the rare occasions when there were interested clients. It was also the equivalent of three months' work.

"You may not realize it, madam, but you are insulting me."

She swung round and, for a fraction of a second, Jaime Astarloa glimpsed a flash of anger in her violet eyes. It would not, he thought ruefully, be very hard to imagine her with a foil in her hand.

"Isn't it enough?" she asked insolently.

He gave a faint smile. Had that remark come from a man, the man would soon be receiving a visit from his seconds. However, Adela de

Otero was a woman and much too beautiful. Again he regretted finding himself involved in this awkward scene.

"My dear lady," he said serenely, icily polite, "the thrust in which you are so interested has the exact value I attribute to it and not a penny more. Besides, I only teach it to those I deem worthy, a right which I zealously preserve. It had never occurred to me to speculate on it, far less to haggle over the price like some vulgar merchant. Good evening."

He took his top hat, gloves and walking stick from the maid and went down the stairs without another word. From the second floor he heard the notes of Chopin's Polonaise being wrested from the piano with furious determination.

Parry in quarte. Good. Parry in tierce. Good. Semi-circular parry. Again, please. That's it. En marchant and advance. Good. Withdraw and break off. To me. Engage in quarte, that's it. Take "time" in quarte. Good. Parry in low quarte. Excellent, Don So-and-So. Paquito has talent. He just needs time and discipline.

Several days passed. Prim was still waiting to pounce and Queen Isabel was setting off to do some sea-bathing in Lequeitio, which was highly recommended by her doctors to relieve the skin disease she had suffered from since childhood. She was accompanied by her confessor and her consort, with a large cortège of flatterers, duchesses, tittle-tattlers, servants and the usual hangers-on from the royal palace. Don Francisco de Asís twirled the ends of his moustache and simpered over the shoulder of his faithful secretary Meneses, and Marfori, the Foreign Secretary, went about bragging to all and sundry, flaunting the spurs he had won for his prowess in the bedroom, the spurs of a chicken *royale à la mode*.

On either side of the Pyrenees, émigrés and generals were openly plotting, all of them brandishing aspirations. The deputies – third-class passengers – had approved the Ministry of Defence's final budget, knowing full well that most of it was to be used in a vain attempt to calm the ambitions of the military, who were paid for their loyalty to the Crown in promotions and privileges, going to bed as moderates and waking up as liberals, according to the vagaries of the promotions ladder. Meanwhile, Madrid spent the afternoons sitting in the shade, leafing through clandestine newspapers, with a wine jug close to hand. On the corners, sellers cried their wares: *Horchata de chufa*, delicious *horchata de chufa*!

The Marqués de los Alumbres refused to go away for the summer and he and Jaime Astarloa kept up their daily ritual of fencing followed by a glass of sherry. In the Café Progreso, the marvels of a federal republic were proclaimed by Agapito Cárceles, whilst the more temperate Antonio Carreño sketched masonic signs and threw himself wholeheartedly behind unitarianism, although without entirely discounting a proper constitutional monarchy. Don Lucas protested loudly every afternoon, and the music teacher stroked the marble table top and stared out of the window with sad, gentle eyes. As for the fencing master, he could not rid his mind of the image of Adela de Otero.

Someone was knocking at the door. Jaime Astarloa had returned from his morning walk and was freshening up a little before going down to eat at his usual tavern in Calle Mayor.

He was in his shirtsleeves, rubbing his face and hands with cologne in order to try and gain some relief from the heat, when he heard the doorbell and stopped, surprised. He wasn't expecting anyone. He quickly ran a comb through his hair and put on an old silk dressing gown, a souvenir of better days, the left sleeve of which had long needed darning. He left the bedroom, crossed the small living room, which also served as his office and, opening the door, found himself face to face with Adela de Otero.

"Good morning, Señor Astarloa. May I come in?"

There was a touch of humility in her voice. She was wearing a low-cut, sky-blue dress with white lace at the cuffs, neck and hem. On her head she wore a picture hat of fine straw adorned with a bunch of violets that matched her eyes. In her hands, covered by gloves made of the same lace as that on her dress, she carried a diminutive blue parasol. She was much more beautiful than she had seemed in her elegant rooms in Calle Riaño.

The fencing master hesitated for a moment, disconcerted by this unexpected apparition.

"Of course, madam," he said, still not quite recovered from his surprise. "I mean, of course, please . . . do come in."

He gestured for her to enter, although, after the abrupt way in which their conversation some days before had ended, the young woman's presence was making him feel distinctly uncomfortable. As if guessing his state of mind, she smiled at him.

"Thank you for receiving me, Don Jaime," she said, and her violet eyes looked at him from beneath long lashes, only increasing the fencing master's disquiet. "I was afraid that . . . but then, I expected no less of you. I am glad to see that I was not mistaken."

Jaime Astarloa took a while to realize that she had been afraid he would slam the door in her face and the thought startled him. He was, above all else, a gentleman. On the other hand, the young woman had, for the first time, addressed him by his Christian name, and that did nothing to calm his mind; to hide his confusion, he resorted to his habitual courtesy.

"Please come in, madam."

With a gallant gesture he invited her to cross the small hallway and go into the living room. Señora de Otero stopped in the middle of the dark, crowded room, looking curiously round at the objects that constituted Jaime Astarloa's history. Completely unabashed, she ran a finger along the backs of some of the many books filling the dusty oak bookshelves: a dozen old treatises on fencing, bound copies of Dumas, Hugo, Balzac. There were also a few volumes of Plutarch's *Parallel Lives*, a much-read Homer, Novalis's *Heinrich von Ofterdingen*, several titles by Chateaubriand and Vigny, as well as various memoirs and technical treatises analysing the military campaigns of the First Empire; most were written in French. Don Jaime excused himself for a moment and, going into the bedroom, exchanged his dressing gown for a frock coat, hurriedly tying his tie. When he returned to the living room, the young woman was studying an old oil painting, grown dark with the years, hanging on the wall between ancient swords and rusty daggers.

"Is he a member of your family?" she asked, pointing to the thin, youthful, rather severe face looking back at them from within the frame. The man was dressed in the fashions of the early part of the century, and his pale eyes regarded the world as if he found it not entirely convincing. His broad brow and his air of dignified austerity gave him a marked resemblance to Jaime Astarloa.

"He's my father."

Adela de Otero looked from the portrait to Don Jaime and back again at the portrait, as if to test the truth of his words. She seemed satisfied.

"A handsome man," she said, in that pleasant, slightly hoarse voice. "How old was he when he sat for the painting?"

"I don't know. He died when he was thirty-one, two months before I was born, fighting against Napoleon's troops."

"Was he a soldier?" The young woman seemed genuinely interested in the story.

"No, he was an Aragonese gentleman, one of those upright men who hate being told what to do. He took to the hills with a group of other men and carried on killing Frenchmen until they killed him." A tremor of pride shook the fencing master's voice. "They say he died alone, hunted down like a dog, berating in excellent French the soldiers who came for him with their bayonets."

She remained for a moment with her eyes fixed on the portrait, as she had done all the while he was speaking. She bit her lower lip thoughtfully, then she turned slowly to face him.

"I am aware that my presence here disturbs you, Don Jaime."

He avoided her gaze, not knowing what to say. Adela de Otero removed her hat and put it down, along with the parasol, on the paper-strewn table. She was wearing her hair caught up at the back of her neck, as she had on their first meeting. It struck Jaime Astarloa that her blue dress added an unusual note of colour to the room's otherwise austere décor.

"May I sit down?" Charm and seduction. It was clear that this was not the first time she had made use of these weapons. "I was out for a walk, and this heat is stifling."

Don Jaime muttered a hurried excuse for his lack of consideration, showing her to a leather armchair, worn and cracked with use. He drew up a footstool for himself, placed it at a reasonable distance from her, and sat there stiff and circumspect. He cleared his throat, determined not to allow himself to be dragged into terrain whose dangers he could all too easily foresee.

"What can I do for you, Señora de Otero?"

His cold, courteous tone only accentuated the lovely stranger's smile. For, although he knew her name, thought Don Jaime, everything else about this woman was veiled in mystery. Regretfully, what had at first been only a spark of curiosity inside him was rapidly growing, gaining ground. He struggled to control his feelings, awaiting a reply. She did not speak at first, but took her time with what seemed to the fencing master almost exasperating calmness. She gazed about the room, as if hoping to find in it signs by which she could evaluate the man she had before her. Don Jaime took the opportunity to study the features that had filled his thoughts in recent days. Her mouth was full and well formed, like a cut made by a knife in a fruit with red, mouth-watering flesh. He thought again that the scar at the corner of her mouth, far from marring her looks, gave her a special attractiveness, hinting at dark violence.

From the moment that she had appeared at his door, Jaime Astarloa had resolved, whatever her arguments might be, to restate his initial refusal. He would never take on a woman pupil. He expected pleas, feminine eloquence, the deployment of the subtle tricks peculiar to the fair sex, an appeal to certain feelings . . . Nothing would move him, he promised himself. Were he twenty years younger, he might have proved more selfishly flexible, won over perhaps by her undoubted powers of fascination. But he was too old for such things to change his mind. He expected nothing from that beautiful applicant; at his age, the feelings that her proximity aroused in him might be momentarily troubling, but they were, without a doubt, controllable. Jaime Astarloa would politely refuse, unmoved by what seemed to him a childish, female caprice. He was entirely unprepared for the question that came next: "How would you respond, Don Jaime, if, during a bout, your opponent made a doublé attack in tierce?"

The fencing master thought he must have misheard. He made a gesture as if to ask her to repeat what she had said, but he stopped halfway, surprised and confused. He drew a hand across his forehead, then placed both hands on his knees and sat looking at Adela de Otero as if demanding an explanation. This was ridiculous.

"I'm sorry?"

She was watching him, amused, with a mischievous gleam in her eyes. She spoke with disconcerting firmness.

"I would like your expert opinion, Don Jaime."

He sighed, shifting about on his footstool. All this was devilishly unusual.

"You're really interested?"

"Of course."

Don Jaime raised a hand to his mouth and gave an embarrassed cough.

"Well, I don't know how far . . . I mean of course, if you find the subject . . . A doublé attack in tierce, you said?" After all it was just a question, albeit a strange one coming from her. Or perhaps not so strange, after all. "Well, I suppose that if my opponent tried to attack in tierce, I would parry and then respond with a half-thrust. Do you understand? It's fairly elementary."

"And if he responded to your half-thrust by parrying and disengaging immediately in quarte?"

He looked at the young woman, this time with evident amazement. She had given the correct sequence.

"In that case," he said, "I would parry in quarte, and attack immediately in quarte." This time he omitted the "Do you understand?" It was obvious that Adela de Otero did. "That is the only possible response."

She threw her head back in unexpected gaiety, as if she were about to laugh out loud, but instead she merely smiled silently. She made a face and looked at him: "Do you want to disappoint me, Don Jaime? Or are you trying to catch me out? You know perfectly well that

that is far from being the only possible response, it may not even be the best one."

His discomfiture was obvious. He could never have imagined having such a conversation. Something told him that he was entering unfamiliar country, but, at the same time his professional curiosity drove him irresistibly on. He decided to lower his guard slightly; just enough to follow the game and see where it was leading.

"Would you care to suggest some alternative, dear lady?" he asked, just sceptically enough not to appear rude. The young woman nodded, almost vehemently, and her eyes glinted in a way that gave Jaime Astarloa much food for thought.

"I can suggest at least two," she replied with a certainty entirely lacking in conceit. "You could parry in quarte, but cut over the enemy's blade and then thrust in quarte over his arm. Does that seem correct to you?"

Don Jaime had to acknowledge forlornly that this was not only correct, it was brilliant.

"But you mentioned another option," he said.

"I did." While Adela de Otero was speaking, she moved her right hand as if reproducing the movements of the foil. "Parry in quarte and respond with a flanconnade. I'm sure you'll agree that any blow is always much faster and more effective if performed in the same line as the parry. Both should form a single movement."

"The flanconnade is not an easy move," said Don Jaime, now genuinely interested. "Where did you learn it?"

"In Italy."

"Who was your teacher?"

"His name is irrelevant." The young woman smiled to soften her refusal to answer his question. "Let's just say that he was considered amongst the best in Europe. He taught me the nine thrusts, their various combinations and how to parry them. He was a patient man." She emphasized the adjective with a pointed look. "And he didn't consider it a dishonour to teach his art to a woman."

Don Jaime preferred to ignore the allusion.

"What is the main risk involved in performing a flanconnade?" he asked, looking her in the eyes.

"Receiving a riposte in seconde."

"And how would you avoid it?"

"By making a froissement in reverse."

"How do you parry a flanconnade?"

"With a seconde or a low quarte. Anyone would think this was an examination, Don Jaime."

"It *is* an examination, Señora de Otero."

They sat regarding each other in silence, as weary as if they really had been fencing with foils. He took a good look at the young woman, noticing for the first time how strong her right wrist was, though without losing any of its feminine grace. The expression in her eyes and the gestures she made while describing the fencing moves were equally eloquent. Jaime Astarloa knew, from experience, how to recognize a talented fencer. Silently he reproached himself for having allowed his prejudices to blind him.

Of course, up to this point, everything had been theoretical and he realized that now he needed to try out her practical skills. Touché. That complicated young woman was about to achieve the impossible: to awaken in him, after thirty years in the profession, the desire to see a woman fence. To see *her* fence.

Adela de Otero was watching him gravely, awaiting his verdict. Don Jaime cleared his throat.

"I have to confess, in all honesty, that I am very surprised."

The young woman didn't reply, nor did she make any gesture. She remained utterly impassive, as if his surprise were something she had expected from the start.

Jaime Astarloa had come to a decision, although in his heart of hearts, he preferred not to question, for the moment, the ease with which he had surrendered.

"I'll expect you tomorrow at five. If the trial lesson proves satisfactory, we will arrange a date to teach you the two hundred escudo thrust. Try to come . . . ", he indicated her clothes, experiencing a sudden awkward rush of modesty. "I mean, try to come dressed in an appropriate fashion."

He expected a cry of joy, a clapping of hands or something of the sort, one of the usual manifestations to which the female nature seems so inclined. But he was disappointed. Adela de Otero merely gave him a long, silent look, and, although Don Jaime could not have said why, an absurd shiver ran through his body.

The light from the oil lamp cast flickering shadows about the room. Jaime Astarloa reached out his hand to work the mechanism of the wick, raising it a little until the brightness grew. With his pencil he drew another two lines on the sheet of paper, forming the vertex of an angle, and joined the two ends with an arc. Seventy-five degrees, more or less. That was the margin within which one should move the foil. He noted the figure down and sighed. A half-thrust in quarte without disengaging; perhaps that was the right path to take. And then what? The opponent would, logically speaking, parry in quarte. Would he though? Well, there were plenty of ways to force it. Then he would have to riposte immediately in quarte, perhaps with a half-thrust, with a false attack without disengaging. No, that was too obvious. Don Jaime put the pencil down and imitated the movement of the foil with his hand, studying his shadow on the wall. He thought glumly how absurd it was that he always ended up with familiar, classical moves that could easily be predicted and avoided by an opponent. The perfect thrust was something else. It had to be as swift and precise as a bolt of lightning, unexpected, impossible to parry. But what was it?

On the shelves, the gold lettering on the spines of the books gleamed softly in the light from the oil lamp. The pendulum of the clock on the wall swung monotonously back and forth, its gentle tick-tock the only sound filling the room now that his pencil was no longer moving across the page. He lightly thumped the table a few times, sighed deeply and looked out of the open window. The Madrid rooftops were now nothing but a confusion of shadows, barely hinted at by the pale light of a sliver of moon, fine as a silver thread.

He would have to abandon that opening in quarte. He picked up his pencil again – it was gnawed at one end – and drew more lines and arcs. Perhaps by opposing a counter parry of tierce, with the wrist pronated, and with his weight on his left thigh . . .

It was risky, for it exposed the person performing it to a thrust to the face. The solution, therefore, consisted in throwing your head back and disengaging in tierce. But when to do it? Of course, at the moment when your opponent raised his foot, a lunge in tierce or quarte over the arm. He drummed his fingers on the piece of paper, exasperated. This was all leading nowhere; the response to both moves was to be found in any treatise on fencing. What else could he do after disengaging in tierce? He drew more lines and arcs, noted down degrees, consulted notes and books open on the table. None of the options seemed appropriate; none provided the basis he needed for his thrust.

He got abruptly to his feet, pushing back his chair, and picked up the oil lamp to light him as far as the fencing gallery. He set it down on the floor next to one of the mirrors, took off his dressing gown and picked up a foil. Sinister shadows appeared on his face, lit from below, as if on the face of a ghost. He made various moves directed at his own image. Counter parry in tierce. Disengage. Counter parry. Disengage. Three times he managed to touch his twin reflection moving simultaneously on the surface of the mirror. Counter parry. Disengage. Perhaps two false attacks one after the other, yes, but then what? He ground his teeth with rage. There must be a way!

In the distance, the post office clock struck three. The fencing master stopped, expelling the air from his lungs. It was all utterly ridiculous. Not even Lucien de Montespan had managed it.

"The perfect thrust doesn't exist," that maestro of maestros used to say when anyone asked him the question. "Or, to be exact, there are many. Any thrust that hits home is the perfect thrust, but that's all. Any thrust can be parried given the right movement. Thus, a fight between two seasoned fencers could go on for ever. What happens is that Fate, which enjoys spicing things up with a dash of the unforeseen, determines that everything must have an end and forces one of the combatants, sooner or later, to make a mistake. It is therefore merely a matter of concentrating on keeping Fate at bay, long enough for the other man to make a mistake first. Anything else is pure illusion."

Jaime Astarloa had never been convinced. He still dreamed of the master stroke, the Astarloa stroke, his Grail. That one ambition, to discover the unpredictable, infallible move, had stirred his soul ever since he was a youth, in the distant days when he was at the military academy preparing to enter the army.

The army. How different his life might have been! A young officer with a free place as the orphan of a hero of the War of Independence, with his first billet in the Royal Guard in Madrid, the same regiment in which Ramón María Narváez had served. Lieutenant Astarloa had had a promising career, cut short almost before it began by an act of youthful folly. All because of a pale mantilla, beneath which he had glimpsed two dark, shining eyes and a slender white hand gracefully fluttering a fan. All because a certain young officer fell head over heels in love and because, as usually happens in this sort of story, there was a third party, a rival insolent enough to get in the way. There was a cold, misty morning, the clash of swords, a cry and a red stain on a sweat-soaked shirt, a stain that spread before anyone could stem the flow. There was a pale young man, staring stunned and incredulous at the scene, surrounded by the grave faces of colleagues advising him to flee, to preserve the freedom that the tragedy placed at risk. Then there was the frontier one rainy evening, a train travelling north-east through green fields, beneath a leaden sky. There was a miserable boarding house next to the Seine, in a grey, unfamiliar city which people called Paris.

A chance acquaintance, a fellow exile who had a good position there, recommended Jaime as a student-cum-apprentice to Lucien de Montespan, who was, at the time, the most prestigious fencing master in France. Intrigued by the young duellist's story, Monsieur de Montespan took him on after discovering in him an unusual talent for the art of fencing. Jaime Astarloa's only tasks at first were those of a steward; he offered towels to the clients, maintained the weapons and ran other small errands entrusted to him by the maestro. Later, as he progressed, he was still assigned only secondary tasks, but this time directly related to fencing. Two years later, when Montespan moved to Austria and Italy, Jaime Astarloa went with him. He had just turned twenty-four and instantly fell under the spell of Vienna, Milan, Naples and, above all, Rome, where they both spent a long period in one of the most famous *salles d'armes* in that city on the Tiber. Montespan's fame soon spread in Rome, where his sober, classical style, following the pure lines of the old school of French fencing, contrasted with the somewhat anarchic fantasy and freedom of movement of which Italian fencing masters were so enamoured. It was in Rome that, thanks to his personal gifts, Jaime grew into both a perfect society gentleman and a consummate fencer alongside his teacher, to whom he was bound by ties of affection and for whom he carried out the duties of aide and secretary. Monsieur de Montespan entrusted him with the students of lesser rank or those who had to be initiated in the basic moves before the prestigious maestro took them on himself.

In Rome, Jaime fell in love for the second time and there too he had his second duel with a bare blade. This time the two were unconnected; the love affair was passionate and without serious consequences, finally burning itself out quite naturally. As regards the duel, it took place according to the strictest rules of the social code in vogue at the time, with a Roman aristocrat who had publicly voiced his doubts about Lucien de Montespan's professional credentials. Before the old teacher could send for his seconds, young Astarloa had anticipated him, sending his own seconds to the accuser, a certain Leonardo Capoferrato. The matter was resolved in a dignified manner, with foils in a pine forest in Lazio, and with perfect, formal classicism. Capoferrato, who had a reputation as a formidable fencer, had to acknowledge that, whatever his opinion of Monsieur de Montespan, his aide and student, Signor Astarloa, had proved himself more than capable of putting two inches of steel in Capoferrato's side, inflicting a wound to the lung which, though not fatal, was nonetheless quite serious.

Thus passed three years that Jaime Astarloa would always remember with singular pleasure. In the winter of 1839, however, Montespan experienced the first symptoms of the illness which, a few years later, would take him to the grave, and he resolved to return to Paris. Jaime Astarloa did not want to leave his mentor and they both returned to the French capital. Once there, Montespan advised him to set himself up on his own account, promising to sponsor his entry into the closed society of *maîtres d'armes*. After a reasonable period of time, Jaime Astarloa, at the age of just twenty-seven, satisfactorily passed the exam of the Paris Academy of Arms, the most famous of all the academies, and obtained the diploma that would allow him, thenceforth, to exercise his chosen profession freely. He thus became one of the youngest teachers in Europe, and although his youth aroused some suspicion amongst more distinguished clients, who were inclined to choose teachers whose age seemed a guarantee of knowledge, Jaime's own efforts and Monsieur de Montespan's cordial recommendations saw that Jaime soon acquired a good number of pupils of high social standing. In his salon he hung the ancient coat of arms of the Astarloa family: a silver anvil on a field vert, with the motto "To me". He was Spanish, he had a sonorous, gentlemanly name and a perfect right to display a coat of arms. Besides, he wielded the foil with diabolical skill. With all these things in his favour, the success of the new fencing master was pretty much assured in the Paris of the time. He earned good money and grew in experience. At that time too, he perfected – even then searching for the master stroke – a thrust that he had invented and whose secret he guarded jealously, until the day when, at the insistence of friends and clients, he was forced to include it in the repertoire of master strokes that he offered to his students. This was the famous two hundred escudo stroke, which enjoyed notorious success amongst the duellists in high society, who would gladly pay that sum of money when they were in need of some decisive move with which to settle duels against experienced opponents.

While he remained in Paris, Jaime Astarloa maintained a close friendship with his old teacher, whom he visited often. They still fenced together frequently, although the disease had now taken a firm hold on Montespan's body. Thus the day came when Lucien de Montespan was hit six times in a row, without his foil so much as brushing his pupil's chest once. The sixth time it happened, Jaime Astarloa stopped as if thunderstruck and threw his foil to the floor, muttering an apology. His old teacher merely smiled sadly.

"So," he said, "the student can now outdo his teacher. You have nothing more to learn. Congratulations."

He never said anything more about it, but that was the last occasion on which they crossed steel. A few months later, when the young man visited him, Montespan received him by the fire where he was sitting at a table with a heater placed underneath it. Three days earlier, he had closed his fencing academy, recommending all his clients to go to Jaime Astarloa. The laudanum he had been taking was no longer enough to relieve the pain, and he sensed his death was approaching. He had just heard that his former pupil had a new challenge facing him, a duel with foils with a certain individual who was working as a fencing master despite not possessing a diploma from the Academy. Doing so incurred the wrath of qualified fencing masters and unpleasant disputes resulted. This was just such a case and the Academy, which was very particular about this sort of thing, had resolved to put an end to the matter. Defending the corporate honour had fallen upon the youngest of its members, Jaime Astarloa.

Teacher and former pupil talked long and hard about the subject. Montespan had obtained some valuable information about the man who was at the heart of the quarrel, one Jean de Rolandi, and brought the Academy's chosen paladin up to date on his opponent's tricks. Rolandi was a good fencer, though nothing extraordinary; he had certain technical faults that could be used against him. He was left-handed and, although that presented a certain danger to an opponent who, like Jaime Astarloa, was used to men who fought with their right hand, Montespan was sure that the young man would emerge from the duel triumphant.

"You must bear in mind, my boy, that a left-handed swordsman is sometimes less able to take 'time' correctly or perform a flanking move because of his difficulty in forming a straight opposition. With this Rolandi, your guard has to be in quarte outside. Do you agree?"

"I do, Maestro."

"As regards thrusts, remember that, according to my information, when he moves his left hand he does not keep his guard very well. Although, at first, he tends to have his wrist two or three inches higher than his opponent's, in the heat of the fight he often lowers his wrist. As soon as you see him do that, you must immediately deal him a thrust in 'time'."

Jaime Astarloa frowned. Despite his former teacher's disdain for him, Rolandi was, nevertheless, a skilful fencer.

"I've been told that he parries well at a short distance."

Montespan shook his head.

"Nonsense. The people who say that are worse than Rolandi. Worse than you. Don't tell me you're worried about this fool."

The young man reddened at the remark.

"You have always taught me never to underestimate any opponent."

The old man smiled slightly: "You're quite right, and I also taught you never to overestimate them either. Rolandi is left-handed, that's all. While that could prove dangerous to you, it is also an advantage that you must make the most of. He lacks precision. All you have to do is to take 'time' whenever you see him lower his wrist, or whenever he moves to cover himself, parry, surprise or retreat. In any of those circumstances, anticipate his movements while he's moving his wrist or raising his foot. If you can get in a thrust before, you will have hit him before he has stopped moving because you will have performed one movement while he is performing two."

"I'll do it, Maestro."

"I'm quite sure you will," replied the old man, satisfied. "You are the best student I ever had, the coolest and calmest whether with a foil or with a sabre in your hand. In the duel that awaits you I know that you will show yourself worthy of your name and of mine. Restrict yourself to direct, simple thrusts, to simple, circular and semi-circular parries, and, above all, to counter parries and two counter parries in quarte. And don't hesitate to use your left hand in parries if you think it necessary. Dandies advise against it because they say it's inelegant, but in duels, where your life is at stake, you

42

must rule out nothing that might serve as a defence, as long, of course, as it doesn't contravene the rules of honour."

The encounter took place three days later in the Bois de Vincennes between the fort and Nogent, before a large crowd gathered at a safe distance. The affair was public knowledge, indeed it had become something of a social event; even the newspapers knew about it. A group of curious onlookers had congregated there, kept back by the police, who had been sent to do just that. There were laws prohibiting duels, but since the reputation of the French Academy of Arms was at stake, the authorities had agreed to let the duel proceed. Someone criticized the fact that the paladin chosen for such a worthy task was a Spaniard, but Jaime Astarloa was, after all, a member of the Paris Academy and had lived for a long time in France, and his mentor was the renowned Lucien de Montespan: a triple-pronged argument that soon convinced even the reluctant. Amongst the public and the seconds, who were solemn-faced and dressed in black, were all the fencing masters of Paris, as well as some who had travelled in from the provinces to witness the event. Only Montespan was missing, for his doctors had advised him not to go.

Rolandi was dark and slightly built, with small, lively eyes. He was about forty and had sparse, curly hair. He knew the public did not favour him and he would gladly not have been there. Events, however, had developed in such a way that he had no choice but to fight; if he did not, he would be made to look ridiculous, and that shame would pursue him throughout Europe. He had been refused the title of *maître d'armes* on three occasions, despite his skill with both the foil and the sabre. Of Italian origin and a former soldier in the cavalry, he gave fencing lessons in a wretched little room in order to feed his wife and four children. While preparations were under way, Rolandi kept casting nervous glances at Jaime Astarloa, who remained calm and distant. Astarloa was wearing close-fitting black trousers and a loose white shirt that only emphasized his thinness. One of the newspapers covering the event had called him "the young Quixote". He was at the peak of his profession, and knew that he had the support of the fraternity of the Academy's *maîtres d'armes*, the grave, black-clad group of men waiting a few yards away, aloof from the crowd, and sporting walking sticks, medals and top hats.

The public had expected a titanic struggle, but they were disappointed. The fight had barely started, when Rolandi made the fatal mistake of lowering his hand a few inches while preparing a thrust with which to surprise his adversary. Jaime Astarloa lunged forward with a thrust in "time" into that tiny opening, and his foil slipped cleanly along and outside Rolandi's arm, entering unopposed beneath his armpit. The unfortunate man fell backwards, dragging the foil with him in his fall, and as he writhed on the grass, a few inches of bloody steel could be seen protruding from his back. The doctor present could do nothing to save his life. From the ground, still impaled on the foil, Rolandi gave his killer a strange, dark look and died vomiting blood.

When he received the news, Montespan merely murmured, "Good", without looking up from the logs crackling on the fire. He died two days later before his pupil – who had left Paris in order to allow the fuss caused by the affair to die down – could see him again.

On his return, Jaime Astarloa learned from friends of his old teacher's death. He listened in silence, with no sign of sorrow, and afterwards went for a long walk along the banks of the Seine. He stopped for some while by the Louvre, watching the dirty waters slipping downstream. He stood there, motionless, until he lost all sense of time. Night had already fallen when he came to again and began the walk back home. The following morning, he learned that in Montespan's will he had been left the only fortune his former teacher had possessed: his old weapons. He bought a bunch of flowers, hired a carriage and asked to be driven to Père Lachaise cemetery. There, on the anonymous grey gravestone beneath which his teacher's body lay, he placed the flowers and the foil with which he had killed Rolandi.

All that had happened almost thirty years ago. Jaime Astarloa looked at his reflection in the mirror in the fencing gallery. Bending down, he picked up the oil lamp and carefully studied his face, line by line.

Montespan had died when he was fifty-nine, only three years older than he himself was now, and the last memory he had of his teacher was of an old man huddled in front of a fire. He smoothed his white hair. He didn't regret having lived, having loved and having killed; he had never done anything to dishonour the image he had of him-self; he had enough memories stored up to justify his life, although they were his only legacy. His one regret was that he had no one to leave his weapons to when he died, as Lucien de Montespan had. With no one's arm to give them life, they would just be useless objects and end up in the dingy corner of some miserable antique shop, covered in dust and rust, silenced for ever, as dead as their owner. And there would be no one to place flowers on his grave.

He thought of Adela de Otero and felt a pang of anxiety. She had come into his life too late. All she could do was to wrest a few words of muted tenderness from his dry lips.

III

Uncertain "Time" on a False Attack

*"Unless certain that a period of fencing 'time' has been gained,
the fencer should be wary of counter-attacking on an attack
which may, or may not, be false."*

Half an hour before, he looked at himself in the mirror for the sixth time, and was pleased with what he saw. Few men of his acquaintance looked as he did at his age. From a distance he could have been taken for a young man, given his slenderness and agility, preserved through the continual exercise of his profession. He had shaved himself carefully with his old, ivory-handled English razor and had taken even more pains than usual over trimming his thin grey moustache. His white hair, slightly curled at the nape of his neck and at the sides, was combed back sleekly; his parting, high on the left, was as straight as if he had drawn it with the aid of a ruler.

He was in an excellent mood, as excited as a cadet wearing his uniform for the first time and on his way to his first assignation. Far from feeling awkward, he was revelling in that almost forgotten sensation. He picked up his one bottle of delicately perfumed eau-de-cologne, sprinkled a few drops on his hands, then gently patted his cheeks. The lines around his grey eyes grew deeper as he smiled to himself.

He was sure that nothing untoward would result from this particular assignation. Jaime Astarloa was too conscious of the reality of the situation to harbour any foolish illusions. However, there was no denying that there was something extremely attractive about it all. He had taken on a woman student for the first time in his life and, as

Adela de Otero was the student in question, the situation had a quality which, without quite knowing why, he described to himself as "aesthetic". He had already come to terms with the fact that his new client belonged to the opposite sex; once his initial resistance had been overcome, once he had swept his prejudices into a corner, whence he could only just hear their feeble protests, their place had been taken by the pleasant feeling that something new was happening in his, until then, monotonous existence. He was happy to abandon himself to what he fancied was a harmless adventure in the autumn of his life, a subtle game involving newly recovered emotions, one in which he would be the only real player.

At a quarter to five, he made one last inspection of the house. Everything was in order in the living room, which also served as a reception room. The caretaker, who cleaned the rooms three times a week, had carefully polished the mirrors in the fencing gallery, where the heavy curtains and the open shutters created a pleasant atmosphere of golden shadows. At ten minutes to five, he took one last look in the mirror and made a few hurried adjustments to his clothes in order to correct what seemed to him some imperfection in his dress. He was wearing what he usually wore when he was working at home: a shirt, close-fitting fencing breeches, stockings and soft leather shoes – all in immaculate white. For the occasion he had donned a rather old-fashioned dark blue jacket, worn with use, but comfortable and light, which he knew gave him an air of casual elegance. Around his neck he wore a fine white silk scarf.

When the small wall clock was about to strike five, he went and sat down on the sofa in his living room, crossed his legs and distractedly opened a book that was lying on the small table next to him, a shabby edition in quarto of the *Mémoriale de Sainte-Hélène*. He turned a few pages without taking in what he was reading, then looked at the hands on the clock: seven minutes past five. He briefly pondered women's lack of punctuality, only to be gripped by the fear that she might have changed her mind. He was just beginning to get worried when someone knocked at the door.

Those violet eyes were looking at him again, amused and ironic.

"Good afternoon, Maestro."

"Good afternoon, Señora de Otero."

She turned to her maid, who was waiting on the landing. Don Jaime recognized the dark young woman who had opened the door to him in Calle Riaño.

"It's all right, Lucía. Come back for me in an hour."

The servant handed her mistress a small travelling bag, then curtsied and went back down to the street. Adela de Otero removed the long pin from her hat and placed the hat and her parasol in Don Jaime's solicitous hands. Then she took a few steps about the room, stopping as she had before by the portrait on the wall.

"He was a handsome man," she said, as she had the previous day.

The fencing master had thought long and hard about how he should receive the lady, deciding in the end on an attitude of strict professionalism. He cleared his throat, indicating to her that he was not there to discuss his ancestors' physical features, and, with a gesture that was intended to be both cool and courteous, he invited her to go straight into the gallery. She gave him a brief look of amused surprise and then slowly nodded, like an obedient student. The tiny scar in the right-hand corner of her mouth retained the enigmatic smile that Don Jaime found so troubling.

When they reached the gallery, the maestro drew back one of the curtains so that the light streamed in, multiplied by the large mirrors. The sun's rays fell directly on the young woman, framing her in a golden halo. She looked about her, clearly pleased with the atmosphere in the room. A violet gemstone glittered on her muslin dress. It occurred to the fencing master that Adela de Otero always wore something that matched her eyes, which she certainly knew how to show off to the best advantage.

"It's fascinating," she said, with genuine admiration. Don Jaime in turn looked at the mirrors, the old swords, the wooden floor, and shrugged.

"It's just a fencing gallery," he protested, secretly flattered.

She shook her head and regarded her own image in the mirrors.

"No, it's more than that. In this light and with the old weapons on the walls, with the curtains and everything . . . ", her eyes lingered too long on those of the fencing master, who, rather embarrassed, looked away. "It must be a pleasure to work here, Don Jaime. It's all so . . . "

"Prehistoric?"

She pursed her lips, missing the joke.

"No, it's not that," she said, fumbling for the right word. "It's so . . . decadent." She repeated the word as if it gave her a special pleasure. "Yes, decadent in the most beautiful sense of the word, like a flower fading in a vase or a fine antique engraving. When I first met you, I imagined that your rooms would be something like this."

Jaime Astarloa shuffled his feet uneasily. The nearness of the young woman, her utter self-assurance bordering almost on impudence, the vitality she seemed to exude, produced in him a strange confusion. He decided not to allow himself to fall under the spell and tried to get back to the reason that had brought them there. To this end, he expressed the hope that she had brought appropriate clothing with her. Adela de Otero reassured him by showing him her small travelling bag.

"Where can I change?"

Don Jaime sensed a provocative note in her voice, but, annoyed with himself, dismissed the idea. Perhaps he was beginning to get too drawn into the game, he thought, mentally preparing himself to reject with the utmost rigour the first signs of an old man's folly. Gravely he showed the young woman the door of a small room set aside for such things and suddenly developed an intense interest in testing out the firmness of one of the floorboards. When she walked past him towards the changing room, she looked at him out of the corner of her eye and he thought he caught a faint smile, but immediately convinced himself that it was merely the small scar that fixed her mouth with that deceiving look. She pulled the door to, but left it open about two inches. Don Jaime swallowed hard, trying to keep his mind a blank. The small crack drew his gaze like a magnet. He kept his eyes fixed on the toes of his shoes, struggling against that murky magnetism. He heard the rustle of petticoats and, for a second, an image crossed his mind of dark skin in the warm shadows. He immediately banished the vision, feeling utterly despicable.

"For the love of God," the thought burst out in the form of a plea, although he wasn't quite sure to whom the plea was addressed, "she is, after all, a lady."

Then he walked over to one of the windows, raised his face to the light and tried to fill his mind with sun.

Adela de Otero had changed her muslin dress for a simple, light riding skirt in brown, short enough not to get in the way of her feet, and long enough for only a few inches of white-stockinged ankle to remain uncovered. She had put on flat fencing shoes, which gave her movements a grace normally found only in ballerinas. To complete the outfit she wore a plain, round-necked, white linen blouse that buttoned up at the back. It was close-fitting enough to emphasize her bust, which Don Jaime fancied was tantalizingly soft. When she walked, her low shoes gave her gait a lithe animal beauty, combining the masculine quality that Don Jaime had noticed in her before with a lightness of movement that was at once firm and supple. In those flat shoes, thought the fencing master, the young woman moved like a cat.

She levelled her violet eyes at him, trying to gauge the effect of her appearance. Don Jaime did his best to remain inscrutable.

"Which foil do you prefer?" he asked, half-closing his eyes, dazzled by the light that seemed to fold her in a voluptuous embrace. "French, Spanish or Italian?"

"French. I like to have my fingers free."

With a slight bow, he congratulated her on her choice. He too preferred the French foil, with no crossbar, with the grip unimpeded as far as the guard. He went over to one of the racks of weapons on the wall and studied them thoughtfully. Estimating the young woman's height and the length of her arms, he chose the appropriate foil, an excellent weapon with a blade made of Toledo steel, as flexible as a reed. Adela de Otero took the weapon and studied it attentively; she closed her right hand about the grip, appreciatively weighed the foil in her hand and then, turning to the wall, she tried the blade against it, pressing it so that it curved until the point was about twenty inches from the guard. Satisfied with the quality of the steel, she turned to Don Jaime. With the frank admiration of someone who knows how to appreciate the quality of such a weapon, she stroked the well-tempered metal with her fingers.

Jaime Astarloa handed her a padded plastron and solicitously helped her to put it on, fastening the hooks at the back. As he did so, he accidentally brushed the fine fabric of her blouse with the tips of his fingers and smelled the sweet scent of rosewater. He completed his task rather hurriedly, disturbed by the proximity of that beautiful bent neck, of the smooth skin offering itself up to him in all its warm nakedness beneath her hair, caught up by a mother-of-pearl comb. As he fastened the final hook, he noticed with dismay that his hands were shaking; to hide this, he immediately occupied himself in unbuttoning his own jacket and made some banal comment about the usefulness of the plastron in fencing bouts. Adela de Otero, who was drawing on her leather gloves, looked at him rather oddly, bemused by this sudden, uncalled-for loquacity.

"Don't you ever use one, Maestro?"

Jaime Astarloa smoothed his moustache and smiled benignly.

"Sometimes," he replied. Then, removing his jacket and his scarf, he went over to the rack and chose a French foil with a square grip, slightly inclined in quarte. With the foil under his arm, he went and stood opposite the young woman, who was waiting for him on the piste, very erect and with the point of her weapon resting on the floor by her feet, which were at right angles, the heel of her right foot facing the ankle of her left, impeccably positioned to place herself on guard. Don Jaime studied her for a few moments, regretting that he could not fault her position. He nodded approvingly, put on his gloves and indicated the masks lined up on a shelf. She shook her head disdainfully.

"I think you should cover your face, Señora de Otero. As you know, in fencing . . . "

"Perhaps later."

"That would be running a needless risk," insisted Don Jaime, taken aback by his new client's coolness. She doubtless knew that a careless stroke, delivered too high, could mark her face irrevocably. Adela de Otero seemed to guess his thoughts: she smiled, or perhaps it was the little scar that smiled.

"I commend myself to your skill, Maestro, not to be disfigured."

"I'm honoured by your confidence in me, madam, but I would feel happier if . . . "

The flecks of gold in the young woman's eyes glinted strangely as they had before.

"We'll fight our first bout with our faces uncovered," she said, as if introducing that extra risk made it all the more attractive to her. "Just this once, I promise."

He could not get over his surprise; the young woman was devilishly stubborn and extremely proud.

"Madam, I accept no responsibility. I would hate it if . . . "

"Please."

Don Jaime sighed. He had lost that first skirmish. It was time to pass on to the foils.

"We'll say no more."

They saluted, preparing themselves for the bout. Adela de Otero covered herself with absolute correctness; she held the foil with just the right degree of firmness, her thumb on the grip, her ring finger and little finger close together, keeping the guard at chest height and the point of the foil slightly higher than the wrist. She stood in the orthodox Italian fashion, offering the fencing master only her right profile, foil, arm, shoulder, thigh and foot all in one line, her knees slightly bent, her left arm raised with the wrist apparently limp. Don Jaime admired the graceful picture which the young woman presented, ready for attack like a cat about to pounce. Her eyes were narrowed, almost feverishly bright; her jaw was set. Her lips, beautiful despite the scar, were now just a thin line. Her whole body seemed to be tensed, like a spring about to be released; and Don Jaime, taking all this in with one professional glance, realized with some disquiet that, for Adela de Otero, this was much more than a capricious, eccentric pastime. He had merely to place a weapon in her hands for her to become an aggressive opponent. Accustomed to understanding the human condition through just that kind of attitude, Jaime Astarloa sensed that this mysterious woman was the guardian of some fascinating secret. That is why, when he held out his foil and stood on guard before her, he did so with the same calculated care that he would have taken when facing an opponent with an unprotected foil. He sensed that danger was lurking somewhere and that this game was far from being an innocent diversion. His professional instinct never deceived him.

They had only to cross swords for him to see that Adela de Otero had had an excellent teacher. He made a couple of feints to test his opponent's reactions, discovering that she replied calmly, keeping her distance and remaining on the defensive, conscious that her opponent was a man extraordinarily well versed in combat. Don Jaime could categorize someone at once, merely by observing the positions they took up and by testing the firmness of their steel, and this young woman certainly knew how to fence. She behaved with a curious combination of aggression and absolute calm; she was perfectly ready to lunge forward, but she was cool enough not to underestimate a formidable opponent, however often he appeared to offer her opportunities to deliver a decisive thrust. That is why Adela de Otero remained prudently in quarte, trying to rest her defence on the upper third of her foil, quick to take avoiding action when the teacher changed tactics and came too close. Like all expert fencers, she did not look at the blades, but into her opponent's eyes.

Don Jaime made a half-thrust in tierce, intending it to be a false attack before he attacked in quarte; he did so more than anything to test the young woman's reaction because he still did not wish to touch her with his foil. To his surprise, she stood firm, and he saw the tip of the enemy foil flash only a few inches from his belly when, with unexpected speed, she unleashed a low thrust in seconde, letting out a soft grunt from between pursed lips. He retreated, not without some embarrassment, furious with himself for having been so careless. The young woman recovered herself, took two steps back and then advanced one, again in quarte, her lips pressed together and looking into her opponent's eyes through half-closed lids, in a pose of absolute concentration.

"Excellent," murmured Don Jaime loud enough for her to hear, but she showed no satisfaction at his praise. There was a vertical line between her eyebrows, and a bead of sweat ran down from her fore-head to her cheek. The skirt did not seem greatly to encumber her movements; she held the foil with her arm slightly bent, aware of Don Jaime's slightest gesture. She was less beautiful like that, he thought; she was still attractive, but now her beauty lay in the tension with which her body seemed to vibrate. There was something mannish about her, but also something dark and wild.

Adela de Otero did not move sideways, she kept the line and maintained the correct measure on which purists were so keen and which Don Jaime himself recommended to his pupils. He advanced three steps, and she responded by retreating three. He made a thrust in tierce, and the young woman opposed him with an impeccable counter parry in quarte, describing a small circle with her foil around the enemy blade, which was turned aside by the manoeuvre. Silently he admired the clean execution of that defence, considered to be the most important of the principal parries; anyone who mastered it knew all there was to know about fencing. He waited for her to lunge immediately in quarte, which she did; he neutralized the attack and delivered a thrust over her arm, which would have hit home had he not deliberately stopped about an inch short. The young woman noticed this, stepped back without lowering her foil and looked at him, eyes blazing.

"I'm not paying you so that you can just toy with me as if I were one of your beginners, Don Jaime." Her voice trembled with ill-contained anger. "If you're going to hit me, then do so."

He stammered an apology, amazed at her furious reaction. She merely resumed her frown of concentration, and suddenly lunged forward so violently that he barely had time to interpose his foil in quarte, although the force of the attack obliged him to step back. He attacked in quarte to keep his distance, but she continued her assault, engaging, attacking and advancing with extraordinary speed, marking each movement with a hoarse cry. Less troubled by the nature of the attack than by the young woman's passionate determination, Don Jaime continued to retreat, staring, as if hypnotized, at the terrible expression contorting his opponent's face. He broke ground and she followed him, advancing. He broke ground again, but she advanced again, engaging and thrusting in quinte. He again drew back and this time she engaged in quinte and attacked in seconde. "Enough is enough," thought Don Jaime, determined to put an end to this absurd situation. But the young woman still had time to engage in tierce and attack in quarte over the arm before he had completely recovered himself. With considerable difficulty, he managed to extricate himself from that particular imbroglio and, standing firm, waited for her to present her foil horizontally in order to disarm her with a short, sharp blow on the blade. Almost simultaneously, he raised his foil and held the protected tip to Adela de Otero's throat. Her weapon fell to the floor and she jumped back, staring at the threatening foil as if a serpent were about to bite her.

They exchanged a measured, silent look. To his surprise, the fencing master noticed that the young woman no longer appeared angry. The anger that had contorted her features during the fight gave way to a smile in which there was a flicker of irony. He realized that she was glad to have given him a hard time, and this irritated him.

"What were you trying to do? In a fight without protected foils, something like that could have cost you your life, madam. Fencing isn't a game."

She threw her head back and let out a joyful laugh, like a little girl who has perpetrated some magnificent piece of mischief. Her cheeks were flushed with the physical exertion, and there were tiny beads of sweat on her upper lip. Even her eyelashes seemed damp and it crossed Don Jaime's mind – though he immediately dismissed the thought – that this was how she must look after making love.

"Don't be angry with me, Maestro." Her voice and face had changed completely; they were now full of sweetness, giving her a honeyed charm, a warm beauty. She was still breathing hard, her breast rising and falling beneath the protective plastron. "I just wanted to show you that there was no need for you to treat me with paternal care. When I have a foil in my hand, I can't bear being treated with kid gloves, the way men usually treat women. As you see, I am perfectly capable of putting up a good fight," she added, in a tone in which he thought he could hear a touch of menace. "And a sword thrust is a sword thrust, whoever deals it out."

Jaime Astarloa had no choice but to bend before that argument: "In that case, madam, I am the one who should apologize."

She, in turn, saluted graciously.

"I accept your apology." Her hair, caught up at the back of her neck, had come undone slightly, and one black lock brushed her shoulders; she raised her arms and pinned it back with the mother-of-pearl comb. "Shall we continue?"

Don Jaime nodded, picked up her foil from the floor and handed it back to her. He was amazed at the young woman's courage; during the bout the metal button that protected the tip of his foil had several times come dangerously close to her face and yet, at no point had she shown any sign of fear or concern.

"Now we really must use masks," he said. And Adela de Otero agreed. They both put on their protective masks and stood in the on-guard position. Don Jaime regretted that the metal mesh almost completely obscured the young woman's face. He could, however, still see the gleam in her eyes and the white line of her teeth when she opened her mouth to take a deep breath before making a lunge. This time, the bout proceeded without incident; the young woman fenced with absolute serenity, executing the moves impeccably and moving with great precision. Although she never managed to touch her opponent, he needed all his skill to avoid a couple of thrusts that would certainly have reached their target against someone less skilful than himself. As the metallic clash of foils filled the gallery, Don Jaime was thinking that Adela de Otero was easily a match for the worthiest fencers of his acquaintance. For his part, still holding back slightly, despite the young woman's express wishes, Jaime Astarloa finally found himself obliged to take her seriously. On two occasions he was forced to touch his opponent in order not to be touched himself. In all, Adela de Otero received five hits to the chest, which was not many, given the quality of her veteran opponent.

When the clock struck six, they both stopped, overcome by the heat and by exhaustion. She took off her mask, wiping away the sweat with the towel that Don Jaime handed to her. Then she looked at him questioningly, awaiting his verdict.

He was smiling.

"I would never have imagined it possible," he confessed frankly, and the young woman half-closed her eyes with satisfaction, like a cat receiving a caress. "How long have you been practising fencing?"

"Since I was eighteen." Don Jaime tried to work out her age from that information, and she guessed his intention. "I'm now twenty-seven."

He made a gesture of gallant surprise, as if to say that he had thought she was much younger.

"It really doesn't bother me," she said. "I've always thought it stupid to try to hide your age, or to pretend to be younger than you are. Denying your age is like denying your life."

"A wise philosophy."

"Just common sense, Maestro, just common sense."

"That's not a very feminine quality," he said with a smile.

"You'd be surprised how many feminine qualities I lack."

Someone knocked at the door and Adela de Otero looked annoyed.

"It must be Lucía. I told her to come back for me in an hour."

Don Jaime excused himself and went to open the door. It was, indeed, the maid. When he returned to the gallery, the young woman was already getting changed in the changing room. Again she had left the door slightly open.

He returned the foils to their racks and picked up the masks from the floor. When Adela de Otero reappeared, she was once more in her muslin dress and was brushing her hair, gripping the mother-of-pearl comb between her teeth. Her long hair came below her shoulders; it was very black and glossy.

"So, when will you teach me your sword thrust?"

Jaime Astarloa had to acknowledge that she had every right to learn the two hundred escudo thrust.

"The day after tomorrow, at the same time," he said. "My services include learning how to perform the thrust and how to parry it too. With your experience, you'll need only two or three lessons to master it completely."

She looked pleased.

"I think I'll enjoy practising with you, Don Jaime," she said warmly, as if uttering a spontaneous confidence. "It's a pleasure fighting with someone so . . . so delightfully classical. You obviously belong to the old French school: body erect, legs at full stretch and lunging only when absolutely necessary. There are not many fencers like you around any more."

"Alas not, madam."

"I noticed too", she added, "that you have a special quality in a fencer. It's what the experts call – what is it now? – yes, *sentiment du fer*. Is that right? Apparently only the most talented of fencers have it."

Don Jaime nodded vaguely, as if the matter were of no importance, although deep down he was flattered by the young woman's perspicacity.

"It's merely the product of a lot of hard work," he said. "It's a kind of sixth sense that allows you to extend your sense of touch from the fingers down to the very tip of the foil itself. It's a special instinct that warns you of your opponent's intentions and sometimes allows you to predict his moves a fraction of a second before they happen."

"I'd like to learn that too," said the woman.

"Impossible. It's a question of practice. There's no secret to it, no one can buy it with money. In order to get it, you need a whole lifetime, a lifetime like mine."

She seemed suddenly to remember something.

"As regards your fee," she said, "would you rather be paid in cash or with an order drawn on a bank, the Bank of Italy, for example? Once I've learned the thrust, I would like to continue practising with you for some time."

He protested politely. Given the circumstances, it would be a pleasure to offer his services to the lady with no further reward, etc. It was therefore improper to speak of money.

She looked at him coldly and made it quite clear that if she was using the professional services of a fencing master, they would be paid for. Then, regarding the matter as closed, she again caught up her hair at the back of her neck with rapid, precise movements, pinning it in place with the comb.

Jaime Astarloa put on his jacket and accompanied his new client to the living room. The maid was waiting on the stairs, but Adela de Otero seemed in no hurry to leave. She asked for a glass of water and lingered for a moment, looking with frank curiosity at the titles of the books lining the shelves.

"I would give my best foil to know who your fencing master was, Señora de Otero."

"And which is your best foil?" she asked without looking round, while she ran a finger delicately along the spine of a copy of Talleyrand's *Memoirs*.

"A Milanese foil, forged by D'Arcadi."

The young woman pursed her lips as if considering the matter, amused.

"It's a tempting offer, but I can't accept. If a woman is to preserve some attraction, she must surround herself with a little mystery. Let's just say that my teacher was a good one."

"I can see that. And you were an excellent pupil."

"Thank you."

"It's absolutely true. Anyway, if you'll allow me to venture an opinion, I would say that he was an Italian. Some of your movements are characteristic of that honourable school."

Adela de Otero raised one finger delicately to her lips.

"We'll talk about that another day, Maestro," she said in a low voice, like someone confiding a secret. She looked around her and, pointing to the sofa, asked, "May I sit down?"

"Please do."

With a rustle of skirts, she sat on the worn brown leather. Jaime Astarloa remained standing, feeling slightly awkward.

"Where did you learn to fence, Maestro?"

He looked at her mockingly.

"I find your impudence charming, madam. You refuse to enlighten me about your young life, then immediately interrogate me about mine. That's not fair."

She gave him a seductive smile.

"One can never be too unfair with men, Don Jaime."

"That's a very cruel response."

"And a very sincere one too."

He looked at her thoughtfully.

"Doña Adela," he said after a moment, suddenly serious, and with such overwhelming simplicity that his words were far from being mere polite flattery, "I would give anything to be able to send my card and my seconds to the man who inspired such bitter thoughts in you."

She looked at him, amused at first, then surprised when she realized that he was not joking. She started to say something but stopped, pleased, her lips half-open, as if savouring what she had just heard.

"That", she said after a moment, "is the most gallant compliment I have ever heard in my life."

Jaime Astarloa leaned on the back of a chair. He was frowning, somewhat embarrassed. The truth is, it had not been his intention to appear gallant, he had merely put his feelings into words. Now he was afraid that it might have seemed ridiculous – in a man of his age.

She noticed his embarrassment and, coming to his aid, returned quite naturally to the initial topic of conversation.

"You were going to tell me how you began fencing, Maestro."

Don Jaime smiled gratefully and pretended reluctantly to lower his guard.

"When I was in the army."

She looked at him with renewed interest.

"You were a soldier?"

"Yes, for a brief period of my life."

"You must have cut an elegant figure in uniform. You still do."

"Madam, please don't pander to my vanity. We old men are very susceptible to that kind of thing, especially when it comes from a charming young woman, whose husband no doubt . . . "

He left the words hanging in the air, in vain. Adela de Otero merely looked at him as if waiting for him to finish the phrase. After a moment, she took a fan from her handbag and held it between her fingers, without opening it. When she spoke, the expression in her eyes had hardened.

"Is that how you see me? As a charming young woman?"

He stammered, confused:

"Of course," he said after a moment, as coolly as he could.

"Is that how you would describe me to your friends at your club – a charming young woman?"

Jaime Astarloa drew himself up as if he had been insulted.

"Señora de Otero, it is my duty to inform you that I have neither club nor friends. And I feel it only right to add that in the unlikely event that I should find myself in such circumstances, I would never stoop so low as to mention a lady's name."

She gave him a long look as if trying to judge the sincerity of his words.

"Besides," he added, "a moment ago you described me as cutting an elegant figure, and I took no offence. Neither did I ask you if that is how you would describe me to your female friends over tea."

Adela de Otero laughed and he followed suit. Her fan had slipped to the floor and he hurriedly picked it up. He returned it to her, still with one knee on the floor. At that moment, their faces were only a few inches apart.

"I have no friends and I never take tea," she said, and Don Jaime was able to gaze at his leisure into those violet eyes, which he was seeing close to for the first time. "Did you never have any friends? I mean true friends, people to whom you could entrust your life."

He got up slowly. Replying to that question required no great effort of memory.

"Once, but it wasn't a friendship exactly. I had the honour of spending several years with Lucien de Montespan. He taught me everything I know."

Adela de Otero repeated the name under her breath; it was clearly not a name she was familiar with. Jaime Astarloa smiled.

"Of course, you're too young." He stared into space for a moment, then said, "He was the best fencing master of his day. In his prime, there was no one to beat him." He thought for a moment about what he had said. "Absolutely no one."

"Did you work in France?"

"Yes. I worked for eleven years as a *maître d'armes*. I returned to Spain in 1850."

She looked at him hard, as if she derived a certain morbid satisfaction out of extracting these nostalgic memories from him.

"You probably missed your own country. I know that feeling myself."

Jaime Astarloa did not reply at once. He knew perfectly well that the young woman was forcing him to talk about himself, something he was not, by nature, inclined to do. Nevertheless, a strange attraction emanated from Adela de Otero which invited him, sweetly, dangerously, to confide ever more.

"Yes, there was an element of that," he said at last, surrendering to her magic. "But in fact there was more to it, something more complex. You could say it was a kind of flight."

"A flight? You don't seem like the sort of person to run away."

Don Jaime smiled, troubled. He felt memories rising to the surface and that was rather more than he wanted to concede to Adela de Otero.

"I was speaking figuratively, well . . . ", he seemed to change his mind, "perhaps not entirely. Perhaps it really was a flight."

She bit her lower lip, interested.

"Tell me about it, Maestro."

"Perhaps another time, madam, another time. The truth is, it is not a story I care to recall." He stopped, as if he had just thought of something. "And you're wrong when you say that I don't seem like someone who would run away. We all run away from something sometime. Even I."

Adela de Otero remained thoughtful, her lips parted, regarding him as if taking his measure. Then she folded her hands on her lap and said sympathetically:

"Perhaps one day you'll tell me – your story, I mean." She paused to observe the fencing master's obvious embarrassment. "I don't understand how someone of your reputation . . . I mean no offence . . . but you do seem to have known better times."

Jaime Astarloa stiffened proudly. Perhaps, as the young woman had just said, it had not been her intention to offend him, but nevertheless she had.

"Ours is a dying art, madam," he replied, his *amour propre* wounded. "Duels with foils are now rare events, given that the pistol is so much easier to handle and does not require such rigorous discipline. Fencing has become a frivolous pastime." He savoured the scorn in his own words. "Now they call it a sport, as if it were on a par with performing gymnastics in your undershirt!"

She opened her fan; it had mother-of-pearl ribs and was decorated with hand-painted white flowers, a stylized version of almond blossom.

"You, of course, refuse to see it like that . . . "

"Of course. I teach an art and I do so exactly as I was taught to, seriously and with respect. I'm a traditionalist."

The young woman clicked the fan shut and shook her head absently. Perhaps there were images parading through her mind that only she could see and interpret.

"You were born too late, Don Jaime," she said at last, in a neutral voice. "Or perhaps you simply did not die at the right moment."

He looked at her, making no attempt to hide his surprise.

"It's odd that you should say that."

"What?"

"About dying at the right moment." He made an evasive gesture, as if apologizing for his continued existence. The turn the conversation had taken seemed to amuse him, but it was clear that he was not joking. "In this century and after a certain age, dying a proper death is becoming increasingly difficult."

"I would love to know what you consider a proper death."

"I don't think you would understand."

"Are you sure?"

"No, I'm not. You might, but it doesn't matter. These are not things one can talk about to . . . "

"A woman?"

"To a woman."

Adela de Otero closed her fan and raised it slowly until it touched the scar on her mouth.

"You must be a very lonely man, Don Jaime."

He looked at her hard. There was no amusement in his grey eyes now; his eyes had become opaque.

"I am." His voice sounded tired. "But I am the only one to blame for that. Actually loneliness has a kind of fascination; it's a state of egotistical inner grace that you can achieve only by mounting guard on old, forgotten roads that no one travels any more. Do I seem like an absurd old man to you?"

She shook her head. Her eyes were gentle now.

"No, I'm just appalled at your lack of common sense."

Jaime Astarloa made a face.

"One of the many virtues I am glad not to possess, madam, is common sense. You have doubtless realized that already . . . But I wouldn't want to give you the impression that there is some moral justification behind it. Let's just say it is a purely aesthetic matter."

"One can't dine out on aesthetics, Maestro," she murmured, with a mocking expression on her face, as if thinking thoughts that she preferred not to put into words. "That, I can assure you, is something I know only too well."

Don Jaime looked shyly down at his shoes; his expression was that of a boy who has just confessed to some misdemeanour.

"If you do, I am truly sorry," he said in a low voice. "As for myself, I would just say that, because of what I am, I can at least look myself in the face when I stand before the mirror each morning to shave. And that, madam, is more than many men I know can do."

The first street lamps were beginning to be lit, illuminating stretches of the road with gas light. Armed with long poles, the city employees carried out the task in a leisurely fashion, stopping every now and then at a tavern to slake their thirst. Over towards the Palacio de Oriente there was still a remnant of light, above which you could see the silhouette of the rooftops near the Teatro Real. The windows of the houses, open to the warm evening breeze, were lit by the flickering light from oil lamps.

Jaime Astarloa murmured a "Good evening" as he passed a group of neighbours chatting on the corner of Calle Bordadores, sitting out in the cool on wicker chairs. That morning, near the Plaza Mayor, there had been a brawl involving students, nothing much according to his acquaintances at the Café Progreso, who had told him about the incident. According to Don Lucas, a group of troublemakers shouting, "Prim, freedom, down with the Bourbons!" had been forcibly dispersed by the police. Of course, Agapito Cárceles's version differed greatly from that provided – in a scornful voice and with a libertarian sigh – by Don Lucas, who insisted on seeing troublemakers rather than patriots thirsting for justice. The forces of oppression, which were all that remained for the vacillating monarch and her awful entourage to rely on – Cárceles's voice took on a sarcastic tone here and he gave a malicious smile – had, once again, crushed the sacred cause with blows and swords, etc. As Don Jaime could see for himself, however, occasional pairs of mounted Civil Guards were still patrolling the area, shadowy figures beneath their shiny patent leather tricorn hats, auguring no good.

When he reached the palace, he saw the halberdiers standing guard there and then crossed to the balustrade overlooking the gardens. The Casa de Campo was just a large, dark smudge; on the horizon, the night was squeezing out the last faint line of blue light. Here and there, like Don Jaime, a few strollers stood watching the last flicker of daylight burning out in that moment of placid sweetness.

Without quite knowing why, he felt himself drifting into a melancholy mood. He was, by nature, more inclined to take pleasure in the past than to ponder the present, and he preferred to savour his private nostalgias alone; but that usually happened undramatically, without bitterness; on the contrary, it left him in a state of agreeable absorption that might best be described as "bittersweet". He took conscious pleasure in this and when, by chance, he resolved to give some concrete form to these thoughts, he described them to himself as his sparse personal baggage, the only wealth he had managed to store up in his lifetime, and which would go down with him into the grave, extinguished along with his spirit. Enclosed in that baggage was a whole universe, a lifetime of carefully preserved sensations and memories. Jaime Astarloa relied on this to conserve what he defined as serenity: peace of mind and soul, the only fragment of wisdom to which human imperfection could aspire. His whole life lay before him, smooth, broad and definitive, as untroubled by uncertainty as a river flowing to the sea. And yet all it had taken was the chance appearance of a pair of violet-coloured eyes for the fragility of that inner peace to reveal itself in all its disquieting reality.

He had yet to find out if he could mitigate the disaster, considering that, when all was said and done – since his spirit was far removed from passions which once would have revealed themselves immediately – he now found inside himself only a feeling of autumnal tenderness, veiled with a gentle sadness. "Is that all?" he wondered, half-relieved, half-disappointed, whilst he leaned on the balustrade enjoying the spectacle of triumphant shadows filling the horizon. "Is that all I can now hope to feel?" He smiled, thinking about himself, about his own image, about his now declining powers, about his spirit, which, though old and tired, in some way was rebelling against the indolence imposed on it by the slow degeneration of his physical organism. And in that feeling overwhelming him, tempting him with its sweet danger, he recognized the feeble swan song proffered, as a pathetic, last-ditch rebellion, by his still proud spirit.

IV

The Short Lunge

"The short lunge normally exposes anyone who executes it without judgement or prudence. Moreover, it must never be performed on encumbered, uneven or slippery ground."

Amidst the heat and the rumours, the days passed slowly. Don Juan Prim was busy tying conspiratorial knots by the banks of the Thames whilst long lines of prisoners snaked their way across fields seared by the sun, en route to prisons in Africa. Jaime Astarloa had no interest in all this, but it was impossible to ignore the effects. There was a great stir in the group he met with at the Café Progreso. Agapito Cárceles brandished, like a flag, a back number of *La Nueva Iberia*. A much-talked-about editorial, bearing the headline "The Last Word", revealed certain secret agreements reached in Bayonne between the exiled parties of the left and the Liberal Union, with a view to the abolition of the monarchy and the election by universal suffrage of a constituent assembly. It was fairly old news, but *La Nueva Iberia* had been the first to let the cat out of the bag. The whole of Madrid was talking about it.

"Better late than never," said Cárceles, waving the newspaper provocatively beneath Don Lucas Rioseco's sulky moustaches. "Who was it said that such a pact was against nature? Who?" He brought his fist down exultantly on the printed page, already fairly well thumbed by the other members of the group. "Those traditional obstacles we were talking about have their days numbered, gentlemen. Revolution is just around the corner."

"Never! Revolution, never! Still less a republic." Despite his indignation, Don Lucas was somewhat overwhelmed by the news. "At the very most, and I mean at the very most, Don Agapito, Prim will already have come up with some alternative solution in order to retain the monarchy. The Conde de Reus would never condemn the country to the paralysis of revolution. Never! He is, after all, a soldier, and every soldier is a patriot. And since every patriot is a monarchist, therefore . . . "

"I will brook no insults," roared Cárceles excitedly. "I demand you withdraw that statement, Señor Rioseco."

Caught by surprise, visibly nonplussed, Don Lucas looked at his antagonist.

"I didn't insult you, Señor Cárceles."

Purple with rage, the journalist appealed to the other members as witnesses: "He says he didn't insult me, but you all heard this gentleman state quite clearly, in the most gratuitous and uncalled-for fashion, that I am a monarchist."

"I didn't say that you . . . "

"Can you deny it now, you, Don Lucas, who call yourself a man of honour? Go on, deny it and may history be your judge!"

"I do deny it and I am a man of honour, Don Agapito. And I don't give a damn about history. Besides, that's got nothing to do with it. Dammit, you have a terrible knack for making people lose their thread. What the devil was I talking about?"

Cárceles's accusing finger was levelled at the third button on Don Lucas's waistcoat.

"Sir, did you or did you not just state that all patriots are monarchists?"

"I did."

Cárceles gave a sarcastic laugh, like a prosecuting counsel about to send a convicted, self-confessed criminal to the executioner's block.

"Am I a monarchist? Am I, gentlemen?"

All those present, including Jaime Astarloa, were quick to assure him that they would never dream of saying so. Cárceles turned triumphantly back to Don Lucas: "You see!"

"What do I see?"

"I am not a monarchist and yet I am a patriot. You have insulted me and I demand satisfaction."

"You are no patriot, Don Agapito, not even when you're drunk!"

"I . . . ?"

At that point the ritual intervention by the other members of the group became necessary to avoid Cárceles and Don Lucas coming to blows. Once things had calmed down, the conversation returned to speculations about an eventual successor to Isabel II.

"Perhaps the Duke of Montpensier . . . ," said Antonio Carreño quietly, "although they say that Napoleon III has vetoed him."

"You still can't rule out the possibility of an abdication in favour of the Infante Don Alfonso," said Don Lucas, adjusting his monocle, which had fallen out during the recent scuffle.

Cárceles leapt in again as if someone had insulted his mother: "Puigmoltejo? You're dreaming, Señor Rioseco. No more Bourbons. That's all over with. *Sic transit gloria borbonici* and other such Latin phrases, which I will refrain from repeating. We Spaniards have suffered quite enough under the grandfather and the mother. I'll say nothing about the father for lack of proof."

Antonio Carreño stepped in with the common sense of a tenured civil servant, a post that rendered him invulnerable to unemployment no matter which way the wind blew.

"You must recognize, Don Lucas, that the patience of the Spaniards has been tried beyond endurance. Some of the Palace scandals caused by Isabel would make even the most brazen blush."

"That's a slander."

"Well, slander or not, in the lodges we consider that things have overstepped the bounds of tolerance."

Don Lucas, his face flushed with monarchist fervour, was making a desperate defence beneath Cárceles's mocking eyes. He turned to Jaime Astarloa, in a plea for help.

"Do you hear that, Don Jaime? Say something, for God's sake. You're a reasonable man."

Don Jaime shrugged and continued calmly stirring his coffee with a teaspoon.

"My business is fencing, Don Lucas," he said.

"Fencing? Who can think about fencing when the monarchy is in danger?"

Marcelino Romero, the music teacher, took pity on the beleaguered Don Lucas. He stopped munching his toast and made some innocent remark about how very Spanish, how very charming the Queen was – surely no one could deny that. Carreño gave a sardonic little laugh, whilst Cárceles rounded on the pianist in loud indignation: "Being 'very Spanish' is hardly enough of a qualification to rule over a country, sir! That requires patriotism", he gave a sideways glance at Don Lucas, "and a sense of shame."

"She's certainly got plenty to be ashamed of," put in Carreño with a wink.

Don Lucas struck the floor with his stick, impatient with such excesses.

"It's so easy to condemn," he exclaimed, shaking his head sadly. "It's so easy to make firewood out of the poor tottering tree. And that *you* should do so, Don Agapito, you who were a priest . . . "

"Now, stop right there!" said Cárceles. "That should be said in the pluperfect."

"You were, though, however much you may dislike the fact," insisted Don Lucas, delighted to have found a way of irritating his colleague.

Cárceles placed a hand on his breast and called upon Heaven itself to be his witness.

"I renounce as a black symbol of obscurantism the habit I once wore as an obsessed young man."

Antonio Carreño nodded gravely, in silent homage to such rhetorical skills.

Don Lucas continued on the same theme: "But you were a priest, Don Agapito, and you should know better than anyone that charity is the greatest of Christian virtues. You must be generous and act with charity when judging the historic figure of our sovereign."

"Your sovereign, Don Lucas."

"Call her what you will."

"I'll call her everything under the sun: capricious, fickle, superstitious, uncultivated and other things I won't mention."

"I will not put up with any more of your impertinence."

The other members of the group were again obliged to call for calm.

Neither Don Lucas nor Agapito Cárceles would ever have harmed a fly, but this was all part of the liturgy repeated every afternoon.

"We must bear in mind", said Don Lucas, twirling his moustaches, and trying to ignore Cárceles's jeering look, "the unhappy marriage of our sovereign Queen to Don Francisco de Asís, made with a complete disregard for any mutual physical attraction. Conjugal differences, which are public knowledge, encouraged the activities of court cliques and unscrupulous politicians, of favourites and parasites. They, and not the poor Queen, are the people responsible for the sad situation in which we find ourselves now."

Cárceles had kept silent long enough: "Try telling that to the patriots in prison in Africa, to those deported to the Canaries or the Philippines, to all the emigrants flocking into other parts of Europe!" Filled with revolutionary rage, he crumpled up his copy of *La Nueva Iberia*. "The present government of Her Most Christian Highness makes the previous lot look good by comparison, which is quite an achievement. Can you not see what is happening? Even politicians and matadors who have not a drop of democratic blood in their veins have been sent into exile merely because they were under suspicion, or had given less than wholehearted support to the loathsome policies of González Bravo. Just take a good look, Don Lucas, take a good look: from Prim to Olózaga, not to mention Cristino Martos and the others. As you see, even the Liberal Union, as we've just read, changed their tune as soon as old O'Donnell was pushing up the daisies. Isabel's only support now is amongst the divided and ruined forces of the Moderates, who are in chaos because power is slipping from their grasp and they don't know which way to turn. Your monarchy is taking in water, Don Lucas, fore and aft."

"The fact is, Prim is ready to strike," whispered Carreño confidentially, with a lack of originality that was greeted with derisive laughter by the others. Cárceles changed the direction of his implacable artillery.

"As our friend Don Lucas pointed out a little while ago, Prim is a soldier. A more or less glorious soldier, but a soldier nonetheless. I don't trust him an inch."

"The Conde de Reus is a Liberal," protested Carreño.

Cárceles brought his fist down hard on the marble table top, nearly spilling the coffee in the cups.

"A Liberal? Forgive me if I laugh, Don Antonio. Prim, a Liberal! Any real democrat, any proven patriot like yours truly, should, on principle, distrust any plans a soldier might have, and Prim is no exception. Have you forgotten his authoritarian past, his political ambitions? In the end, although circumstances currently oblige him to do his plotting amidst the British fog, every general needs a king in his hand if he is to continue being the jack. Let's see, gentlemen, how many military uprisings have we had so far this century? And how many of them have been called in order to proclaim a republic? You see? Nobody is going graciously to hand over to the people what only the people can demand and take for themselves. There's something about Prim, gentlemen, that I don't trust. I'm convinced that he'll arrive with a king up his sleeve. The great Virgil already said as much: *Timeo Danaos et dona ferentes.*"

A lot of noise was coming from Calle Montera. A group of passers-by had formed a crowd outside the window and were pointing towards the Puerta del Sol.

"What's happening?" asked Cárceles eagerly, forgetting about Prim. Carreño had gone over to the door. Indifferent to all these political upsets, the cat was dozing in its corner.

"There seems to be a party going on," said Carreño. "Let's go and see!"

They all went out into the street. Groups of onlookers were gathering in the Puerta del Sol. There were carriages and policemen advising passers-by to take another route. Several women came hurrying up the street, looking flushed and harassed and glancing fearfully over their shoulders. Jaime Astarloa went over to a policeman.

"Is anything wrong?" he asked.

The policeman shrugged; it was clear that events went beyond his powers of analysis.

"I'm not quite sure, sir," he said, visibly embarrassed, touching his cap when he saw the distinguished appearance of the person addressing him. "It seems they've arrested about half a dozen generals.

They say they're taking them to the military prison at San Francisco."

Don Jaime told his colleagues what he had heard and the news was greeted with exclamations of consternation. The triumphant voice of the irrepressible Agapito Cárceles rang out in the middle of Calle Montera: "Gentlemen, it's just as I said! Now they're showing their hand. These are the death throes of blind repression!"

She was standing before him with a foil in her hand, watching his every move.

"It's very simple. Now watch carefully."

Jaime Astarloa raised his foil and crossed it with hers, so lightly that the touch was like a metallic caress. "The two hundred escudo thrust begins with what we call counter-time: a false attack that presents your opponent with an opening in quarte, in order to provoke him into attacking in that position. That's it. Respond in quarte. Perfect. I parry with a counter parry of tierce, do you see? I disengage and attack, still keeping that opening in order to lure you into opposing me with a counter parry of tierce and then attacking immediately in quarte again. Fine. As you can see, so far, no secret."

Adela de Otero stopped, thoughtful, her eyes fixed on his foil.

"Isn't it dangerous to offer the same opening to your opponent twice?"

Don Jaime shook his head.

"Not at all, madam. Provided you have mastered the counter parry of tierce, which you have. My thrust does inevitably involve some risk, but only if the person using it is not skilled and expert in our art. I would never think of teaching it to an apprentice fencer because I'm convinced that he would get himself killed the first time he tried to use it. Do you understand now my initial reserve when you did me the honour of requesting my services?"

The young woman gave him a charming smile.

"I'm sorry, Maestro. There was no way you could know . . . "

"Indeed I couldn't. And I still can't quite understand how you . . . " He broke off, looking at her, absorbed. "Anyway, that's enough talking. Shall we go on?"

73

"Please do."

"Right." He avoided her eyes as he spoke. "As soon as your opponent attacks for the second time, at the precise moment when your blades touch, you must bend with this counter parry, like this, attacking immediately in quarte outside the arm. Do you see? Your opponent will normally resort to a parade de pointe volante, bending his elbow and raising his foil to an almost vertical position to fend off the attack. That's it."

Jaime Astarloa stopped again, with the point of his foil resting on Adela de Otero's right shoulder. He felt his heart beat faster when he made contact with her skin, he seemed to be able to feel her through the steel, as if the foil were merely an extension of his hand. "*Sentiment du fer*," he murmured to himself as an imperceptible shudder ran through him. The young woman looked sideways at the foil, and the scar on her mouth deepened as she smiled. Embarrassed, the fencing master raised the steel an inch. She seemed to know what he was feeling.

"Right, now comes the decisive moment," Don Jaime went on, forcing himself to recover the concentration which, for a few moments, had vanished completely. "Rather than make a full thrust, when your opponent has begun the movement, you hesitate for a second, as if you were making a false attack with the intention of performing a different thrust. I'll do it slowly so that you can see: like this. You make it impossible for your opponent to complete the parry; instead, he is interrupted halfway, for he prepares to parry the other thrust, which he thinks is about to follow."

There was a jubilant gleam in Adela de Otero's eyes. She had understood.

"And that's where your opponent makes his mistake!" she said gleefully, relishing the discovery.

He made a gesture of benevolent complicity.

"Exactly. That is where the mistake arises which gives victory to us. Watch. After that briefest of hesitations, we continue the movement, at the same time shortening the distance between us, like this, to avoid him stepping back, and leaving him very little room for manoeuvre. At that point, you give your wrist a quarter of a turn – that's it – so that the point of your foil lifts about two inches. You see how simple it is? Done properly, you can easily hit your opponent at the base of the neck, by the right clavicle. Or, if you want to settle the matter, in the middle of the throat."

The tip of his foil brushed the young woman's throat, and she looked at him with her mouth half-open, her eyes flashing with excitement. Jaime Astarloa studied her; her nostrils were flared and she was breathing hard, her chest rising and falling beneath her blouse. She was radiant; she was like a child who had just unwrapped a marvellous gift.

"That's excellent, Maestro. Incredibly simple," she said in a whisper, giving him a look of warm gratitude. "Incredibly simple!" she repeated thoughtfully, looking in fascination at the foil in her hand. She seemed entranced by the new, fatal dimension which the steel blade had just acquired.

"I suppose that's where its merit lies," remarked Don Jaime. "In fencing, it's simplicity that requires inspiration, the complex moves are just technique."

She smiled happily.

"I know a secret thrust which doesn't appear in any of the treatises on fencing," she murmured, as if the thought gave her enormous pleasure. "How many other people know it?"

Don Jaime made a vague gesture.

"I don't know. Ten, possibly twelve. Perhaps a few more. But then what happens is that one person shows it to another person, and after a while it loses its efficacy. As you've seen, it's very easy to parry once you do know it."

"Have you used it to kill anyone?"

He looked at her, startled. It was not the kind of question one expected from a lady.

"I hardly think that's relevant, madam. With all due respect, I really don't think that matters." He paused, while his mind went back in time to the distant memory of a poor wretch bleeding to death in a field, with nobody able to do anything to staunch the blood pouring from his throat. "And even if I had, I would not feel particularly proud of the fact."

Adela de Otero made a doubtful face, as if that were debatable. And a worried thought crossed Jaime Astarloa's mind: there was a touch of dark cruelty in those violet-coloured eyes.

Luis de Ayala was the first to raise the matter. He had heard certain rumours.

"It's unprecedented, Don Jaime. A woman! And you say she's a good fencer?"

"Excellent. No one was more surprised than I."

The Marquis leaned towards him, visibly interested.

"Is she beautiful?"

Jaime Astarloa made a face that was intended to be neutral.

"Extremely."

"You are a devil, Maestro!" Luis de Ayala wagged a finger at him, and gave a knowing wink. "And where did you find this jewel?"

Don Jaime protested weakly. It was absurd to think that at his age, etcetera. It was an exclusively professional relationship. I'm sure Your Excellency will understand.

Luis de Ayala understood all too well.

"I must meet her, Don Jaime," he said.

Don Jaime gave an ambiguous response. He wasn't at all happy at the prospect of the Marqués de los Alumbres meeting Adela de Otero.

"Of course, Excellency, whenever you like. There's no problem at all."

Luis de Ayala took his arm; they walked beneath the leafy willows in the garden. It was hot even in the shade, and the Marquis was wearing only light cashmere trousers and an English silk shirt, with gold cufflinks bearing a coat of arms.

"Is she married?"

"I don't know."

"Do you know where she lives?"

"I went there once, but I saw only her and a female servant."

"She lives alone, then!"

"That is the impression I got, but I can't be sure." Don Jaime was beginning to feel troubled by this interrogation and he was trying desperately to change the subject without appearing to be impolite to his client and protector. "The fact is that Doña Adela doesn't talk very much about herself. As I told Your Excellency before, our relationship is, of course, exclusively professional, that of teacher and student."

They stopped by one of the stone fountains: a chubby-cheeked angel pouring water from a jar. A few sparrows flew off as they approached. Luis de Ayala watched them disappear amongst the branches of a nearby tree and then turned to Don Jaime. The two men could not have been more different: the strong, vigorous physicality of the Marquis was in marked contrast to the lean distinction of the fencing master. Anyone seeing them would have thought that Jaime Astarloa was the aristocrat.

"It is never too late, though, to revise certain apparently immutable principles," said the Marquis with a wicked wink. Don Jaime started, clearly piqued.

"I would rather you did not to continue down that particular road, Excellency." There was an edge to his voice. "I would never have accepted the young woman as a client, had I not seen that she had undoubted talent. You can be absolutely sure of that."

Luis de Ayala sighed, and adopted a friendly but teasing tone.

"Progress, Don Jaime. The magic word. New times, new customs, they affect us all. Not even you are safe."

"With the greatest respect, Don Luis, I believe you are mistaken." It was evident that Don Jaime was greatly perturbed by the turn the conversation had taken. "You may consider this whole story to be the professional caprice of an old fencing master – an aesthetic matter if you like. But there's a vast difference between saying that and imagining that such a thing opens the gate to progress and to new customs. I'm too old to consider seriously any major changes in my way of thinking. I believe myself safe both from the follies of youth and from giving too much importance to what is, I believe, a purely professional activity."

The Marquis smiled approvingly at Don Jaime's measured words.

"You're right, Maestro. I owe you an apology. Besides, you have never been one to defend progress . . . "

"Never. I have spent my whole life trying to preserve a certain idea of myself, and that is all. You have to cling to a set of values that do not depreciate with time. Everything else is the fashion of the moment, fleeting, mutable. In a word, nonsense."

The Marquis looked at him hard. The light tone of their discussion had vanished.

"Don Jaime, your kingdom is not of this world. And I say that with the greatest respect, with all the respect I bear you. I have long felt honoured by your friendship and yet I am still surprised every day by this peculiar obsession of yours with duty, a duty that is not dogmatic, religious, or moral. It is, and this is what is so unusual these days when everything can be bought, a duty to yourself, imposed by your own will. Do you know what that means?"

Jaime Astarloa gave a stubborn frown. This new direction made him feel even more uncomfortable than had the previous one.

"I neither know nor care, Excellency."

"That is exactly what is so extraordinary about you, Maestro, that you neither know nor care. Shall I tell you something? Sometimes I wonder if in this poor Spain of ours the roles have not been sadly switched, and if nobility does not, by rights, belong to you instead of to many of my acquaintances, including myself."

"Please, Don Luis . . . "

"No, let me speak. My grandfather, may he rest in peace, bought the title because he grew rich trading with England during the war against Napoleon. Everyone knows that. The real nobility, the old nobility, was won not by importing contraband English cloth, but by brave deeds with a sword. Am I right or not? And you're not going to tell me, dear Maestro, that you, with a sword in your hand, are worth less than any of them. Or less than myself."

Jaime Astarloa looked up and fixed Luis de Ayala with his grey eyes.

"With a sword in my hand, Don Luis, I am worth as much as any man."

A breath of warm air shook the branches of the willows. The Marquis looked back at the stone angel and clicked his tongue as if he had gone too far.

"Anyway, you're wrong to isolate yourself, Don Jaime. Allow me, as a friend, to tell you that. There's no profit in virtue, I can assure you, or any fun either. For Heaven's sake, don't imagine that I would presume to give a man your age a sermon. I just mean that it's thrilling to look out into the street and see what's happening around you. Especially in historic times such as these. Have you heard the latest?"

"The latest what?"

"The latest plot."

"It's not really my forte. Do you mean the generals who were arrested?"

"No, that's old news. I'm talking about the agreement reached between the Progressives and the Liberal Union that has just been uncovered. You could see it coming, but they've completely abandoned their stance as the legal opposition and have decided to support the military revolution. Their programme is now to depose the Queen and offer the throne to Montpensier, who has committed the modest amount of three million reales to the enterprise. Deeply hurt, Isabel has apparently decided to exile her sister and her brother-in-law to Portugal. As for Serrano, Dulce, Zabala and the others, they have been deported to the Canary Islands. The supporters of Montpensier are now working on Prim, to see if they can get him to give him his blessing as candidate to the throne, but our brave Catalan soldier is not saying a word. And that's how things stand."

"A fine mess!"

"You can say that again. That's why it's so exciting to follow the details from the sidelines, as I do. What can I say? When it comes to politics and women, you have to taste all the sauces, but you must never let either of them give you indigestion. That is my philosophy, and here I am; I enjoy life and its surprises while they last. And afterwards, who cares! I disguise myself in a peasant's hat and cloak and wander past the stalls during the festival of San Isidro with the same scientific curiosity I felt during the three months I worked in that wretched post as secretary in the Ministry of the Interior bestowed on me by my late Uncle Joaquín. You have to live, Don Jaime. And this from a man who yesterday lost three thousand duros on the casino table, and did so with a scornful smile on his lips which was much commented on by the public. Do you understand?"

Don Jaime smiled indulgently.

"Perhaps."

"You don't seem very convinced."

"You know me well enough, Excellency, to know what I think."

"Yes, I do. You are a man who feels like a foreigner everywhere. If Jesus Christ had said to you, 'Leave everything and follow me', you would have done so gladly. There's nothing you care about enough to regret its loss."

"Apart from a pair of foils. At least allow me that."

"All right, keep the foils. Assuming that you were the type to follow Jesus Christ, or anyone, but that is assuming rather a lot." The Marquis seemed amused by the idea. "I've never asked you if you are a monarchist, Don Jaime. I mean the monarchy as an abstraction, not our pathetic national farce."

"Before, Don Luis, you said that my kingdom was not of this world."

"Nor of the next, I'm sure. The fact is I unreservedly admire your ability to remain on the margins."

Don Jaime looked up; he was studying the clouds in the distance, as if there were something familiar about them.

"Perhaps I'm too selfish," he said. "An old egotist."

Don Luis pulled a face.

"That often has a price, my friend, a very high price."

Jaime Astarloa turned the palms of his hands up in a gesture of resignation.

"You can get used to anything, especially when you have no option. If you have to pay, you pay; it's just a question of attitude. At a particular moment in your life you adopt a certain position, whether mistaken or not. You decide to be like this or that. You burn your boats and then all you can do is defend that position, come hell or high water."

"Even though you're clearly living out a mistake?"

"Especially then. That's where aesthetics comes in."

The Marquis gave a broad smile, revealing his perfect teeth.

"The aesthetics of the mistake. That would make a fine academic thesis. There would certainly be plenty to say on the subject."

"I don't agree. Indeed, I don't think there's much to say about anything."

"Apart from fencing."

"Apart from fencing, of course." Jaime Astarloa fell silent, as if that were the end of the matter. But after a moment, he shook his head and pressed his lips together. "Pleasure isn't only to be found outside, as Your Excellency said a moment ago. It can also be found in remaining faithful to certain personal rituals, especially when everything stable seems to be collapsing around you."

The Marquis observed in an ironic tone, "I think Cervantes had something to say about that. Except that you are a gentleman who has no need to set out on the road, because you carry your windmills inside you."

"And I'm an introspective, egotistical gentleman, don't forget that, Your Excellency. The man from La Mancha wanted to right wrongs, all I want is to be left in peace." He remained thoughtful for a while, analysing his feelings. "I don't know if that is compatible with honesty, but, I am trying to be honest, I assure you, or at least honourable – anything, indeed, that has its roots in the word 'honour'," he added simply. No one would have taken his tone to be that of a conceited man.

"A most unusual obsession, Maestro," said the Marquis, genuinely surprised. "Especially these days. Why that word above all others? I can think of dozens of alternatives: money, power, ambition, hatred, passion . . . "

"I suppose because one day I chose that word and not another. Perhaps by chance, or because I liked the sound of it. Perhaps, in some way, I related it to the image of my father, for I was always proud of the way he died. A good death justifies anything, any life."

"That idea of death", said Ayala, smiling, eager to prolong his conversation with the fencing master, "has a suspicious whiff of Catholicism about it. The good death as the gateway to eternal salvation."

"If you're hoping for salvation, or whatever, it has very little merit in it. I was referring to the final battle on the threshold of eternal darkness, with oneself as the only witness."

"You're forgetting about God."

"He doesn't interest me. God tolerates the intolerable; he is irresponsible and inconsistent. He is not a gentleman."

The Marquis looked at Don Jaime with real respect.

"I have always maintained, Maestro," he said, after a silence, "that nature organizes things in such a way that she makes cynics out of lucid men in order that they may survive. You are the only proof I have of the wrongness of my theory. And perhaps that is what I like about you, even more than our fencing bouts. It reconciles me to certain things that I would have sworn existed only in books. You're my sleeping conscience."

They both fell silent, listening to the sound of the fountain; the soft breeze again shook the branches of the willows. Then Don Jaime thought about Adela de Otero, gave a sideways glance at Luis de Ayala and noticed inside himself a disagreeable murmur of remorse.

Indifferent to the political turmoil taking place in the capital that summer, Jaime Astarloa kept punctually to the arrangements made with his clients, including the three hours a week devoted to Adela de Otero. There was nothing questionable about these sessions, they kept strictly to the technical side of things, which was the reason for their relationship. Apart from these bouts, in which the young woman continued to fence with consummate skill, they spoke only briefly about inconsequential issues. The almost intimate conversation they had had on the afternoon of her second visit to his apartment was never repeated. In general, she merely asked Don Jaime precise questions about fencing, to which he replied with great pleasure and considerable relief. For his part, Don Jaime suppressed, with apparent ease, any interest he had in learning more about his client, and when he occasionally touched on the subject, she either ignored him or ingeniously sidestepped the question. The only thing he could ascertain was that she lived alone, that she had no near relatives, and that she was trying, for reasons whose secret she alone possessed, to remain on the margins of the social life which, given her situation, one would have expected her to enjoy in Madrid. He knew that she possessed a considerable fortune, verging on the lavish, yet she had a second- rather than a first-floor apartment in Calle Riaño, and that she had obviously lived for some years abroad, possibly in Italy, or so he assumed from certain details and expressions he picked up during his conversations with her. Otherwise, there was no way of knowing if she was single or a widow, although her way of life seemed more suited to the second hypothesis. Her easy manner, the scepticism evident in all her remarks about men, were not what one would expect in a young single woman. It was clear that this woman had loved and suffered; Jaime Astarloa was old enough to recognize the aplomb which, even in youth, it is possible to achieve only by experiencing and surviving intense personal pain. In that respect, he was unsure whether or not it would be fair to describe her, in the vulgar terminology of the day, as an adventuress. Perhaps she was; yet she seemed so unusually independent that it was difficult to place her amongst the ranks of the more conventional women of the fencing master's acquaintance. Nevertheless, something told him that to label her an adventuress was to oversimplify.

Despite Adela de Otero's reticence about herself, the relationship he had with her could, in general terms, be regarded as satisfying. Her youth and personality, which were enhanced by her beauty, produced in Jaime Astarloa a state of healthy animation that grew with each passing day. She treated him with a respect not exempt from a strange coquetry. He enjoyed their skirmishing, so much so that, as time passed, he waited ever more eagerly for the moment when she would appear in the gallery, always with the same small travelling bag beneath her arm. He was used now to her leaving the door of the changing room ajar, and he would go in there as soon as she had left, to breathe in the sweet smell of rosewater, which hung in the air like a reminder of her presence. And there were moments, for example, when they looked too long into each other's eyes, when a violent bout of fencing brought them close to physical contact, in which only by dint of great self-discipline did he manage to conceal, beneath a layer of paternal courtesy, the unsettling effect she had on his mind.

The day came when, during a bout, she lunged forward with such force that she hurled herself against Don Jaime's chest. He felt the weight of her body, warm and supple in his arms, and out of pure reflex action he grasped her round the waist, to help her recover her balance. She quickly drew herself up, but her face, covered by the metal mesh of the mask, remained turned for a moment towards his, so close that he could feel her breathing and feel her shining eyes looking at him intensely. Back in the on-guard position again, he was so affected by what had happened that she hit him twice on the chest before he could even think about putting himself properly on defence. Happy to have successfully carried out two attacks, she moved back and forth on the piste, harrying him with lightning-quick thrusts, with improvised attacks and feints, bursting with joy, like a young girl giving herself heart and soul to a game she loved. His calm restored, Don Jaime observed her while he kept her at arm's length, tapping her foil, which clinked against his when she stopped for a moment, sagely studying her opponent's defence while she sought an opening into which she could lunge forward with speed and courage. He had never loved her so much as at that moment.

Later, when she emerged from the changing room in her street clothes, she seemed shaken. She was pale and unsteady on her feet. She passed a hand across her forehead, dropped her hat on the floor and had to use the wall for support. He went over to her, concerned.

"Are you all right?"

"I think so," she said faintly. "It's just the heat."

She leaned on his proffered arm. Her head was bent, and her cheek almost brushed his shoulder.

"It's the first sign of weakness I've ever seen in you, Doña Adela."

A smile lit up the young woman's pale face.

"Consider it a privilege, then," she said.

He accompanied her back to the living room, enjoying the light pressure of her hand on his arm, until she withdrew it in order to sit down on the old, worn leather sofa.

"You need a tonic. Perhaps a sip of brandy."

"Don't bother. I feel much better now."

Don Jaime insisted and walked over to a cupboard. He came back with a glass in his hand.

"Please, drink a little of this. It's good for the blood."

She sipped a little of the brandy and grimaced. He opened the shutters and the window to let in more air and then sat down opposite her, at a safe distance. They remained for a while in silence. On the pretext that he was concerned about her, Don Jaime was looking at her more insistently than he would have dared to in normal circumstances. He stroked the place on his arm where she had rested her hand; he could still feel the pressure of it there.

"Take another sip. It seems to be doing you good."

She nodded obediently. Then she gave him a grateful smile, resting the glass of cognac in her lap, though she had barely touched it. The colour was beginning to return to her cheeks, and she indicated with a lift of her chin the objects filling the room.

"You know," she said in a low, confiding voice, "your house is just like you. Everything is so lovingly preserved that it exudes comfort and a feeling of safety. Here you seem to be safe from everything, as if time had stopped. These walls contain . . . "

"A whole life?"

She pretended to applaud, pleased that he had come up with the right words to complete the sentence.

"Your life," she replied seductively.

Jaime Astarloa got up and walked about the room, silently contemplating the objects she was referring to: the old diploma from the Paris Academy; the coat of arms carved in wood with the motto "To me"; a pair of antique duelling pistols in a glass case; the framed insignia of a Lieutenant of the Royal Guard on a background of green velvet . . . He ran his hand gently over the spines of the books lined up on the oak shelves. Adela de Otero was watching him intently, with her lips half open, trying to capture the distant music of the objects surrounding the fencing master.

"It's a beautiful thing to refuse to forget," she said after a few moments.

He made a helpless gesture, implying that no one can choose his own memories.

"I'm not sure that 'beautiful' is the right word," he said, indicating the walls covered with books. "Sometimes I feel as if I were in a cemetery. It's a very similar feeling, all symbols and silence." He considered what he had just said and smiled sadly. "The silence of all the ghosts that you've left behind you. Like Aeneas fleeing Troy."

"I know what you mean."

"You do? Yes, perhaps. I'm beginning to think that you really do."

"The ghosts of the people we could have been and weren't . . . Isn't that what it is? The people we dreamed of being, until we were forced to wake from the dream." She was talking in a monotone, as if reciting from memory a lesson learned long ago. "The ghosts of those whom once we loved but never had, of those who loved us and whose hopes we destroyed out of malice, stupidity or ignorance."

"Yes, I see you understand perfectly."

Her scar intensified the sarcasm of her smile: "And why shouldn't I? Or do you believe, perhaps, that only men have a Troy they have left burning behind them?"

He sat looking at her, not knowing what to say. She had closed her eyes, listening to far-off voices that only she could hear. Then she blinked, as if waking from a dream, and her eyes met those of the fencing master.

"Yet", she said, "there's no bitterness in you, Don Jaime, no rancour. I'd like to know where you get the strength to remain so intact, so as not to fall on your knees and beg for mercy. You always have that look of the eternal foreigner about you, as if you were somehow absent. It's as if, in your determination to survive, you were storing up strength inside you, like a miser."

He shrugged.

"It's not me," he said in a low voice, almost shyly. "It's my fifty-six years of life, with all the good and ill there was in them. As for you . . . " He stopped, unsure.

"As for me . . . " Her violet eyes had grown inexpressive, as if a veil covered them. Don Jaime shook his head innocently, like a child.

"You're very young. You're at the beginning of everything."

She raised her eyebrows and let out a mirthless laugh.

"I don't even exist," she said.

Jaime Astarloa stared at her, confused. She leaned forward to put the glass down on the table. As she did so, he saw her strong, beautiful neck, bare beneath the mass of jet-black hair caught up at the nape. The last rays of sun were falling on the window, which framed a rectangle of reddish clouds. The reflection of one of the panes flickered on the wall and was gone.

"It's odd," he murmured. "I always prided myself that, after a reasonable period of time spent crossing swords with a person, I somehow knew him. It's not difficult, just a question of exercising one's sense of touch to get inside someone. Everyone reveals who he is when he fences."

"Maybe," she murmured absently, in a dull voice.

He picked up a book at random; then, after holding it for a moment in his hands, he returned it to its place.

"That isn't the case with you," he said. She seemed slowly to come back to herself; her eyes showed a flicker of interest.

"I'm serious," he said. "With you, Doña Adela, all I have seen is your vigour, your aggression. Your movements are unhurried and sure, too agile for a woman, too graceful for a man. You give off a feeling of magnetism, of contained, disciplined energy, and sometimes a dark, inexplicable anger, about whom or what I don't know. Perhaps the answer lies beneath the ashes of that Troy you appear to know so well."

Adela de Otero seemed to be thinking about his words.

"Go on," she said.

He shrugged.

"There's not much more to say," he confessed apologetically. "As you see, I am capable of observing all this, but I can't get to what lies behind it. I'm just an old fencing master with no pretensions to being a philosopher or a moralist."

"You're not doing badly for an old fencing master," remarked the young woman with a wry smile. There was a kind of languid tremor beneath her smooth skin. Outside, the sky above the rooftops of

Madrid was growing dark. A cat walked along the window sill, sly and silent, glancing into the room, which was beginning to fill with shadows, then continuing on its way.

She moved, and there was a rustle of skirts.

"At the wrong time," she said thoughtfully and mysteriously, "on the wrong day . . . in the wrong city." She leaned forward slightly and gave a fleeting smile. "A pity," she added.

Don Jaime looked at her, disoriented. Seeing his expression, the young woman gently opened her lips, then, with a gracious gesture, patted the space on the sofa by her side.

"Come and sit here, Maestro."

From his place by the window, Jaime Astarloa shook his head. The room was nearly dark, veiled in greys and shadows.

"Have you ever loved anyone?" she asked. Her features were beginning to disappear in the encroaching darkness.

"Several people," he said in a melancholy voice.

"Several?" the young woman seemed surprised. "Ah, I see. No, Maestro, I mean have you ever *loved*?"

In the west, the sky was rapidly growing dark. Don Jaime glanced at the unlit oil lamp. Adela de Otero did not seem troubled by the gradual fading of the light.

"Yes, once, in Paris. A long time ago."

"Was she beautiful?"

"Yes. As beautiful as . . . you. Besides, Paris made her even more beautiful: the Latin Quarter, the fitting rooms of elegant shops on the rue St-Germain, dances in La Chaumière and Montparnasse . . . "

The memories came with a pang of nostalgia that made his stomach contract. He turned again to the lamp.

"I think we should . . . "

"Who left whom, Don Jaime?"

He smiled sadly, conscious that she could no longer see his face.

"It was rather more complicated than that. After four years, I forced her to choose. And she did."

The young woman was now a motionless shadow.

"Was she married?"

"Yes, and you are a most intelligent young woman."

"What happened then?"

"I sold everything I had and came back to Spain. It was all a long time ago now."

In the street, with pole and stick, someone was lighting the lamps. The feeble glow of gaslight came in through the open window. She got up from the sofa and walked through the darkness to his side. She stood there, next to the window.

"There's an English poet," she said in a low voice, "Lord Byron."

Don Jaime waited in silence. He could feel the warmth emanating from the young body at his side, almost brushing his own. His throat was dry, tight with the fear that she might hear his heart beating. Her voice was quiet, like a caress: "The Devil speaks truth much oftener than he's deem'd. He hath an ignorant audience."

She drew closer to him. The glow from the street lit up the lower part of her face, her chin and mouth.

There was a profound silence that seemed to last an eternity. Only when that silence became unbearable, did she speak again: "There's always a story to tell."

She spoke in such a low voice that Don Jaime had to guess at her words. She was so close that he could almost feel on his skin the delicate smell of rosewater. He realized that he was beginning to lose his head and sought desperately for something that would anchor him in reality. He reached out his hand to the lamp and lit it with a match. The smoking flame trembled in his hands.

He insisted on accompanying her to Calle Riaño. It was too late, he said, not daring to look her in the eye, to be out alone trying to find a carriage. So he put on a jacket, picked up his walking stick and top hat, and went down the stairs ahead of her. At the door he stopped and, after a brief hesitation that did not escape her, offered her his arm with all the icy courtesy he could muster. The young woman leaned on him and, as they walked along, she turned now and then to glance at him out of the corner of her eye, with a look of concealed mockery. Don Jaime hired a calash whose driver was dozing, leaning against a lamp-post; they got in, and Don Jaime gave the address. The carriage went down Calle Arenal, turning to the right when it reached the Palacio de Oriente. Don Jaime remained silent, his hands resting on the handle of his walking stick, vainly trying to keep his mind a blank. What might have happened did not happen, but he was not sure if he should congratulate himself or despise himself. As for what Adela de Otero might be thinking at that moment, he had absolutely no desire to know. However, one certainty floated in the air: that night, at the end of a conversation which should have brought them closer, something had been broken between them, definitively and for ever. He did not know what, but that was the least of it; there was the unmistakable noise of pieces shattering to the ground about him. The young woman would never forgive him for his cowardice – or for his resignation.

They rode in silence, each occupying a corner of the red-upholstered seat. Sometimes, when they passed beneath a lamp-post, a fragment of light spilled into the carriage, allowing Don Jaime to catch a glimpse of his companion's profile, absorbed in the contemplation of the shadows filling the streets. He would like to have said something to relieve the unease tormenting him, but he feared that he would only make matters worse. The whole thing was utterly absurd.

After a while, Adela de Otero turned to him.

"I've been told, Don Jaime, that you have people of quality amongst your clientèle. Is that right?"

"It is."

"People from the nobility too? I mean counts, dukes and all that."

Jaime Astarloa was relieved to embark on a topic of conversation completely different from that which had taken place in his house a while before. She was doubtless conscious that things might have gone too far. Perhaps, sensing his awkwardness, she was trying to break the ice after that embarrassing situation in which she too had played some part.

"Some yes," he replied, "but not many, I confess. The days are long gone when a *maître d'armes* of some prestige could set himself up in Vienna or St Petersburg and be named captain of an imperial regiment. The nobility today have little interest in practising my art."

"And who are the honourable exceptions?"

Don Jaime shrugged.

"Two or three. The son of the Conde de Sueca, the Marqués de los Alumbres . . . "

"Luis de Ayala?"

He looked at her, making no attempt to conceal his surprise.

"Do you know Don Luis?"

"I've heard people talk about him," she said with perfect indifference. "I've heard that he's one of the best swordsmen in Madrid."

He nodded, pleased.

"He is."

"Better than me?" Now there was a note of interest in her voice.

He snorted, finding himself in a tight spot: "You have completely different styles."

Adela de Otero adopted a frivolous tone: "I would love to fence with him. They say he's a most interesting man."

"I'm afraid that's impossible."

"Why? I don't see what the difficulty is."

"Well, I mean . . . "

"I'd like to have a couple of bouts with him. Have you taught *him* the two hundred escudo thrust as well?"

Don Jaime shifted uneasily in his seat. He was beginning to feel worried by the fact that he was worried.

"Your request, Doña Adela, is a little . . . um . . . irregular," he said, frowning. "I don't know if the Marquis . . . "

"Are you very close?"

"Well, he honours me with his friendship, if that's what you mean."

She took his arm, with such girlish enthusiasm that Jaime Astarloa found it hard to recognize the young woman who, only half an hour before, had been talking to him in the grave intimacy of his living room.

"There's no problem, then!" she exclaimed, satisfied. "Tell him about me; tell him the truth, that I'm good with a foil, and I'm sure he'll want to meet me: after all, a woman who fences . . . "

Don Jaime stammered a few unconvincing excuses, but she returned to the charge again and again: "By now, Maestro, you must be aware that I know no one in Madrid, apart from you. I'm a woman and I can't go knocking on doors with my foil under my arm."

"I should hope not!" Don Jaime's exclamation arose this time from his sense of decorum.

"You see? I would die of embarrassment."

"It's not just that. Don Luis de Ayala is very strict in matters of fencing. I don't know what he would think if a woman . . . "

"You took me on, Maestro."

"Exactly. I'm a fencing master by profession. Don Luis de Ayala's profession is being a marquis."

The young woman let out a brief laugh, mischievous and gay.

"The first time you visited me at home, you said that you refused as a matter of principle . . . "

"Professional curiosity got the better of me."

They crossed Calle de la Princesa and drove by the Palacio de Liria. A few smartly dressed passers-by were walking in the cool, beneath the tremulous light of the street lamps. A bored watchman touched his cap at the calash, believing that it was heading for the residence of the Duke and Duchess of Alba.

"Promise you'll tell the Marquis about me!"

"I never promise anything that I'm not prepared to do."

"Maestro, anyone would think you were jealous."

Jaime Astarloa felt a wave of heat rising to his head. His face was hidden, but he was sure that he had flushed bright red to his ears. He sat with his mouth open, unable to articulate a word, feeling a strange knot forming in his throat. "She's right," he said to himself in a rush, "she's quite right. I'm behaving like a little boy." He breathed deeply, ashamed of himself, and banged on the floor of the calash with the tip of his walking cane.

"Very well, I'll try, but I'm not promising anything."

She clapped her hands like a happy child and, leaning towards him, she squeezed his hand. Too warmly, perhaps, to be out of mere gratitude for his granting her wish. And he thought that Adela de Otero was, without the slightest doubt, a most disconcerting woman.

Jaime Astarloa reluctantly kept his word, tactfully approaching the subject during a fencing session at the house of the Marqués de los Alumbres: "A young fencer, you know who I mean, indeed you yourself evinced some curiosity about her once. You know how young people like to break with tradition and all that. She's undoubtedly an enthusiast for our art, gifted, with a good hand. If it were anyone else, I would never dare to mention it. If you think . . . "

Luis de Ayala stroked his waxed moustache with great satisfaction. Of course. He'd be delighted.

"And she's beautiful, you say?"

Don Jaime felt irritated with himself and cursed what he deemed to be his ignoble role as procurer. On the other hand, what Adela de Otero had said in the carriage kept coming back to him, with painful persistence. At his age, it was ridiculous to discover that he could still be pricked by jealousy.

The introductions took place in Don Jaime's gallery when, two days later, the Marquis just happened to be passing at the time when Adela de Otero was having her fencing lesson with Don Jaime. They exchanged the usual courtesies and Luis de Ayala – who was sporting a mauve satin tie with a diamond tiepin, embroidered silk socks and an impeccably waxed moustache – humbly asked if he might watch. He leaned against the wall, arms folded, and adopted the grave expression of a connoisseur, whilst the young woman, with absolute aplomb, gave one of the best displays of fencing that Don Jaime had ever seen from a student. From his corner, the Marquis burst into applause, obviously completely charmed.

"Madam, it has been an honour to watch you."

Her violet eyes fixed on Ayala's with such intensity that the Marquis loosened his collar with his finger. In them there was a spark of defiance, of provocative promise. At the first opportunity, the Marquis went over to the fencing master and said quietly: "What a fascinating woman!"

Don Jaime watched all this with an ill humour that he struggled to hide beneath an attitude of cold professionalism. When the bout was over, Luis de Ayala launched into a long technical conversation with the young woman, while the fencing master returned the foils, plastrons and masks to their places. The Marquis was offering, with exquisite gallantry, to accompany her to her house. His phaeton, along with his English coachman, were waiting outside in the street and it would be a pleasure to place them at her entire disposal. They obviously had a lot to talk about, given their mutual love of fencing. Perhaps later that evening at nine, she would care to go to the concert in the gardens in the Campos Elíseos. The Society of Music Teachers, conducted by Gaztambide, was performing Rossini's *La Gazza Ladra* and a medley from *Roberto el Diablo*. Adela de Otero bowed graciously and accepted, charmed. Her face was still flushed from her exertions, which only made her look even more seductive.

While she was changing, with the door closed this time, Luis de Ayala invited Don Jaime to come too, out of pure politeness, but without much enthusiasm, since it was obvious that he was not keen for him to accept. Feeling that he would be the odd man out in the party, Don Jaime declined and merely smiled awkwardly, in dumb anguish. The Marquis was a formidable opponent and Jaime Astarloa sensed that he had lost the game before even daring to begin. The Marquis and Adela de Otero walked off together arm in arm, talking animatedly, and Don Jaime listened in painful impotence as their footsteps disappeared down the stairs.

He paced about the house all day like a caged lion, cursing loudly. On one occasion he stopped and looked at his face in the mirrors in the gallery.

"What else did you expect?" he asked himself scornfully.

In the mirror, the grey-haired image of an old man made a bitter face.

Several days passed. Gagged by the censors, the newspapers could only hint at political difficulties. It was said that Don Juan Prim had obtained permission from Napoleon III to take the waters in Vichy. Troubled by the proximity of the conspirator, González Bravo's government made its unease known, through various channels, to the

94

Emperor of France. In London, while he was packing his bags, Prim held intense meetings with his fellow conspirators and managed to persuade various important people to open their purse strings for the Cause. A revolution without sufficient financial backing ran the risk of being a botched job, and the hero of Castillejos, having got his fingers burned with previous failures, was not prepared to take any chances.

In Madrid, González Bravo repeated, with a certain raffish charm, the words he had pronounced on the day he took up his post in Congress: "As a government, we vow to resist revolution; we have confidence in the country, and the conspirators will find that we will stand our ground. It is not I who preside over the Council of Ministers, but the ghost of General Narváez."

However, the ghost of the great man from Loja did not give a damn about the rebels. Seeing the way the land lay, the generals, who before had been quite happy to put the people to the sword, now passed en masse over to the side of the revolution, although they were still not prepared to show their cards until the thing was done. Quietly soaking in Lequeitio, far from the hotbed of Madrid, Isabel II was uncertain what to do, and as a last resort she turned to General Pezuela, the Conde de Cheste, who stroked the pommel of his sabre and made fervent vows of loyalty to her.

"If we have to die defending the royal chamber, so be it; that, after all, is what we are here for."

Trusting for the moment in his bizarre promise, the government press tried to calm the country by publishing endless news items about how everything was continuing to function normally. A popular song had become fashionable in pro-government papers:

Lots of people live quite happily on hope,
and lots of donkeys eat green grass . . .

Jaime Astarloa had lost a client. Adela de Otero no longer came to her fencing lessons. She was seen about Madrid, invariably accompanied by the Marqués de los Alumbres: walking in the Retiro Gardens, riding in a carriage along the Prado, at the Teatro Rossini or in a box at the Zarzuela. This caused great cluckings amongst the cream of

Madrid society, who tapped one another with their fans and discreetly elbowed one another, asking who this young woman was who had so obviously set her cap at that rake Luis de Ayala. Nobody knew where she had sprung from, nothing was known about her family, and she seemed to have no social contacts at all, apart from the Marquis. The sharpest tongues in Madrid spent two weeks in arduous speculations and investigations, but, in the end, they had to declare themselves defeated. All they could say for certain about the young woman was that she had recently arrived from abroad, which doubtless explained why she did certain things which were improper in a lady.

Somewhat muted versions of these rumours reached Don Jaime's ears, and he took them all in with due stoicism. He even imposed this exquisite prudence on the daily fencing bouts he continued to have with Luis de Ayala. He never showed the slightest curiosity about the young woman's life and the Marquis did not seem inclined to keep him up to date. Only once, while both were savouring their usual glass of sherry after a couple of bouts, the aristocrat placed a hand on his shoulder and, smiling in a friendly, confidential manner, said: "Maestro, I owe my happiness to you."

Don Jaime accepted the remark with the necessary aplomb and that was that. A few days later, the fencing master received the second money order signed by Adela de Otero in payment of his fees for the last few weeks. It was accompanied by a brief note:

I regret to say that I no longer have time to continue our very interesting fencing sessions. I would like to thank you for your kindness and to assure you that I will never forget you.
Yours sincerely,
Adela de Otero

He frowned as he re-read the letter several times. Then he put it down on the table, picked up a pen and did his sums. He immediately took out some writing paper and dipped his pen in the inkwell:

Dear Madam,
I note with surprise that in the second money order which you sent me you include payment for nine fencing sessions this month,

when, in fact, I only had the pleasure of taking you for three.
I am, therefore, returning to you the excess amount of three
hundred and sixty reales.

Yours faithfully,
Jaime Astarloa
Fencing Master

He signed the letter and then threw the pen down on the table in
irritation. A few drops of ink spattered Adela de Otero's letter. He
waved it about in the air so that the blots could dry, then studied the
young woman's edgy handwriting, for the strokes were long and
sharp as daggers. He was not sure whether to tear it up or to keep it,
but finally decided to keep it. When his pain had lessened, that
piece of paper would be just another memory. Mentally, Don Jaime
consigned it to the overflowing trunk of his nostalgias.

That afternoon, the meeting at the Café Progreso broke up earlier
than usual. Agapito Cárceles was hard at work on an article which he
had to deliver that evening and Carreño assured them that he had an
extraordinary meeting to go to at the San Miguel lodge. Don Lucas
had gone home early, complaining of a slight summer cold, so Jaime
Astarloa was left alone with Marcelino Romero, the piano teacher.
They decided to take a walk, now that the heat of the day had given
way to a warm evening breeze. They strolled down the Carrera de San
Jerónimo; Don Jaime doffed his hat when they passed acquaintances
of his near Lhardy's and at the door of the Athenaeum. Romero was
his usual placid, melancholy self and walked along staring at the tips
of his toes, sunk in his own thoughts. He was wearing a crumpled
cravat and his hat was pushed too far back on his head. The cuffs of
his shirt were distinctly grubby.

The Paseo del Prado was seething with people strolling beneath the
trees. On the wrought-iron benches, soldiers and maidservants were
exchanging compliments and jokes whilst enjoying the last of the
sun. A few elegant gentlemen, either in the company of ladies or out
with a group of friends, walked back and forth between the fountains

97

of Cibeles and Neptune, affectedly swinging their walking sticks and raising a hand to their hats whenever a respectable or interesting woman rustled past. Open carriages drove down the sandy central avenue in the reddish evening light, carrying women wearing hats and parasols of every conceivable hue. A ruddy-faced Colonel from the Engineers, his chest emblazoned with heroic hardware, and wearing a sash and sabre, was placidly smoking a cigar while he talked in a low voice with his adjutant, a buck-toothed Captain, who kept gravely and cautiously nodding; they were clearly talking about politics. The Colonel's wife followed a few steps behind, her ample flesh precariously corseted into a dress thick with lace and ribbons, while the maid, in apron and cap, shepherded a flock of about half a dozen children of both sexes, all lace edgings and black stockings. In the square, a couple of fops with brilliantined hair parted in the middle were twirling their waxed moustaches and casting furtive glances at a young woman, who, beneath the vigilant gaze of her governess, was reading a volume of short poems by Campoamor, oblivious of the expectation aroused in the two inquisitive observers by her small, slender foot and two tempting inches of delicate ankle encased in white stocking.

The two friends walked calmly along, enjoying the pleasant temperature; the fencing master's old-fashioned elegance presented a stark contrast to the pianist's rumpled appearance. Romero eyed a man selling ice-cream wafers, who was spinning the wheel of his machine, surrounded by children. Romero turned glumly to his friend and asked: "How are you off for money, Don Jaime?"

Don Jaime gave him a friendly, mocking look.

"Don't tell me you want to buy a wafer."

The music teacher blushed. Most of his students had gone away on holiday and he was down to his last penny. In summer, he usually lived by scrounging discreetly off his friends.

Don Jaime put a hand in his waistcoat pocket.

"How much do you need?"

"Twenty reales will do."

Don Jaime took out a silver duro and slipped it into the hand that his friend held shyly out to him. Romero muttered a hurried excuse:

"My landlady . . . "

Jaime Astarloa cut short the explanation with an understanding gesture; he was familiar with his situation. His friend sighed gratefully.

"We're living in difficult times, Don Jaime."

"We are indeed."

"A time of anxiety and unrest . . . " The pianist raised a hand to his heart, feeling for a non-existent wallet. "A time of solitude."

Jaime Astarloa grunted non-committally. Romero interpreted that as a sign of agreement and seemed to find it comforting.

"Love, Don Jaime, love," he went on, after a moment of sad reflection. "That is the only thing that can make us happy and, paradoxically, it is also the thing that condemns us to our worst torments. To love is to be enslaved."

"You're only a slave if you expect something from others," said Don Jaime, giving his friend such a piercing look that the latter blinked, confused. "Perhaps that's where you make your mistake. If you need nothing from anyone, then you're free. Like Diogenes in his barrel."

The pianist shook his head; he didn't agree.

"A world in which we expected nothing from anyone would be an inferno, Don Jaime. Do you know what the worst thing is?"

"The worst thing, I find, is always a very personal matter. What is the worst thing for you?"

"For me, it's the absence of hope. To feel that one has fallen into a trap and . . . I mean, there are terrible moments when it seems that there is simply no way out."

"There are traps with no way out."

"Don't say that."

"I would remind you, though, that no trap is successful without the unconscious complicity of the victim. Nobody forces the mouse to look for the cheese in the mousetrap."

"But the search for love, for happiness . . . Why, I myself . . . "

Jaime Astarloa turned rather brusquely towards his friend. Without quite knowing why, he felt irritated by his friend's melancholy expression, so like that of a hunted fawn. He felt tempted to be cruel.

"Then kidnap her, Don Marcelino," he said.

The other man's Adam's apple rose and fell rapidly, as he swallowed hard.

"Who?"

There was alarm and panic in the question, as well as a plea, which the fencing master chose to ignore.

"You know perfectly well who I mean. If you really love the good woman, then don't just languish beneath her balcony for the rest of your life. Go in there and throw yourself at her feet, seduce her, trample her virtue, drag her out of there by force. Shoot the husband, or yourself! Either do something heroic or simply make a complete and utter fool of yourself, but for God's sake, do something. After all, you're only forty!"

His unexpected, brutal eloquence had erased from Romero's face the slightest sign of life. The blood had drained from his cheeks, and for a moment he looked as if he were going to turn tail and run.

"I'm not a violent man," he stammered at last, as if that justified everything.

Jaime Astarloa gave him a hard look. For the first time, the pianist's shyness did not inspire compassion in him, only disdain. How different everything would have been had Don Jaime met Adela de Otero when he was Romero's age.

"I'm not talking about the violence that Cárceles preaches at our meetings," he said. "I mean the violence that is born of personal courage," he indicated his own chest. "Here."

Romero had moved from concern to distrust; he toyed nervously with his cravat, whilst avoiding his friend's eyes.

"I'm against all kinds of violence, personal or collective."

"Well, I'm not. There are very subtle shades of violence, I can assure you. A civilization that renounces the possibility of resorting to violence in thought or deed destroys itself. It becomes a flock of sheep, which will get their throats cut by the first person to come along. The same thing happens with men."

"And what about the Catholic Church? The Church is against violence and during the two thousand years of its existence it has never once had to resort to it."

"Don't make me laugh, Don Marcelino. Christianity was sustained by Constantine's legions and by the swords of the crusaders, and the Catholic Church by the Inquisition's bonfires, by the galleys at Lepanto and by the Habsburgs' infantrymen. Who do you think will support your cause?"

The pianist lowered his eyes.

"I'm disappointed in you, Don Jaime," he said after a moment, digging the tip of his walking stick into the sandy ground. "I never suspected that you shared Agapito Cárceles's views."

"I don't share anyone's views. Quite apart from anything else, I couldn't care less about the principle of equality, which our friend defends with such brio. But now that you mention the subject, I can tell you that I would rather be governed by a Caesar or a Bonaparte, whom I could always try to assassinate if I didn't care for him, than have my tastes, customs and the company I keep decided by the vote of the shopkeeper on the corner. The tragedy of our century, Don Marcelino, is its lack of genius, comparable only to its lack of courage and its lack of good taste. Doubtless this is due to the irresistible rise of shopkeepers all over Europe."

"According to Cárceles, those shopkeepers' days are numbered," said Romero with a touch of timid rancour; the husband of his beloved was a well-known grocer.

"All the worse for us, because we know only too well what he offers as an alternative. Do you know what the problem is? We find ourselves in the last of the three generations history chooses to repeat every now and then. The first generation needs a god, and so they invent one. The second erects temples to that god and tries to imitate him. And the third uses the marble from those temples to build brothels in which to worship their own greed, lust and dishonesty. And that is why gods and heroes are always, inevitably, succeeded by mediocrities, cowards and imbeciles. Good afternoon, Don Marcelino."

Without the slightest twinge of remorse, Don Jaime stood there, leaning on his walking stick while he watched the wretched pianist depart, his head sunk between his shoulders, doubtless on his way to resume his desperate patrol beneath the balcony in Calle Hortaleza.

Jaime Astarloa remained for a while watching the passers-by, although still absorbed in thoughts about his own situation. He knew very well that some of the things he had said to Romero could easily be applied to himself, and knowing that made him feel far from happy. After a while, he decided to go home. He walked in leisurely fashion up Calle Atocha and stopped at his usual pharmacist to replenish his supply of alcohol and liniment. The lame assistant who served him was his usual friendly self, enquiring after his health.

"I can't complain," said Don Jaime. "These remedies, as you know, are for my students."

"Are you not going away for the summer? The Queen is already in Lequeitio. The whole court will be there, unless Don Juan Prim steps in. Now there's a man for you!" The assistant slapped his lame leg proudly. "You should have seen him at the Battle of Castillejos, riding along as calmly as if he were out for a Sunday trot on an August afternoon, and all the while the Moors were closing round us like devils. I had the honour to be by his side then, and to be wounded for my country. When I got hit on the leg by a stone, Don Juan turned and looked at me and he said in that Catalan accent of his: 'Why, that's nothing, boy.' I gave three loud cheers as they carried me off on a stretcher. He probably still remembers me!"

Don Jaime went out into the street with the package under his arm, past the Palacio de Santa Cruz and under the arches to the Plaza Mayor, where he remained for a few moments amongst the crowd of people listening to the martial music of a military band beneath the equestrian statue of Felipe III. He was walking out onto Calle Mayor, intending to have supper at Pereira's before going home, when he stopped short, as if someone had struck him a blow. On the other side of the street, leaning out of a carriage window, was Adela de Otero. She didn't notice him, being occupied in a discreet dialogue with a middle-aged gentleman wearing a tailcoat and top hat, holding a walking stick, and resting nonchalantly on the frame of the carriage window.

Don Jaime did not move, but watched the scene. The gentleman, with his back to him, was turned towards the young woman and talking in a low, restrained voice. She was unusually serious, now and then shaking her head. She murmured a couple of grave remarks, and her companion nodded. Don Jaime was about to continue on his way, but curiosity got the better of him, and he stayed where he was, trying to silence any scruples he had about allowing himself to indulge in such an unequivocal, unworthy act of espionage. He listened hard to capture some fragment of the conversation, but all in vain. The speakers were too far away.

The gentleman still had his back to him, but Don Jaime was sure that he did not know him. Adela de Otero suddenly made a negative gesture with the fan she was holding and then began to say something, meanwhile looking vaguely down the street. She suddenly noticed Jaime Astarloa, who began to raise his hand to his hat by way of greeting. His gesture was interrupted halfway, though, when he saw the extraordinary look of alarm in the young woman's eyes. She hurriedly withdrew her head and hid inside the carriage, while the gentleman, clearly worried, half-turned towards Don Jaime. She must have shouted an order, because the coachman, who had been lounging in his seat, suddenly jumped and whipped the horses into a trot. The stranger drew back and walked rapidly away in the opposite direction, swinging his stick. Don Jaime only saw his face for a moment, but caught a glimpse of long sideburns and a thin, neat moustache. He was an elegant man of medium height and distinguished appearance; he was carrying an ivory walking stick and seemed to be in a great hurry.

Don Jaime gave a great deal of thought to the incident that he had witnessed, but found himself incapable of interpreting it. He went over and over it in his mind while he ate his frugal supper and, even back in the solitude of his rooms, he continued to struggle vainly to throw light on the mystery. He felt a need to know who that man was.

However, something else intrigued him still more. When she saw him, Jaime Astarloa had glimpsed an expression he had never seen before on her face. There was no surprise or irritation, which would have been understandable, on her finding herself observed with such frank impertinence. What he had seen was something much darker and more troubling, so much so that it took him a while to be sure that his intuition was not deceiving him; for what he had seen in Adela de Otero's eyes, for a fraction of a second, was fear.

He woke suddenly, sitting up anxiously in bed. His body was drenched in sweat from the terrible nightmare which, even with his eyes now open to the darkness, remained fixed upon his retina. A cardboard doll was floating face down, as if drowned. Its hair was entangled with the lilies and slimy weeds floating on the surface of stagnant, green water. He was bending over the doll with exasperating slowness and when he picked it up, he saw its face – the glass eyes had been torn from their sockets. The sight of those empty sockets made a shudder of horror run through him.

He remained upright for hours, unable to get back to sleep until the first light of day filtered through the shutters on the windows.

Luis de Ayala had seemed restless for some days. He found it hard to concentrate on their bouts, as if his thoughts were far from fencing.

"Touché, Excellency."

The Marquis gave a sad, apologetic shake of his head.

"I'm not having much luck, Maestro."

His usual good cheer had given way to a strange melancholy. He was often abstracted and he rarely joked. At first, Don Jaime put it down to the volatile political situation. Prim had been seen in Vichy and then had mysteriously disappeared. The whole court was spending the summer in the north, but the main political and military personalities were still in Madrid, waiting. Winds were blowing that augured nothing but ill for the monarchy.

One morning, during the dying days of August, when the fencing master made his daily visit, Luis de Ayala excused himself: "I'm not in the mood today, Don Jaime. My hand's not steady enough."

He suggested that they go for a walk in the garden. They strolled beneath the willows, along the gravel path that led past the water singing in the fountain with the stone angel. A gardener was working some way off, amongst clumps of flowers drooping in the heat of the morning.

They walked for a while, exchanging trivial remarks. When they came to a wrought-iron shrine, the Marqués de los Alumbres turned to Jaime Astarloa with a casual air that was soon belied by his words: "Maestro, I would be interested to know how you met Adela de Otero."

Don Jaime was surprised, for this was the first time since the day when he had introduced them both that Luis de Ayala had mentioned her name in his presence. Nevertheless, as coolly and briefly as he could, Don Jaime told him what he knew. The Marquis listened in silence, nodding now and then. He seemed worried. Then he asked if Don Jaime knew any of her social contacts, friends or relatives, and the fencing master repeated what he had said during the conversation they had had weeks before. He knew nothing about her, apart from the fact that she lived alone and was an excellent fencer. For a moment, he was tempted to tell the Marquis about the mysterious meeting he had witnessed near the Plaza Mayor, but decided instead to say nothing. He did not want to betray what, given the young woman's attitude, must be a secret.

The Marquis was also interested to find out if Adela de Otero had mentioned his name before he met her at Don Jaime's house, and if at any time she had shown a particular interest in meeting him. After a slight hesitation, Don Jaime said that she had, and he gave a brief summary of their conversation in the hired carriage on the night when he had taken her home.

"She knew that you were an excellent fencer and insisted on meeting you," he said honestly, although he sensed that there must be an unusual reason behind Luis de Ayala's curiosity. Nevertheless, he remained discreet, expecting no clarification on the part of the Marquis, who was smiling now with a Mephistophelian air.

"I see that what I've said amuses you," said Jaime, rather annoyed, thinking that he saw in his client's face a mocking allusion to the unpleasant role of procurer which Don Jaime had been obliged to play in the matter.

The Marquis immediately caught Don Jaime's meaning: "Don't misunderstand me, Maestro," he said affectionately. "I was thinking about myself. You may not believe it, but this story has, I assure you, acquired quite fascinating depths. In fact," he added, smiling again, as if amused at his own thoughts, "you have just confirmed a couple of ideas that have been going through my head lately. Our young friend is, indeed, an excellent fencer. Let's see now how good she is at hitting the target."

Jaime Astarloa fidgeted, embarrassed. The unexpected turn the conversation had taken plunged him into a sea of confusion.

"I'm sorry, Excellency, I don't quite understand . . . "

The Marquis made a gesture asking him to be patient.

"Calm down, Don Jaime, all in good time. I promise I will tell you everything . . . later. When I have solved a little matter that is still pending."

Don Jaime fell into an uneasy silence. Did this have anything to do with the mysterious conversation he had witnessed weeks before? Was there some amorous rivalry? Whatever it was, Adela de Otero was no business of his. Not any longer, he said to himself. He was just about to open his mouth to say something to alter the course of the conversation, when Luis de Ayala placed a hand on his shoulder. He looked unusually serious.

"Maestro, I'm going to ask you a favour."

Don Jaime drew himself up, the very image of honesty and integrity.

"At your orders, Excellency."

The Marquis hesitated for a moment, then seemed to overcome any remaining scruples he might have. He lowered his voice.

"I need to give something to you for safekeeping. Until now I have kept it with me, but for reasons which I will soon explain, I feel it necessary to find a temporary hiding place for it. Can I count on you?"

"Of course."

"It's a file containing papers which are of vital importance to me. You may not believe it, but there are very few people whom I could trust with this matter. You need merely keep them in some suitable place in your house until I ask for them back. They're in an envelope sealed with my personal seal. Naturally, I have your word of honour that you will not look at the contents, and that you will maintain absolute silence on the subject."

Don Jaime frowned. All this was very strange, but the Marquis had mentioned the words "honour" and "trust". There was no more to be said.

"You have my word."

The Marquis smiled and seemed suddenly to relax.

"You have my eternal gratitude, Don Jaime."

Don Jaime said nothing, wondering if the matter had anything to do with Adela de Otero. The question burned on his lips, but he managed to keep his thoughts to himself. The Marquis trusted in his honour as a gentleman and that was all that was needed. There would be time enough, Ayala had promised him, for explanations.

The Marquis took a beautiful Russian leather cigar case from his pocket and drew out a long Havana cigar. He offered one to Don Jaime, who declined courteously.

"It's your loss," said the Marquis. "They're from Vuelta Abajo in Cuba, a taste I inherited from my late Uncle Joaquín. Nothing like the cheap rubbish you can buy in the tobacco shops here."

With that the matter seemed closed. Don Jaime, however, had one question to ask: "Why me, Excellency?"

Luis de Ayala paused in lighting his cigar and looked at Don Jaime over the flame of his match.

"For one simple reason, Don Jaime. You are the only honest man I know."

Applying the flame to his cigar, the Marquis inhaled the smoke with sensuous pleasure.

V

Glissade

"The glissade or coulé is one of the surest attacks in fencing,
obliging one to cover oneself."

Madrid was sleeping out the siesta, lulled by the last heat of summer. The political life of the capital continued, though becalmed in the quiet of a sultry September, beneath leaden clouds, through which filtered only a suffocating summer torpor. The pro-government press hinted that the exiled generals in the Canaries were still quiet, but denied that the conspiratorial tentacles had reached the navy which, contrary to ill-intentioned, subversive rumours, remained, as always, loyal to Her August Majesty. As regards public order, it had been several weeks since there had been any kind of disturbance in Madrid, after the exemplary punishment meted out by the authorities to the leaders of the last popular uprising, who now had more than enough time to ponder their folly in the uninviting shade of Ceuta prison.

Antonio Carreño brought fresh rumours to the gathering at the Café Progreso: "Listen carefully, gentlemen. I have it on good authority that things are on the move."

He was greeted by a chorus of jeering scepticism. Carreño placed his hand on his heart, offended.

"Surely you don't doubt my word . . . "

Lucas Rioseco said that no one doubted his word, only the veracity of his sources; he had been announcing the Second Coming for almost a year now.

Adopting his usual tone of cautious confidence, Carreño beckoned them all towards him over the marble table top: "This time, gentlemen, it's serious. López de Ayala has gone to the Canaries to interview the exiled generals. And, wait for it, Don Juan Prim has disappeared from his house in London. Whereabouts unknown. You know what that means."

Agapito Cárceles was the only one to give any credit to the matter: "It means there's going to be a real rumpus."

Jaime Astarloa crossed his legs. These endless prophecies had come to bore him unspeakably. In a furtive tone, Carreño continued to impart information about the current conspiracy.

"They say that Prim has been seen in Lisbon, disguised as a footman, and that the Mediterranean fleet is only waiting for his arrival to give the cry."

"What cry?" asked the innocent Marcelino Romero.

"What cry do you think, man? The cry of freedom."

Don Lucas gave an incredulous little laugh.

"It's like something out of a Dumas melodrama, Don Antonio, published in instalments."

Carreño fell silent, wounded by the old man's reluctance to believe him. To avenge his colleague, Agapito Cárceles launched into a heated revolutionary harangue directed exclusively at Don Lucas.

"The moment has arrived to take your places at the barricades!" he concluded, like a character out of a play by Tamayo y Baus.

"See you there, then!" proclaimed a needled Don Lucas in an equally theatrical manner. "With you on one side and me on the other, of course."

"Of course! I never doubted for a moment, Señor Rioseco, that your place would be amongst the ranks of repression and obscurantism."

"And most honoured to be there."

"Honour has nothing to do with it. The truth is that the only honourable Spain is a revolutionary Spain. Your meekness is enough to grate on the nerves of any patriot worth his salt, Don Lucas."

"Well, have some camomile tea then."

"Long live the republic!"

"Oh, who cares!"

"Long live the federal state!"

"Fine, man, fine. Fausto! Bring me some toast!"

"Long live the rule of law!"

"The only law this country needs is one that allows for people to be shot while escaping."

Thunder rumbled over the rooftops of Madrid. The heavens opened and a violent rainstorm ensued. On the other side of the street, you could see people running for shelter. Jaime Astarloa sipped his coffee and looked sadly out at the rain beating against the window panes. The cat, which had gone out for a stroll, bounded back in, its fur standing up in damp spikes, a scrawny image of misfortune which fixed the fencing master with suspicious, malevolent eyes.

"Modern fencing technique, gentlemen, tends to do away with the delightful freedom of movement that gives our art its special grace. That very much limits possibilities."

The two Cazorla brothers and Álvaro Salanova were listening attentively, foils and masks beneath their arms. Manuel de Soto was not there; he was spending the summer with his family in the north.

"All this", Jaime Astarloa continued, "greatly impoverishes fencing. For example, some fencers now neglect to take off their masks and to salute their seconds . . . "

"But there are no seconds in fencing bouts, Maestro," said the younger of the Cazorla brothers timidly.

"Exactly, sir, exactly. You have put your finger on the problem. People take up fencing now without thinking about its practical applications in the field of honour. After all, they say, it's a sport, isn't it? That is a complete aberration; it is as if, to give a wild example, priests were to start saying mass in Spanish. That would, of course, be more up to date, more popular, if you like, more in keeping with the times, don't you think? Nevertheless, to give up the lovely, albeit somewhat hermetic sonority of the Latin language would be to tear the ritual out by its deepest roots, degrading it, vulgarizing it. Beauty, beauty with a capital B, can be found only in the cult of tradition, in the rigorous exercise of those gestures and words that have been repeated and preserved by men down the centuries. Do you understand what I mean?"

The three young men nodded gravely, more out of respect for their teacher than out of conviction. Don Jaime raised a hand, executing a few fencing movements in the air, as if he were holding a foil.

"Of course, we mustn't close our eyes to useful innovations," he went on. "But we must always remember that beauty resides in preserving precisely what others allow to fall away. Don't you find a fallen monarch far worthier of your loyalty than one who is still on the throne? That is why our art must maintain its purity, must remain uncontaminated, classical, yes, above all else, classical. Those who restrict themselves to acquiring mere technique deserve our pity. You, my young friends, have the marvellous opportunity to acquire an art. That is something, believe me, that money cannot buy, something that you carry here, in your hearts and in your minds."

He stopped talking and studied the three faces looking at him with reverent attention. He indicated the older Cazorla brother.

"But that's enough talk. You, Don Fernando, will practise with me the circular parry in seconde, croisé of seconde. I remind you that this manoeuvre must be done cleanly; never use it with an opponent who is physically much stronger than yourself. Do you remember the theory?"

The young man nodded proudly.

"Yes, Maestro." And he recited by heart, like a schoolboy, "If I do a circular parry in seconde and I can't find my opponent's foil, I croisé in seconde, disengage and lunge in quarte over the arm."

"Perfect," said Don Jaime, selecting a foil from his collection while Fernando Cazorla put on his mask. "Ready? Let's get down to business then. Of course, we mustn't forget the salute. That's it. You stretch out your arm and raise your fist, like that. Do it as if you were wearing an imaginary hat. You take it off with your left hand, elegantly. Perfect." He turned to the other two lads. "You must remember that the salutes in quarte and tierce are for the seconds and the witnesses. One assumes that such events would normally take place amongst the well born. We can hardly object if two men insist on killing each other over a point of honour, can we? But we can at least demand that they do so as politely as possible."

He crossed his foil with Fernando Cazorla's. The young man flexed his wrist while he waited for Don Jaime to present him with the thrust that would initiate the movement. In the mirrors in the gallery, their images multiplied, as if the room were full of fencers. The fencing master's voice rang out, calm and patient: "That's it, very good. To me. Good. Careful now, circular parry in seconde. No, do it again, please. That's it. Circular parry in seconde. Parry! No, please remember you have to parry in seconde and immediately disengage. Once more, if you wouldn't mind. On guard. To me. Parry. That's it. Croisé. Good. Now. Perfect. Quarte over the arm, excellent." There was real satisfaction in Don Jaime's voice, that of an author contemplating his work. "Let's do it again, but be careful. This time I'm going to attack harder. On guard. To me. Good. Parry. Good. That's it. Croisé. No. You were too slow, Don Fernando, that's why I managed to hit you. Let's start again."

From the street came the noise of some great tumult. They could hear the sound of horses' hooves charging over the cobbles. Álvaro Salanova and young Francisco Cazorla leaned out of one of the windows.

"There's trouble, Maestro!"

Don Jaime interrupted the bout, and joined his students at the window. Sabres and patent leather tricorn hats gleamed in the street. On horseback, the Civil Guard were breaking up a band of demonstrators who were fleeing in all directions. Two shots rang out near the Teatro Real. The young fencers watched the scene, fascinated by the commotion.

"Look at them running!"

"They got a real thrashing!"

"What do you think's happened?"

"Perhaps it's the revolution!"

"No," said Álvaro Salanova, curling his lip in disdain. "There's only half a dozen of them. The Civil Guard will take care of them."

A passer-by was hurriedly seeking shelter in a doorway below. A couple of old ladies in black peered out, like birds of evil omen, cautiously observing the scene. The balconies were packed with people; some cheered on the insurgents, others the guards.

"Long live Prim!" shouted three rather disreputable-looking women, with the impunity allowed them by their sex and by the fact that they were standing on a fourth-floor balcony. "Why don't you string up Marfori?"

"Who's Marfori?" asked Francisco Cazorla.

"A minister," said his brother. "They say that the Queen and he . . . "

Don Jaime deemed that enough was enough, and he closed the shutters, ignoring the murmur of disappointment from his students.

"We're here to practise fencing, gentlemen," he said in a tone that admitted of no argument. "Your parents pay me to teach you something useful, not to spend your time gawping at things that are none of your business. Let's get back to what we were doing." He gave a supremely scornful glance at the closed shutters and stroked the grip of his foil. "We have nothing to do with whatever might be going on out there. We'll leave that to the mob and to the politicians."

They took up their positions again and the metallic clink of foils returned to the gallery. On the walls, the displays of old weapons, rusty and immutable, continued to gather dust. In the fencing master's house, one had only to close the shutters in order for time to stop in its tracks.

It was the concierge who brought him up to date when he passed her on the stairs.

"Good afternoon, Don Jaime. What do you think of the news, then?"

"What news?"

The old woman crossed herself. She was a plump, chatty widow, who lived with her unmarried daughter. She went to mass twice daily at San Ginés and was convinced that all revolutionaries were heretics.

"Don't tell me you don't know what's going on. Haven't you heard?"

Jaime Astarloa raised an eyebrow, indicating polite interest.

"Tell me, Doña Rosa."

The concierge lowered her voice, looking suspiciously around her, as if the walls might have ears.

"Don Juan Prim disembarked yesterday in Cádiz and they say that the navy has rebelled. That's how they repay our poor Queen for all her kindness."

He went up Calle Mayor towards the Puerta del Sol, on his way to the Café Progreso. Even without the concierge's news, it would have been clear that something serious was going on. Excited groups of people were standing in circles commenting on the events of the day, and, from a safe distance, about twenty or so curious onlookers were watching the squadron of soldiers standing guard on the corner of Calle Postas. The soldiers, bayonets fixed and their helmets pulled down over their shaven heads, were under the command of a fierce-looking officer with a beard, who kept pacing up and down, his hand resting on the hilt of his sabre. The soldiers were very young and obviously felt important, basking in the expectation that their presence aroused. A well-dressed gentleman walked past Don Jaime and went over to the Lieutenant.

"What's going on?" he asked.

The soldier swung round with lofty arrogance.

"I am carrying out the orders of my superiors. Now move along."

Looking solemn in their blue uniforms, a few soldiers were confiscating newspapers from the lads who had been selling them, crying their wares amongst the people gathered there; a state of war had been declared; any news relating to the uprising was censored. A few tradespeople, who had learned from the experience of recent unrest in the streets, were shutting up their shops and joining the groups of interested bystanders. The patent leather hats of the Civil Guard could be seen glinting in Calle Carretas. It was said that González Bravo had telegraphed his resignation to the Queen and that the rebellious troops and Prim were advancing on Madrid.

Everyone was at the Café Progreso and Jaime Astarloa was immediately brought up to date. Prim had arrived in Cádiz on the night of the 18th, and on the morning of the 19th, to the cry of "Long live national sovereignty", the Mediterranean fleet had come out in favour of the revolution. Admiral Topete, whom everyone had considered loyal to the Queen, was amongst the rebels. One after the other, the garrisons in the south and east had joined the uprising.

"The unknown factor now", exclaimed Antonio Carreño, "is what the Queen will do. If she doesn't surrender, there'll be civil war, because this isn't just another coup, gentlemen. I have it on good authority. Prim now has a powerful army that's growing larger by the minute. And Serrano is involved too. There's some speculation that a regency has been offered to Don Baldomero Espartero."

"Isabel II will never give in," said Don Lucas.

"We'll see about that," said Agapito Cárceles, who was visibly delighted with the course of events. "It would be better if she did at least try to resist."

The others looked at him, surprised.

"Resist?" said Carreño. "That would lead the country into civil war."

"A blood bath," said Marcelino Romero, glad to be able to contribute something.

"Exactly," said the journalist, beaming. "Don't you understand? It seems perfectly obvious to me. If Isabel goes for half-measures, shows herself ready to negotiate or abdicates in favour of her son, we'll be back to square one. There are a lot of monarchists amongst the rebels, and they'll end up giving us Puigmoltejo, or Montpensier or Don Baldomero, or some other Tom, Dick or Harry. And I'm not having it. That isn't why we've struggled all these years."

"Where exactly did you do your struggling?" asked Don Lucas scornfully.

Cárceles looked at him with republican disdain.

"In the shadows, sir. In the shadows."

"I see."

Cárceles decided to ignore Don Lucas.

"As I was saying," he went on, addressing the others, "what Spain needs is a proper, bloody civil war with plenty of martyrs, with barricades in the street and with the sovereign people attacking the royal palace. We need committees of public safety, and to have those monarchical figureheads and their lackeys", at this point he gave Don Lucas a dark look, "dragged through the streets."

That seemed excessive to Carreño.

"Now, Don Agapito, don't go too far. In the lodges . . . "

But there was no stopping Cárceles.

"The lodges are very half-hearted, Don Antonio."

"Half-hearted? The lodges half-hearted?"

"Yes sir, that's what I said. The revolution may have been unleashed by malcontents amongst the generals, but we must try to ensure that it ends up in the hands of its rightful owners: the people." His face lit up. "The republic, gentlemen! The *res publica*, no less will do. And the guillotine."

Don Lucas let out an angry roar. His monocle was fogged with indignation.

"At last you have removed your mask!" he exclaimed, pointing an accusing finger, tremulous with righteous wrath. "At last you have revealed your Machiavellian face, Don Agapito! Civil war! Blood! The guillotine! That is your true language!"

The journalist looked at him in genuine bemusement.

"I've never used any other language, as far as I know."

Don Lucas made as if to get up, but seemed to think better of it. That afternoon Jaime Astarloa was paying and the coffees were on their way.

"You're worse than Robespierre, Señor Cárceles!" he muttered, overcome. "Worse than that infidel Danton!"

"Now don't go mixing the sheep with the goats, my friend."

"I'm not your friend! It's people like you who have plunged Spain into ignominy!"

"You *are* a bad loser, Don Lucas."

"We haven't lost yet. The Queen has named General Concha as president; now there's a real man. For the moment, he has entrusted Pavía with command of the army that will confront the rebels. And I imagine you have no doubts about the proven valour of the Marqués de Novaliches. You may have counted your chickens too early, Don Agapito."

"We'll see about that."

"We certainly will."

"We're seeing it right now."

"We'll see!"

Bored by the eternal polemics, Jaime Astarloa left earlier than usual. He picked up his hat and cane, said goodbye until the following day and went out into the street, resolved to take a short walk before returning home. On the way, he noticed, with some annoyance, the febrile atmosphere in the streets. The whole business touched him only tangentially. He was beginning to grow sick of the arguments between Cárceles and Don Lucas, as he was of the country in which he was fated to live.

He thought irritably that they could all go hang themselves with their wretched republics and their wretched monarchies, with their patriotic speeches and their stupid café brawls. He would have given anything to have them stop spoiling his life with their disturbances, disputes and upsets, the reasons for which left him utterly cold. All he wanted was for them to leave him in peace. As far as the fencing master was concerned, they could all go to the Devil.

There was a rumble of distant thunder, and the wind gusted along the streets. Don Jaime bent his head and held onto his hat, quickening his step. A few minutes later it began raining hard.

On the corner of Calle Postas, the rain was drenching the soldiers' blue uniforms and running in large drops down their faces. They were still mounting guard like shy country bumpkins, the points of their bayonets brushing their noses, keeping close to the wall, trying to shelter from the rain. From a doorway, the Lieutenant was silently contemplating the puddles, a smoking pipe in the corner of his mouth.

It rained in torrents all that weekend. From the solitude of his room, bent over the pages of a book by the light of an oil lamp, Don Jaime listened to the endless peels of thunder and the lightning crackling across a dark sky rent by flashes which made the nearby buildings stand out in silhouette. The rain beat hard on the roof, and a couple of times he had to get up and place bowls beneath leaks that dripped from the ceiling with irritating, liquid monotony.

He leafed abstractedly through the book he had in his hands and stopped at one particular quotation, which, years before, he had underlined in pencil.

"His feelings reached an intensity hitherto unknown to him. He relived the experiences of an infinitely varied life; he died and was reborn, he loved ardently and passionately and found himself separated once more and for ever from his beloved. At last, towards dawn, when the first light began to dissolve the shadows, a sense of peace began to grow in his soul, and the images became clearer, more permanent . . . "

He smiled with infinite sadness, his finger still on those lines that seemed to have been written not for Heinrich von Ofterdingen, but for himself. In recent years he had seen himself depicted on that page with singular mastery, it was all there. It was probably the most accurate summation of his life that anyone would ever be able to formulate. Nevertheless, in the last few weeks, there had been something missing. The growing peace, the clear, permanent images that he had thought definitive, were becoming clouded again beneath a strange influence that was pitilessly destroying, piece by piece, that calm lucidity in which he had believed he would be able to spend the rest of his days. A new factor had been introduced into his life, a mysterious, unsettling force, which made him ask questions whose answers he struggled to avoid. He could not tell where it was all leading him.

He suddenly shut the book and slammed it down on the table. He became horribly aware of his utter isolation. Those violet-coloured eyes had used him for some unknown end, which, whenever he tried to imagine it, filled him with an irrational feeling of dark fear. And what was worse: those eyes had robbed his old and weary spirit of its peace.

He woke up with the first light of dawn. Lately, he slept badly; his sleep was disturbed, restless. He washed thoroughly and then placed the case containing his razors on a table, next to the mirror and the bowl of hot water. As usual, he lathered up carefully and shaved. He trimmed his moustache with his old silver scissors and then ran a tortoiseshell comb through his still damp white hair. Satisfied with his appearance, he dressed with care, tying a black silk tie about his neck.

From his three summer suits he chose an everyday one, in light brown alpaca, whose long, old-fashioned jacket gave him the distinguished bearing of an ageing dandy from the turn of the century. It is true that the seat of his trousers was somewhat worn with use, but the tails of his jacket concealed it most satisfactorily. He chose the best preserved of his clean handkerchiefs and sprinkled a few drops of eau-de-cologne on it before putting it in his pocket. As he left, he donned a top hat and placed the case bearing his foils under his arm.

It was a grey day, and showers still looked likely. It had been raining all night and a large puddle in the middle of the street reflected the eaves of the houses beneath a heavy, leaden sky. Courteously he greeted the concierge, who was returning home with her basket full of groceries, and crossed the road to have his usual breakfast – hot chocolate and fritters – in a modest little café on the corner. He went and sat down in the back, where he always sat, beneath the glass globe covering a defunct gas burner. It was nine o'clock and there were few customers. Valentín, the owner, came over with a cup of hot chocolate and a paper screw full of fritters.

"No newspapers today, I'm afraid, Don Jaime. What with one thing and another, they haven't come out yet, and I suspect they won't."

Don Jaime shrugged. The absence of a daily newspaper didn't bother him in the least.

"Any news?" he asked, more out of politeness than any real interest.

The owner of the café wiped his hands on his greasy apron.

"It seems the Marqués de Novaliches is in Andalusia with the army, and that he's about to confront the rebels any day now. They say too that Córdoba, which rebelled when the others did, unrebelled the following day, as soon as they caught a glimpse of the government troops. Things are not at all clear, Don Jaime. Heaven knows where it will all end."

Having eaten his breakfast, Don Jaime went out into the street and headed for the house of the Marqués de los Alumbres. He had no idea whether or not Luis de Ayala would want to fence today, given the atmosphere in Madrid, but Jaime Astarloa was, as always, prepared to carry out his part of the agreement. At worst, it would mean a journey made in vain. Since it was getting late, and he didn't want to be delayed by any unforeseen incident in the streets, he got into an unoccupied carriage that was waiting by one of the arches in the Plaza Mayor.

"Palacio de Villaflores."

The coachman cracked his whip, and the two bored nags set off unenthusiastically. The soldiers were still on the corner of Calle Postas, but the Lieutenant was nowhere to be seen. Opposite the post office, a group of curious onlookers were being half-heartedly moved on by some municipal policemen. They worked for the town hall, with the Damoclean sword of dismissal constantly hanging over their heads; they had no idea who would be governing the country tomorrow, and they did not quite know what to do.

The mounted Civil Guard he had seen in Calle Carretas were no longer at their posts. Jaime Astarloa met them further down, with their tricorn hats and their cloaks, patrolling back and forth between the Parliament building and the Fountain of Neptune. With their black moustaches stiff with wax and their sabres in their scabbards, they watched the passers-by with the grim certainty that, whoever won, they would still be the instruments of public order. Regardless of whether the government was Progressive or Moderate, the Civil Guard were never dismissed.

Don Jaime sat back in the carriage, looking abstractedly about him, but as he approached the Palacio de Villaflores, he started and looked out of the window with alarm. There was an unusual amount of activity outside the home of the Marqués de los Alumbres. More than a hundred people were milling around in the street, kept back from the entrance by several guards. They were from all social classes, mostly people from the neighbourhood, along with various others who had nothing better to do. Some of the more daring busybodies had scaled the railings and were peering into the garden. Making the most of all this fuss, a couple of pedlars were meandering in and out amongst the parked carriages, crying their wares.

With a dark presentiment, Don Jaime paid the coachman and hurried over to the gates, pushing his way through the crowd. The onlookers were jostling one another to get a better look, in ghoulish expectation.

"It's terrible, terrible," a few women were saying, crossing themselves.

A grey-haired man, carrying a walking stick and wearing a frock coat, was standing on tiptoe trying to see what was happening. Hanging on his arm, his wife was looking at him questioningly, waiting for news.

"Can you see anything, Paco?"

Another woman was fanning herself, with the air of someone in the know: "It happened during the night. One of the guards told me; he's a cousin of my daughter-in-law. The judge has just arrived."

"It's a tragedy," remarked someone.

"Do you know what happened?"

"His servants found him this morning."

"They say he was no better than he should be."

"That's a lie! He was a gentleman and a Liberal. Don't you remember how he resigned when he was a Minister?"

The woman resumed her furious fanning.

"A tragedy. And he was so handsome, too."

Fearing the worst, Don Jaime went over to one of the guards at the gates. The municipal policeman stopped him with the firmness conferred by the authority of a uniform.

"You can't come in here, sir."

Don Jaime clumsily indicated the case of foils beneath his arm.

"I'm a friend of the Marquis. I have an appointment with him this morning."

The guard looked him up and down and, seeing the gentleman's distinguished appearance, moderated his attitude. He turned to a colleague on the other side of the railings.

"Corporal Martínez! There's a gentleman here who says he's a family friend. It seems he has an appointment."

Sleek and portly behind his golden buttons, Corporal Martínez came over, eyeing Don Jaime suspiciously.

"What's your name?"

"I'm Jaime Astarloa. I have an appointment with Don Luis de Ayala at ten o'clock."

The Corporal gravely nodded and half-opened the gate.

"Would you mind coming with me?"

He followed the guard down the gravelled path, beneath the familiar shade of the willows. There were more municipal police at the door, and a group of gentlemen were talking in the reception room, at the foot of the broad staircase adorned with large urns and marble statues.

"Would you mind waiting a moment?"

The Corporal went over to the group and, in a low voice, exchanged a few respectful words with a short, dapper gentleman with a dyed, waxed moustache and a wig covering his bald pate. He was dressed with a certain vulgar affectation and wore metal-rimmed glasses with blue lenses, attached by a ribbon to the lapel of his frock coat, on which he wore the insignia of some civil award. He listened to the guard, then turned and looked at the new arrival. Muttering a few words to his companions, he came over to Don Jaime. His astute, watery eyes glinted behind the lenses.

"I am the chief of police, Jenaro Campillo. Whom do I have the honour of addressing?"

"Jaime Astarloa, fencing master. Don Luis and I . . . "

The man interrupted him with a gesture.

"Yes, I know about that." He stared at Don Jaime, as if sizing him up. Then he pointed at the case that Don Jaime had under his arm. "Are those your implements?"

Don Jaime nodded.

"They're my foils. As I said, Don Luis and I . . . I mean, I usually come here every morning." He broke off and looked at the policeman, stunned. He realized that, absurdly, he had only that moment taken in what had happened, as if his mind had blocked it out, refusing to acknowledge something that was all too blindingly obvious. "What has happened to the Marquis?"

The policeman looked at him thoughtfully; he seemed to be weighing the sincerity of the emotions apparent in the fencing master's stunned response. After a moment, he gave a little cough, put his hand in his pocket and drew out a Havana cigar.

"I am very much afraid, Señor Astarloa," he said calmly, as he pierced one end of the cigar with a toothpick. "I am very much afraid that the Marqués de los Alumbres is in no condition to fence today.

From a purely forensic point of view, I would say that he was not at all well."

He made a gesture with his hand as they spoke, inviting Don Jaime to accompany him. Don Jaime caught his breath as he went into a small room which he knew intimately, having been there every day for the last two years: it was the anteroom to the gallery in which he used to practise with the Marquis. On the threshold between the two rooms lay a motionless body, stretched out on the floor and covered by a blanket. A long trail of blood emanated from the blanket and split into two in the middle of the room. There, the trail took two directions, culminating in two coagulated pools.

Jaime Astarloa dropped the case of foils on an armchair and leaned on the back of the chair; he seemed completely at a loss. He looked at his companion as if demanding some explanation for what seemed a cruel joke, but the policeman merely shrugged and lit a match, taking long pulls on his cigar, still watching Don Jaime's reactions.

"Is he dead?" asked Don Jaime. The question was such a foolish one that the policeman raised an ironic eyebrow.

"Completely."

Don Jaime swallowed hard.

"Suicide?"

"Have a look for yourself. I would value your opinion."

Jenaro Campillo breathed out a cloud of smoke, bent over the corpse and uncovered it to the waist, standing back to observe the effect on Jaime Astarloa. Luis de Ayala's face still bore the expression he had worn when surprised by death: he was lying on his back, his right leg bent beneath his left; his half-open eyes were opaque and his lower lip seemed fixed in a last dying grimace. He was in his shirtsleeves, his tie undone. There was a perfect, round hole on the right side of his throat, which passed through to the nape of his neck. That was the source of the stream of blood now creeping across the floor of the room.

Feeling as if he were in a nightmare from which he hoped to awaken at any moment, Jaime Astarloa stared at the corpse, incapable of a single coherent thought. The room, the stiff corpse, the bloodstains, all spun about him. He felt his legs give way. He breathed deeply, not daring to let go of the chair he was leaning on. Then, when he finally managed to impose some discipline on his body and order on his thoughts, the reality of what had happened there hit him suddenly and painfully, as if someone had pierced his very soul. He looked at his companion with horrified eyes; the policeman frowned, returning his gaze with a slight nod; he seemed to guess what Don Jaime was thinking, encouraging him to put it into words. Then Don Jaime bent over the corpse and reached out his hand to the wound as if to touch it, only to stop short. When he stood up, he looked badly shaken, his eyes wide, for he had just come face to face with naked horror. There was no mistaking a wound like that. Luis de Ayala had been killed with a foil, with a single, clean thrust to the jugular: it was the two hundred escudo thrust.

"It would be most useful to me, Señor Astarloa, to know when you last saw the Marqués de los Alumbres."

They were sitting in a room, surrounded by Flemish tapestries and beautiful gilt-framed Venetian mirrors, next to the room in which the corpse still lay. Don Jaime seemed to have aged ten years: he was leaning forward, his elbows on his knees, his face in his hands. His grey eyes, dull and inexpressive, were fixed on the floor. The chief of police's words reached him from afar, amongst the mists of a bad dream.

"On Friday morning." Even his own voice sounded odd to Jaime Astarloa. "We said goodbye shortly after eleven o'clock, after our fencing session."

Jenaro Campillo studied the ash on his cigar for a few moments, as if, at that moment, he were more concerned with the correct burning of his cigar than with the painful matter in hand.

"Did you notice anything that might have led one to expect this misfortune?"

"Not at all. Everything was completely normal, and we parted as we did every day."

The ash on the cigar was about to fall. Carefully holding the cigar between his fingers, the chief of police looked about him in search of an ashtray, but failed to find one. Then, glancing furtively over at the door of the room in which the corpse lay, he decided to flick the ash onto the carpet.

"You often visited the . . . er . . . deceased. Do you have any idea as to the motive for the murder?"

Don Jaime shrugged.

"I don't know. Robbery, perhaps."

The policeman shook his head and took another long pull on his cigar.

"We have already questioned the two servants, as well as the coachman, the cook and the gardener. An initial visual examination seems to indicate that nothing of value was taken." The policeman paused, whilst Jaime Astarloa, not paying attention to what he was saying, was still trying to put his own ideas in order. He felt certain that he had some clues to the mystery; the question was whether to confide what he knew to this man or to tie up a few loose ends himself first.

"Are you listening, Señor Astarloa?"

Don Jaime jumped, blushing, as if the chief of police had seen into his thoughts.

"Of course," he replied hurriedly. "So that rules out theft as the motive for the crime."

The policeman made a cautious gesture, then reached an index finger under his wig to scratch his left ear.

"Partly, Señor Astarloa, but only partly. At least as regards a conventional larceny," he said. "Do you know what a visual examination means?"

"I imagine that it is one made with your eyes."

"Very funny." Jenaro Campillo looked at him darkly. "I'm glad you haven't lost your sense of humour. People die, and you make jokes."

"So do you."

"But I represent the competent authority."

They looked at each other for a moment in silence.

"The visual examination", the policeman went on at last, "confirms that during the night a person or persons unknown entered the Marquis's private apartments and spent some time forcing locks and going through drawers. They also opened his safe, this time with a key. It was a very good safe, by the way, made by Bossom & Son of London. Aren't you going to ask me if anything was taken?"

"I thought you were the one asking the questions."

"That is the custom, but not the rule."

"Was anything taken?"

The chief of police smiled mysteriously, as if Don Jaime had put his finger on the problem.

"You know, that's the odd thing. The murderer, or murderers, stoically resisted the temptation to carry off the considerable quantity of money and jewels contained therein. Strange criminals, I think you'll agree." He sucked on his cigar, then exhaled the smoke, savouring both the aroma and his own reasoning. "To sum up, it's impossible to ascertain if they took anything or not, since we have no idea what he kept in there. We don't even know if they found what they were looking for."

Don Jaime shuddered inwardly, trying to conceal his emotions. He had more than enough reason to think that the murderers had not found what they were looking for: doubtless, it was a certain sealed envelope that was in his house, hidden behind a row of books . . . His mind was working quickly, trying to piece together all the disparate fragments of the tragedy. Recent situations, words, expressions with no apparent connection were now slowly and painfully fitting together so perfectly that he felt a pang of fear. Although he still could not see the whole picture, the first indications made it clear what his role in the events had been. He realized all this with an acute sense of anxiety, humiliation and disgust.

The chief of police was looking at him inquisitively; he was waiting for an answer to a question that Don Jaime, absorbed in his thoughts, had not heard.

"I'm sorry?"

The policeman's shining, bulbous eyes, like those of a fish in an aquarium, were observing him from behind the blue lenses of his spectacles. They seemed almost benevolent, although it was hard to tell if this concern was genuine or merely the product of a professional attitude intended to inspire confidence. After a brief moment of consideration, Don Jaime decided that, despite Jenaro Campillo's manner and his eccentric appearance, he was no fool.

"I was asking, Señor Astarloa, if you could think of any detail that might help me in my investigation."

"I'm afraid not."

"Really?"

"I don't usually play with words, Señor Campillo."

The policeman made a conciliatory gesture.

"Can I speak frankly, Señor Astarloa?"

"Please do."

"Despite the fact that you are one of the people who saw the deceased most often, you are not proving to be of much use to me."

"There are other people he saw regularly too, and you said a moment ago that they could not help you either. I don't know why you should place so much importance on my testimony."

Campillo studied the smoke from his cigar and smiled.

"To tell you the truth, neither do I." He paused thoughtfully. "Perhaps it's because you seem to me an honourable man. Yes, perhaps that's why."

Don Jaime made a dismissive gesture.

"I'm just a fencing master," he replied, trying to sound indifferent. "Our relationship was exclusively professional; Don Luis never made me his confidant."

"You saw him last Friday. Was he upset, worried? Did you notice anything unusual about his behaviour?"

"Nothing that struck me."

"And on the days before that?"

"Perhaps. I didn't notice. I can't really remember. Besides, so many people are on edge at the moment, I probably wouldn't have noticed it anyway."

"Did you talk about politics at all?"

"In my view, Don Luis kept himself apart from all that. He used to say that he liked to observe it from afar; it was a sort of hobby."

The chief of police made a doubtful face.

"A hobby? Hm, I see. Nevertheless, as you no doubt know, the late

Marquis once occupied an important post in the Ministry of the Interior. He was nominated by the Minister himself, who just happened to be his maternal uncle, the late Joaquín Vallespín." Campillo smiled sarcastically, making it clear that he had his own views on nepotism amongst the Spanish aristocracy. "That was some time ago, but such things tend to create enemies. I'm a case in point. When he was Minister, Vallespín blocked my promotion to Superintendent for six months." He clicked his tongue, remembering. "How things change!"

"Maybe, but I don't think I'm the right person to enlighten you on the subject."

Campillo had finished his cigar and was holding the butt between his fingers, not knowing what to do with it.

"There is another, perhaps more frivolous, angle from which we can consider the matter." He opted for throwing the cigar butt into a Chinese porcelain vase. "The Marquis was quite a ladies' man, you know what I mean. Perhaps some jealous husband . . . you see what I'm driving at. Besmirched honour and all that."

Don Jaime blinked. That remark seemed to him in the worst possible taste.

"I'm afraid, Señor Campillo, that I can't be of any help to you on that point either. I will only say, that in my opinion, Don Luis de Ayala was a complete gentleman." He looked at the policeman's watery eyes and then at his wig, which was somewhat awry. That gave him the courage to raise his voice slightly defiantly. "And as regards myself, I hope that I merit exactly the same opinion from you; I would therefore prefer to hear no further sordid gossip on the subject."

Campillo immediately apologized, somewhat embarrassed, slyly adjusting his wig. Of course. Don Jaime mustn't misinterpret his words. It was a mere formality. He would never have dared to insinuate . . .

Don Jaime was barely listening. A silent battle was being waged within him, because he was knowingly withholding valuable information which could perhaps point to the motive for the murder. He realized that he was trying to protect a certain person whose troubling image had come to mind the moment he saw the body in the room.

Protect? If his deductions were right, this wasn't just protection, it was blatant concealment, an act that not only violated the law, but also went against all the ethical principles underpinning his life. He didn't want to rush into anything, he thought; he needed time to analyse the situation.

Campillo was staring at him now, frowning slightly, drumming his fingers on the arm of the chair. At that moment, for the first time, Don Jaime thought that he too might be considered a suspect in the eyes of the authorities. After all, Luis de Ayala had been killed with a foil.

That was when the policeman uttered the words he had been dreading throughout the whole conversation: "Do you know a certain Adela de Otero?"

The fencing master's heart stopped for a moment, then started beating wildly. He swallowed hard before replying.

"Yes," he said, with all the sang-froid he could muster. "She was one of my clients."

Campillo bent towards him, extremely interested.

"I didn't know that. Is she still?"

"No. She dispensed with my services some weeks ago."

"How many weeks?"

"I don't know. About a month and a half."

"Why?"

"I don't know."

The policeman leaned back in his chair and took another cigar from his pocket, all the time looking at Don Jaime as if in deep thought. This time he didn't pierce the cigar with a toothpick, he merely gnawed distractedly at one end.

"Did you know about her . . . friendship with the Marquis?"

Don Jaime nodded.

"Only very superficially," he said. "As far as I know, the relationship began after she stopped attending my classes. I never," he hesitated for a moment before finishing the phrase, "I never saw the lady again."

Campillo lit his cigar amidst a cloud of smoke, which irritated Jaime Astarloa's nose. Tiny beads of sweat shone on Don Jaime's forehead.

"We've questioned the servants," said the policeman after a while.

"Thanks to them, we know that Señora de Otero often visited the house. All agree that the relationship between herself and the deceased was of an . . . er . . . intimate nature."

Don Jaime held the policeman's gaze as if none of this affected him in the least.

"And?" he asked, trying to adopt a distant air. The chief of police gave a half-smile, smoothing the ends of his dyed moustache.

"At ten o'clock last night", he explained almost confidentially, as if the corpse in the other room might hear them, "the Marquis dismissed the servants. We know that he usually did this when he was expecting a visit that might be described as 'romantic'. The servants withdrew to their part of the house on the other side of the garden. They heard nothing suspicious, only the rain and the thunder. This morning, at about seven, when they came into the house, they found their master's body. At the other end of the room there was a foil stained with blood. The Marquis was cold and stiff; he had been dead for several hours. Cold meat."

Don Jaime shuddered, unable to share the chief of police's macabre sense of humour.

"Do they know who the visitor was?"

Campillo gave a disappointed click of the tongue.

"No. We can only deduce that the visitor came in by a discreet door on the other side of the palace, in the cul-de-sac that the Marquis often used as a coach house. Some coach house, I might add: five horses, a berlin, a coupé, a tilbury, a phaeton, an English coachman." He gave a melancholy sigh, implying that, in his opinion, the late Marquis certainly did not stint himself. "But, returning to the subject in hand, I admit that there is nothing to tell us whether the murderer was a man or a woman, whether there was just one or several people. There are no footprints of any kind, despite the fact that it was pouring with rain."

"A difficult situation, it would seem."

"It is. Difficult and unfortunate. What with all the political upheaval we're experiencing at the moment, with the country on the verge of civil war along with everything else, I'm afraid that the investigation may take some time. The murder of a marquis becomes a mere anecdote when the throne is in question, don't you think? As you see, the murderer knew how to choose his moment." Campillo exhaled a large cloud of smoke and looked at the cigar appreciatively. Don Jaime noticed that it was from Vuelta Abajo and bore the same band as those Luis de Ayala used to smoke. Doubtless, in the course of his investigations, this representative of the competent authority had had occasion to ransack the dead man's cigar box. "But let's get back to Doña Adela de Otero, if you don't mind. We don't even know if she's a Señora or a Señorita. Do you happen to know?"

"No. I always called her Señora, and she never corrected me."

"They say she's pretty. A real stunner."

"I suppose a certain class of people might describe her like that."

The policeman ignored the remark.

"And a bit flighty too. I mean this business of the fencing classes . . . "

Campillo gave a knowing wink and Jaime Astarloa decided that he had had all he could take. He stood up.

"As I said before, I know very little about the lady," he said brusquely. "Besides, if you're so interested in her, you can go and question her yourself. She lives at 14 Calle Riaño."

The policeman did not move and the fencing master realized that something was not quite right. Campillo was sitting in his chair looking at Don Jaime, his cigar in his hand. Behind his spectacles, the fish eyes glinted with malicious irony, as if the whole business nonetheless had its funny side.

"Naturally." He seemed delighted with the situation, savouring a joke that he had been reserving till the end. "Of course, how were you to know, Señor Astarloa? You couldn't, of course. Your ex-client, Doña Adela de Otero, has disappeared from her home. Don't you find that an odd coincidence? Someone kills the Marquis and she vanishes without trace, imagine that. It's as if the earth had swallowed her up."

VI

An Attack on the Blade

*"An attack on the blade is one with the help of which your
opponent has gained an advantage."*

Once their official business was over, the chief of police accompanied
Don Jaime to the door, making an appointment to see him the
following day in his office. "If events allow," he added, with a look of
resignation, in a clear allusion to the current crisis in the country. Don
Jaime walked away in sombre mood. He was relieved to escape from
the scene of the tragedy and from that disagreeable interrogation, but,
at the same time, he was confronted by an unpleasant fact: now he
would have time alone to consider recent events and he was not
looking forward to the prospect of giving free rein to his thoughts.

He stopped outside the Retiro Gardens, resting his forehead on
the wrought-iron bars of the gate and gazing in at the trees in the
park. The respect he had felt for Luis de Ayala, the painful shock of
his death, were not enough, however, to fill him with indignation. The
existence of a certain shadowy woman, doubtless in some way
connected with all this, profoundly altered what, in principle, should
be an objective evaluation of the facts on his part. Don Luis had been
murdered and Don Luis was a man whom he had respected. That, he
thought, should be reason enough for him to want the authors of
the crime to get their just deserts. Why, then, had he not been open
with Campillo and told him everything he knew?

He shook his head, discouraged. He was not, in fact, sure that
Adela de Otero was responsible for what had happened. The thought
only lasted a few moments, then withdrew under the weight of

evidence. Why deceive himself? He did not know if the young woman had actually pierced the Marquis's throat with the foil, but it was clear that, directly or indirectly, she had had something to do with it. Her sudden appearance in his life, her interest in meeting Luis de Ayala, her behaviour in recent weeks, her suspicious and opportune disappearance. Everything, down to the last detail, even the last word she had spoken to him, now seemed part of a plan carried out with implacable coldness. Then there was the sword thrust. *His* thrust.

But to what end? He was no longer in any doubt that he had been used as a means to reach the Marqués de los Alumbres. But why? A crime could not be explained away that simply; behind it, there was, there had to be, a motive of sufficient magnitude for the criminal to feel justified in taking such a grave step. By a process of logical deduction, Don Jaime's thoughts flew to the sealed envelope hidden behind the books in his studio. Gripped by a violent excitement, he moved away from the railings and started walking towards the Puerta de Alcalá, quickening his pace. He had to get home, open that envelope and read its contents. The key to everything must lie there.

He stopped a hired carriage and gave his address, although, for a moment, he thought that perhaps it would, after all, be best to place everything in the hands of the police and to watch the matter evolve as a mere spectator. He realized at once that he could not do this. Someone had forced him to play a ridiculous role in this whole business, with the indifference of a puppet-master pulling the strings of a puppet. His old pride rebelled, demanded satisfaction; no one had ever dared to play with him like that, and it left him feeling angry and humiliated. Perhaps he would go to the police later, but first he needed to find out precisely what had happened. He wanted to know if there was time to settle the outstanding bill that Adela de Otero had left him with. It was not really a matter of avenging the Marqués de los Alumbres; what Jaime Astarloa wanted was full satisfaction for his feeling of betrayal.

Lulled by the motion of the carriage, he leaned back in his seat. He was beginning to experience a kind of calm lucidity. Out of a purely professional habit, he began carefully to go over events, employing his usual method: fencing movements. They helped him to impose order on his thoughts when he tried to analyse complex situations. His opponent or opponents had begun with a feint, a false attack. When they came to him, they had quite a different goal in mind; the false attack was merely a way of threatening him with a different thrust from the one they intended to use. Their attack was aimed not at him, but at Luis de Ayala, and Jaime Astarloa had not been quick enough to predict the depth of that movement, but had made the unforgivable mistake of facilitating it.

Everything began to slot into place. Having been successful with their first move, they had proceeded to the second. With the Marquis, it had been relatively easy for the lovely Adela de Otero to do what in fencing is called "forcing an attack": forcing your opponent's foil meant pushing it away at its weakest point, in order to uncover the opponent before lunging. And Luis de Ayala's two weak points were fencing and women.

Then what had happened? The Marquis, a good swordsman, had realized that his opponent was using the appel to lure him out of his defensive position. Being a resourceful man, he had immediately placed himself on guard and entrusted to Don Jaime the probable object of his opponent's moves: that mysterious sealed envelope. Though conscious of the danger, Luis de Ayala was a gambler as well as a fencer. Knowing the style of the man, Don Jaime was sure that the Marquis had pushed his luck too far, not wanting to interrupt the bout until he could see how it was going to end. Doubtless he thought he would be able to deflect the foil at the last moment when the enemy, his game revealed, lunged forwards. That had been his mistake. A veteran fencer like Ayala should have been the first to know that it was always dangerous to resort to the flanconnade as a way of parrying an attack, especially where a woman like Adela de Otero was involved.

If, as Don Jaime suspected, the aim of the attack had been to make off with the Marquis's documents, it was clear that the murderers had failed to complete the movement. By pure chance, the unwitting intervention of the fencing master had frustrated the success of the manoeuvre. What, in principle, should have been settled with a simple thrust in quarte through Ayala's jugular, became one in tierce, a move that could not be carried out with the same facility. The vital question, which now affected his own survival, was to find out whether or not his opponents knew about the decisive role he had played in all this, thanks to the late Marquis's forward thinking. Did they know that the documents were safe in his house? He thought long and hard about the matter, reaching the consoling conclusion that they could not possibly know. Ayala would never have been so unwise as to reveal the secret to Adela de Otero, nor to anyone else. He himself had told Astarloa that he was the only person to whom he could entrust such a delicate task.

The carriage trotted up the Carrera de San Jerónimo. Don Jaime was impatient to reach his house, tear open the envelope and decipher the enigma. Only then would he know what to do next.

It was starting to rain again as he got out of the carriage on the corner of Calle Bordadores. He walked in through the front door, shaking the rain off his hat, and went straight to the top floor, up the creaking staircase with the iron banister, which shook beneath his hand. On the landing, he realized with annoyance that he had left his case of foils behind at the Palacio de Villaflores. He would go and fetch them later on, he thought, as he took the key out of his pocket, turned it in the lock and pushed the door open. Much to his chagrin, he could not help but feel apprehensive as he went into the dark, empty apartment.

He showed his unease by glancing in all the rooms to reassure himself. Inevitably, he was the only person there and he felt ashamed to have allowed his imagination to get the upper hand. He placed his hat on the sofa, took off his jacket and opened the shutters to let in the greyish light from outside. Then he went over to the bookshelf, slipped his hand behind the row of books and removed the envelope which Luis de Ayala had given him.

His hands were trembling, and he felt his stomach contract as he broke the seal. The envelope was folio sized and about an inch thick. He tore the wrapping and removed a folder tied with ribbons; it contained several sheets of manuscript paper. In his haste to undo the knots, the folder fell open and the pages scattered on the floor near the walnut sideboard. Cursing his own clumsiness, he bent down to pick them up. They had an official look about them; most were letters and documents bearing a letterhead. He went and sat down at his desk and placed the papers before him. At first, he couldn't read a single word; he was so keyed up that the lines seemed to dance before him. He closed his eyes and made himself count to ten. Then he took a deep breath and started reading. Don Jaime shuddered as he read some of the signatures.

Ministry of the Interior

To: Don Luis Álvarez Rendruejo
Inspector General of Government Security and Police
Madrid

I am writing to ask you to keep a close watch on the people indicated below, since we have reasonable suspicions that they are conspiring against the government of Her Majesty the Queen.

Given the status of some of the presumed conspirators, I take it for granted that the task will be carried out with all possible discretion and tact and that the results of the investigation will be communicated directly to me.

 Martínez Carmona, Ramón. Lawyer. Calle del Prado, 16, Madrid

 Miravalls Hernández, Domiciano. Industrialist. Calle Corredera Baja, Madrid

 Cazorla Longo, Bruno. Manager of the Bank of Italy. Plaza de Santa Ana, 10, Madrid

 Cañabate Ruiz, Fernando. Railway engineer. Calle Leganitos, 7, Madrid

Porlier y Osborne, Carmelo. Financier. Calle Infantas,
  14, Madrid
To ensure maximum security, I would be grateful if you would
deal with this matter personally.

Joaquín Vallespín Andreu
Minister of the Interior
Madrid, 3 October 1866

To: *Joaquín Vallespín Andreu*
    Minister of the Interior

Dear Joaquín,
I have been thinking about our conversation of yesterday evening,
and your proposal seems acceptable to me. I confess that I have
my reservations about doing anything to benefit this scoundrel,
but the result makes it worthwhile. You get nothing for free
nowadays!
  The business about the mining concession in the Cartagena
mountains has been settled. I spoke to Pepito Zamora and he has
no objections, despite the fact that I've given him no detailed
information. He must think I'm hoping to gain some personal
advantage from it, but that doesn't matter. I'm too old now to
worry about fresh calumnies. By the way, I have made the proper
enquiries and I believe that our man is going to make a killing.
Believe me, I have a nose for such things.
  Keep me informed. Needless to say, the matter should not be
mentioned in the Council of Ministers. Get rid of Álvarez
Rendruejo as well. From now on, you and I can deal with the
matter between us.

Ramón María Narváez
8 November

Ministry of the Interior

To: Don Luis Álvarez Rendruejo
    Inspector General of Government Security and Police
    Madrid

Please give orders for the following people to be detained, under suspicion of conspiring against the government of Her Majesty the Queen:

Martínez Carmona, Ramón
Porlier y Osborne, Carmelo
Miravalls Hernández, Domiciano
Cañabate Ruiz, Fernando
Mazarrasa Sánchez, Manuel María

They should all be detained separately and kept incommunicado.

Joaquín Vallespín Andreu
Minister of the Interior
Madrid, 12 November

General Inspectorate of Prisons

To: Don Joaquín Vallespín Andreu
    Minister of the Interior
    Madrid

Dear Sir,
I am pleased to inform you that the following: Martínez Carmona, Ramón; Porlier y Osborne, Carmelo; Miravalls Hernández, Domiciano and Cañabate Ruiz, Fernando were today admitted into Cartagena prison without incident, awaiting their transfer to prisons in Africa, where they will serve their sentences.
Yours faithfully,

Ernesto de Miguel Marín
Inspector General of Prisons
Madrid, 28 November 1866

To: *Señor Don Ramón María Narváez*
    President of the Council of Ministers, Madrid

Dear General,
I am pleased to be able to send you the results contained in the accompanying report, which reached my hands this very night. I can give you more details if you require them.

Joaquín Vallespín Andreu
Madrid, 5 December
(Only copy)

To: *Don Joaquín Vallespín Andreu*
    Minister of the Interior
    Madrid

Dear Joaquín,
I have only one thing to say: excellent work. What our man has given us represents the most serious blow we can deal the schemer J.P. Under separate cover, I am sending you precise instructions on how to approach the matter. This afternoon, when I return from the Palace, we will go into more detail.

    We have to be firm. There is no other way. As for the soldiers implicated, I am going to recommend that Sangonera uses his toughest measures. We have to teach them a lesson.

    Meanwhile, stand your ground.

Ramón María Narváez
6 December

Ministry of the Interior

To: *Don Luis Álvarez Rendruejo*

Please arrange for orders to be given to detain the following people, on charges of high treason and of conspiring against the government of Her Majesty the Queen:

De la Mata Ordóñez, José. *Industrialist. Ronda de Toledo, 22, Madrid*

Fernández Garre, Julián. *Civil servant. Calle Cervantes, 19, Madrid*

Gal Rupérez, Olegario. *Captain in the Engineers. Jarilla Barracks, Alcalá de Henares*

Gal Rupérez, José María. *Lieutenant in the Artillery. La Colegiata Barracks, Madrid*

Cebrián Lucientes, Santiago. *Lieutenant-colonel in the Infantry. Trinidad Barracks, Madrid*

Ambrona Páez, Manuel. *Commanding Officer in the Engineers. Jarilla Barracks, Alcalá de Henares*

Figuero Robledo, Ginés. *Shopkeeper. Calle Segovia, 16, Madrid*

Esplandiú Casals, Jaime. *Lieutenant in the Infantry. Vicálvaro Barracks*

Romero Alcázar, Onofre. *Administrator of "Los Rocíos" estate, Toledo*

Villagordo López, Vicente. *Commanding Officer in the Infantry. Vicálvaro Barracks*

As regards the military personnel included in this report, you will act in conjunction with the corresponding military authorities, who are already in possession of the appropriate orders issued by His Excellency, the Minister of War.

Joaquín Vallespín Andreu
Minister of the Interior
Madrid, 7 December 1866
(Copy)

General Inspectorate of Government Security and Police

To: Don Joaquín Vallespín Andreu
    Minister of the Interior

Dear Sir,
I am pleased to tell you that this morning the instructions

received yesterday have now been carried out by employees of this department in conjunction with the military authorities, and that all the individuals listed in the same have now been detained.

Yours faithfully,

Luis Álvarez Rendruejo
Inspector General of Government Security and Police
Madrid, 8 December 1866

General Inspectorate of Prisons

To: Don Joaquín Vallespín Andreu
Minister of the Interior

Dear Sir,
I am writing to tell you that, as of today, the following people have been placed in Cádiz prison awaiting deportation to the Philippines.

De la Mata Ordóñez, José
Fernández Garre, Julián
Figuero Robledo, Ginés
Romero Alcázar, Onofre

Yours faithfully,

Ernesto de Miguel Marín
Inspector General of Prisons
Madrid, 19 December 1866

Ministry of War

To: Don Joaquín Vallespín Andreu
Minister of the Interior
Madrid

Dear Joaquín,
This letter is official confirmation that this afternoon Lieutenant-colonel Cebrián Lucientes and Commanding

Officers Ambrona Páez and Villagordo López went into exile in the Canaries on board the steamship Rodrigo Suárez. *Captain Olegario Gal Rupérez and his brother José María Gal Rupérez are still in the military prison in Cádiz awaiting the next embarkation of deportees for Fernando Po.*

Pedro Sangonera Ortiz
Minister
Madrid, 23 December

Ministry of War

To: Don Joaquín Vallespín Andreu
      Minister of the Interior
      Madrid

Dear Joaquín,
It is once again my duty, my painful duty on this occasion, to take up my pen to inform you officially that, since no pardon was given by Her Majesty the Queen, and the period stipulated in his sentence having passed, Lieutenant Jaime Esplandiú Casals was shot at four o'clock by a firing squad in the moat of Oñate castle. He was condemned to death for sedition, high treason and conspiring against Her Majesty's government.
Yours faithfully,

Pedro Sangonera Ortiz
Minister
Madrid, 26 December

This was followed by a series of official notes, along with other brief letters of a confidential nature between Narváez and the Minister of the Interior, bearing later dates and in which they discussed the various activities of Prim's agents in Spain and abroad. Jaime Astarloa deduced from them that the government had been keeping a close eye on the clandestine movements of the conspirators. They were constantly citing names and places, recommending that this man be placed under surveillance or that man detained; they warned of the false name under which one of Prim's agents was to embark from Barcelona. Don Jaime looked back at the other letters to check the dates. The correspondence covered a period of a year and ended abruptly. Don Jaime thought back and realized that the end coincided with the death in Madrid of Joaquín Vallespín, the man on whom the whole file seemed to centre. Vallespín, as he well remembered, had been one of Agapito Cárceles's *bêtes noires* at the Café Progreso; he was a man described as entirely loyal to Narváez and to the monarchy; as an eminent member of the Moderate Party, he had distinguished himself during his time in his post by his determination to take a firm line. He had died of some kind of heart disease, and his funeral had been carried out with due pomp, indeed Narváez himself had led the mourning. Narváez had followed Vallespín to the grave shortly afterwards, thus depriving Isabel II of her main political support.

Jaime Astarloa scratched his head in puzzlement. All this made no sense at all. He wasn't particularly up-to-date on Cabinet machinations, but he had the feeling that these documents, which were the likely cause of Luis de Ayala's death, contained nothing to justify his eagerness to hide them, far less his murder. Don Jaime re-read a few pages with dogged concentration, hoping to discover some clue that might have escaped him on a first reading – in vain. He lingered longest over the somewhat cryptic note that he found in the second part of the file: the brief letter from Narváez to Vallespín addressing him in familiar terms. In it, Narváez referred to a proposal, doubtless put to him by the Minister, which he deemed "acceptable", and which apparently had to do with a matter concerning "a mining concession". Narváez had consulted with someone called Pepito Zamora, presumably the man who was Minister of Mines at the time, José Zamora. But that seemed to be all. There was no clue, no other names. "I have my reservations about doing anything to benefit this scoundrel," Narváez had written. Which scoundrel was he referring to? Perhaps the answer lay there, in that name that appeared nowhere. Or did it?

He sighed. Perhaps, for someone versed in the matter, this would have some meaning, but it did not lead him to any conclusion at all.

He could not understand what it was that made those documents so important and dangerous that people would stop at nothing, not even murder, in order to gain possession of them. Besides, why had Luis de Ayala entrusted them to him? Who wanted to steal them, and why? Then again, how had the Marqués de los Alumbres, who claimed to keep very much on the sidelines in politics, managed to get hold of these papers, which were part of the private correspondence of the late Minister?

At least there was a logical explanation for that. Joaquín Vallespín Andreu was a relative of the Marqués de los Alumbres, his uncle, Don Jaime seemed to recall. The government post that Ayala had held during his brief experience of public life had been offered to him by Andreu during one of Narváez's last governments. Did the dates coincide? Don Jaime could not quite remember, although Ayala's brief stint at the ministry might have come later. The important thing was that the Marqués de los Alumbres could have obtained the documents while he was carrying out his official duties, or perhaps on the death of his uncle. That was reasonable enough, even very likely. But, in that case, what did they mean exactly and why such interest in keeping them secret? Were they so very dangerous, so very compromising that a justification could be found in them for murder?

He got up from the table and walked about the room, weighed down by this grim story, which completely defied his analytical abilities. It was all so devilishly absurd, especially the involuntary role that he had played in the tragedy, and was still playing, he thought with a shudder. What did Adela de Otero have to do with that web of conspiracies, official letters and lists of names? And not one of the names was familiar to him. He did remember reading something in the newspaper about the events mentioned, or else he had heard remarks about them at the café, before and after every attempt Prim made to take power. He even remembered the execution of that poor Lieutenant, Jaime Esplandiú. But nothing else. He was up a blind alley.

He thought of going to the police, handing the file over to them and forgetting all about the matter. But it wasn't that simple. He remembered with a sense of great unease the interrogation he had been submitted to that morning by the chief of police as they stood over Ayala's body. He had lied to Campillo by concealing the existence of the sealed envelope. And if those documents did compromise someone, they were equally compromising for him, since he had been the innocent depository. Innocent? The word made him curl his lip. Ayala was not alive to explain the whole imbroglio, and innocence was something for the judges to decide.

He had never felt so confused. His honest nature rebelled against the lie, but did he have any choice? A prudent instinct counselled him to destroy the folder, to extricate himself from the nightmare, if, that is, there was still time. That way no one would know anything. No one, he thought apprehensively, but neither would he. And he needed to know what sordid story lay at the back of all this. He had a right to know, and the reasons for that were many. If he did not uncover the mystery, he would never regain his peace of mind.

He would decide what to do with the documents later on, whether to destroy them or to hand them over to the police. Now what he had to do was crack the code. It was clear, though, that he could not do so alone. Perhaps someone more versed in political matters . . .

He thought of Agapito Cárceles. Why not? He was a colleague, a friend and, in addition, he was a passionate follower of political events in the country. The names and facts contained in the file would be doubtless familiar to him.

He hurriedly collected up the papers, hid them behind the row of books again, picked up his walking stick and top hat and left the house. As he stepped out into the street, he consulted his watch: it was nearly six in the evening. Cárceles would probably be at the Café Progreso. It was nearby, in Calle Montera, barely ten minutes away, but Don Jaime was in a hurry. He hailed a carriage and asked the driver to take him there as quickly as possible.

He found Cárceles in his usual corner of the café, deep in a monologue about the evil role that the Austrians and the Bourbons had played in the fate of Spain. Opposite him, wearing a crumpled scarf about his neck and his eternal air of incurable melancholy, Marcelino Romero was looking at him, not listening, sucking distractedly on a sugar cube. Contrary to his custom, Don Jaime dispensed with formalities. Apologizing to Don Marcelino, he took Cárceles to one side and explained the situation to him, albeit through hints and hedged about with all kinds of reservations.

"It's about some documents that I have in my possession, for reasons which are, for the moment, irrelevant. I need someone of your expertise to clarify a few doubts I have. I can, of course, trust in your absolute discretion."

The journalist seemed delighted with the idea. He had finished his lecture on Austrian and Bourbon decadence, and the music teacher was hardly an ideal companion. After making their excuses to Romero, they both left the café.

They decided to walk to Calle Bordadores. Along the way, Cárceles referred in passing to the tragedy at the Palacio de Villaflores, which was the talk of all Madrid. He was vaguely aware that Luis de Ayala had been one of Don Jaime's clients and he demanded details of the event with such acute, professional curiosity that Don Jaime found it very hard to keep the issue at bay with evasive answers. Cárceles, who never missed an opportunity to make some scornful remark about the aristocratic classes, seemed completely unmoved by the death of one of their number.

"Less work for the sovereign people when the time comes," he proclaimed lugubriously, immediately changing the subject when he saw Don Jaime's disapproving look. After a while, though, he returned to the attack, this time to put forward the hypothesis that there was doubtless a woman involved in the Marquis's death. It was clear as day: the Marquis had obviously been bumped off over some matter of honour. After all, hadn't he been killed with a sabre or something of the sort? Perhaps Don Jaime knew.

Don Jaime saw with relief that they were nearly at the door of his apartment. Cárceles, who was visiting the place for the first time, scanned the small living room with some curiosity. When he saw the rows of books, he headed straight for them, studying the titles on the spines with a critical eye.

"Not bad," he said at last with a magnanimous gesture. "Personally, though, I feel there should be a few of those books so fundamental to an understanding of the age in which we live – Rousseau, say, or perhaps a little Voltaire."

Jaime Astarloa did not give a damn about the age he lived in, far less about Agapito Cárceles's outmoded tastes in literary or philosophical material, so he interrupted his friend as tactfully as he could and brought the conversation back to the matter at hand. Cárceles forgot about the books and was clearly keen to tackle the documents. Don Jaime took them from their hiding place.

"Above all, Don Agapito, I trust in your honour as a friend and a gentleman to treat this whole matter with the utmost discretion." He spoke gravely and he could see that his tone of voice appeared to impress the journalist. "Do I have your word?"

Cárceles solemnly raised a hand to his breast.

"Of course you do."

Don Jaime thought that perhaps he was, after all, wrong to trust him, but there was no turning back. He spread the contents of the folder on the table.

"These documents have come into my possession for reasons which I am not at liberty to explain, since the secret is not mine to reveal. They contain some hidden meaning which I cannot uncover and which, because it is of great importance to me, I must understand." There was now a look of absorbed attention on Cárceles's face as he listened to his friend's faltering words. "Perhaps the problem lies in my lack of knowledge of political matters in this country, but the fact is that I am incapable of making any coherent sense of what, obviously, does make sense. That is why I decided to ask you, since you know about these things. I would like you to read these documents, try to deduce what it is all about and then give me your expert opinion."

Cárceles did not move for a few moments, looking hard at Don Jaime, who could see that his companion was impressed. Cárceles licked his lips and looked at the documents on the table.

"Don Jaime," he said at last, with barely concealed admiration. "I would never have imagined that you . . . "

"Nor would I," said Don Jaime, cutting him short. "And to be absolutely honest, I must tell you that these papers are in my hands quite against my will. I have no choice now, however, and I must know what they mean."

Cárceles looked at the documents again, uncertain whether or not to touch them. Undoubtedly he sensed that some grave matter lay behind all this. At last, as if coming to a sudden decision, he sat down at the table and picked them up. Don Jaime remained standing, next to him. Given the situation, he resolved to abandon his usual politeness and to re-read the contents of the folder over his friend's shoulder.

When he saw the letter headings and the signatures on the first letters, the journalist swallowed hard. A couple of times he turned round to look incredulously at Don Jaime, but made no comment. He read on in silence, carefully turning the pages, pausing now and then with a finger on one of the names in the lists. When he was halfway through his reading, he suddenly stopped as if he had had an idea, and hurriedly leafed back to an earlier page. A faint grimace, resembling a smile, appeared on his ill-shaven face. He then continued with his reading, while Don Jaime, who did not dare to interrupt, waited expectantly, on tenterhooks.

"Can you make anything of it?" he asked at last, unable to contain himself any longer. The journalist made a cautious gesture.

"Possibly. But at the moment it's only a hunch. I need to be quite certain that we're on the right track."

He plunged back into his reading, frowning in concentration. After a moment, he slowly nodded, as if he had found the certainty he was looking for. He stopped again and looked up at the ceiling, as though trying to remember.

"There was something . . . " he said in a sombre voice, as if to himself. "I don't quite remember, but it must have been . . . at the beginning of last year. Yes, mines. There was some campaign against Narváez; people said he was in on the deal. Now, what was that . . . ?"

Jaime Astarloa could not remember ever having felt so nervous.

Suddenly, Cárceles's face lit up.

"Of course, how could I have been so stupid!" he exclaimed, striking the table with the palm of his hand. "But I need to check the name. Could it be that . . . ?" He again leafed rapidly back through the pages. "Good God, Don Jaime, did you really not see it? What you have here is an unprecedented scandal! I swear that . . . !"

Someone knocked at the door. Cárceles stopped speaking and looked fearfully towards the hall.

"Are you expecting anyone?"

Don Jaime shook his head, as disconcerted as Cárceles was by the interruption. With unexpected presence of mind, the journalist picked up the documents, looked about him, then jumped nimbly to his feet and stuffed the papers under the sofa, before turning to Don Jaime.

"Get rid of them, whoever they are!" he whispered in his ear. "You and I must talk."

Perplexed, Don Jaime automatically straightened his tie and went to the front door. The knowledge that he was about to have revealed to him the mystery which had brought Adela de Otero to him and had cost Luis de Ayala his life was gradually sinking in, provoking in him a feeling of unreality. For a moment, he wondered if he would suddenly wake up and find that it had all been an absurd joke, the fruit of his imagination.

There was a policeman at the door.

"Don Jaime Astarloa?"

Don Jaime felt the hairs prickle on the back of his neck.

"That's right."

The policeman cleared his throat. He had gypsy features and a scrappy beard.

"The chief of police, Don Jenaro Campillo, sent me. Would you mind accompanying me to a carriage?"

Don Jaime looked at him uncomprehendingly.

"I'm sorry?" he asked, trying to gain time.

The policeman saw his confusion and, smiling, said in a calm voice: "Don't worry, it's just routine. It seems there's some new information relating to the murder of the Marqués de los Alumbres."

Don Jaime blinked, irritated by the inopportuneness of the call. But the policeman had spoken of new information. It could be important. Perhaps they had found Adela de Otero.

"Would you mind waiting a moment?"

"Not at all. Take all the time you want."

He left the policeman at the door and went back into the living room, where Cárceles, who had been listening to the conversation, was waiting.

"What shall we do?" said Don Jaime in a low voice. The journalist made a gesture advising calm.

"You go," he said. "I'll wait for you here. It will give me a chance to read through the whole thing more slowly."

"Have you found something?"

"I think so, but I'm still not sure. I have to go more deeply into it. Off you go now."

Don Jaime nodded. He had no option.

"I'll be as quick as possible."

"Don't rush." There was a somewhat disturbing glint in Agapito Cárceles's eyes. "Has this got anything to do with what I've just been reading?" he said, pointing to the door.

Jaime Astarloa blushed. It was all getting out of control. For a while now a feeling had been mounting in him of crazed exhaustion.

"I'm not sure yet." At this stage, it seemed ignoble to lie to Cárceles. "I mean . . . we'll talk when I get back. I have to put my thoughts in order."

He shook his friend's hand and went out, accompanied by the policeman. An official carriage waited below.

"Where are we going?" he asked.

The policeman had stepped in a puddle and was trying to remove the water from his boots.

"To the morgue," he replied. And settling himself in his seat, he began whistling a popular tune.

Campillo was waiting in an office in the Forensic Institute. There were beads of sweat on his forehead, his wig was awry and his glasses dangled from the ribbon attached to his lapel. When he saw Don Jaime come in, he got up with a polite smile.

"I'm so sorry, Señor Astarloa, that we should be obliged to meet twice in one day and in such distressing circumstances."

Don Jaime looked about him suspiciously. He had to muster all his energy to preserve what remained of his sang-froid, which seemed to be leaking out from every pore in his body. This was all beginning to go beyond the limits of the controlled emotions to which he was accustomed.

"What's happened?" he asked, making no effort to hide his disquiet. "I have an important matter to sort out at home . . . "

Jenaro Campillo made an apologetic gesture.

"I'll only keep you a few minutes, I assure you. I know how tiresome this situation is for you, but, believe me, something most unexpected has happened." He clicked his tongue, as if expressing his own distaste for the whole business. "And what a day for it to happen, too! I've just received some far from reassuring news. There are rebel troops advancing on Madrid. It's rumoured that the Queen may be forced to go over into France, and here they're afraid there may be disturbances in the streets. So you see how things are. But, regardless of these political events, common justice must follow its inexorable course. *Dura lex, sed lex.* Don't you agree?"

"Forgive me, Señor Campillo, but I don't understand. This doesn't seem to me the most appropriate place for . . . "

The chief of police raised a hand, appealing for Don Jaime's patience.

"Would you be so kind as to accompany me?"

He pointed the way. They went down some stairs, then along a dark corridor with white-tiled walls and damp stains on the ceiling. The place was lit by gas lights, whose flames were shaken by a cold draught which made Jaime Astarloa shiver in his light summer jacket. The noise of footsteps disappearing down the other end of the corridor set off sinister echoes.

Campillo stopped by a frosted glass door and pushed it open, inviting his companion to go in first. Don Jaime found himself in a small room furnished with old filing cabinets in dark wood. A municipal employee stood up behind his desk when he saw them come in. The man was thin, of uncertain age, and his white coat was spattered with yellow stains.

"Number seventeen, Lucio, if you wouldn't mind."

The man picked up a form that was on the table and pushed open one of the swing doors on the other side of the room. Before following him, the policeman took a Havana cigar from his pocket and offered one to Don Jaime.

"Thank you, Señor Campillo. As I told you this morning, I don't smoke."

Campillo raised a reproving eyebrow.

"The spectacle I'm obliged to share with you is not exactly pleasant," he remarked, putting the cigar in his mouth and lighting it with a match. "Cigar smoke often helps one to bear such things better."

"What things?"

"You'll see in a moment."

"Whatever it is, I don't need to smoke."

The policeman shrugged.

"As you wish."

They went into a low but spacious room, the walls covered in the same white tiles and with identical damp stains on the ceiling. In one corner there was a large sink with a tap that kept dripping.

Don Jaime stopped involuntarily, while the intense, all-pervading cold penetrated to his very entrails. He had never before visited a morgue, nor had he imagined that it would be so desolate and gloomy. Half a dozen large marble tables were lined up in the room; on four of them there were sheets, beneath which he could see motionless human forms. He closed his eyes for a moment, filling his lungs, only to breathe out again at once with a groan of digust. There was a strange smell floating in the air.

"Phenol," said the policeman. "It's used as a disinfectant."

Don Jaime nodded silently. His eyes were fixed on one of the bodies stretched out on a marble table. Protruding from the lower end of the sheet were two human feet. They were yellowish in colour and seemed to glow blue in the gaslight.

Jenaro Campillo followed his gaze.

"You know him already," the policeman said with a casualness which, to Don Jaime, seemed monstrous. "It's this one over here that interests us."

With his cigar he indicated the next table, again covered by a sheet. Beneath it lay a smaller, more delicate figure.

The policeman exhaled a dense cloud of smoke and brought Don Jaime to a halt by the covered corpse.

"It appeared about mid-morning in the river, more or less at the time that you and I were having our nice little chat in the Palacio de Villaflores. She was probably thrown in there during the night."

"Thrown in?"

"That's what I said," said the policeman with a sarcastic little laugh, as if, despite everything, the matter was not without its humorous side. "I can assure you that this is not a case of suicide, nor an accident. Are you sure you won't follow my advice and have one of these cigars? I'm very much afraid, Señor Astarloa, that it will take you a long time to forget what you're about to see; it's quite shocking. But I need you to complete the identification process, no easy task, especially in this case, as you yourself are about to find out."

While he was talking, he made a sign to the clerk to remove the sheet covering the body. Don Jaime felt a wave of nausea rising up from his stomach; he took in desperate gulps of air in order to control it. His legs buckled under him and he had to lean on the marble table in order to steady himself.

"Do you recognize her?"

Don Jaime forced himself to keep looking at the naked corpse. It was the body of a young woman of medium height, who might have been quite attractive a few hours before. Her skin was the colour of wax, her belly sunk between her pelvic bones, and her breasts, possibly beautiful in life, fell to either side, towards her inert, rigid arms.

"Nice piece of work, eh?" murmured Campillo behind him.

With a supreme effort, Don Jaime looked again at what had once been a face. There were no features, only butchered skin, flesh and bones. There was no nose, and the mouth was just a dark, lipless hole, through which you could see a few broken teeth. In place of eyes there were two empty, reddish sockets. Her black, abundant hair was dirty and tangled, still bearing traces of slime from the river.

Unable to bear the sight any longer, trembling with horror, Don Jaime moved away from the table. He felt the policeman's hand on his arm, the smell of cigar smoke and then the voice that reached him in a low whisper.

"Do you recognize her?"

Don Jaime shook his head. Into his troubled mind came the memory of an old nightmare – a blind doll floating in a puddle – but it was the words which Campillo spoke afterwards that made a mortal cold slip slowly into the furthest corner of his soul: "You should recognize her, Señor Astarloa, despite the mutilation. It's your old client, Doña Adela de Otero."

VII

The Appel

*"To use the appel (striking the ground with the leading foot)
unsettles your opponent and induces a reaction."*

It took him a while to realize that the chief of police had been talking
to him for some time. They had come up from the basement and
were once more at street level, sitting in a small office in the Forensic
Institute. Jaime Astarloa was sitting back in his chair, utterly still,
staring blankly at a faded engraving on the wall, a Nordic landscape
with lakes and fir trees. His hands hung by his sides and an opaque,
expressionless veil seemed to cover his grey eyes.

"The body got caught up in the reeds underneath the Toledo
bridge, on the left bank. It's odd that the current didn't carry her
further when you consider the storm we had last night; that leads
us to believe that she was thrown into the water shortly before dawn.
What I don't understand is why they went to the trouble of carrying
her all the way there, instead of leaving her in her apartment."

Campillo paused and looked inquisitively at Don Jaime, as if
giving him the opportunity to ask a question. Getting no reaction, he
shrugged. He still had his cigar clamped between his teeth and was
cleaning the lenses of his glasses with a crumpled handkerchief he
had taken from his pocket.

"When they told me that a body had been found, I ordered them
to force the door of the house. We should have done it much sooner,
because we found a pretty ugly scene there: signs of struggle, over-
turned furniture, and blood, a lot of blood. There was a great pool of
blood in the bedroom, a trail along the corridor . . . It looked, if

you'll pardon the expression, as if someone had slaughtered a calf."
He looked at Don Jaime, judging the effect of his words; he seemed
keen to ascertain whether or not his description was realistic enough
to shock Don Jaime. He must have decided that it was not, because
he frowned, rubbed more energetically at his spectacles and continued
to list macabre details, all the time watching Don Jaime out of
the corner of his eye. "It seems that they killed her in that . . .
conscientious manner and then took her out under cover of night
to throw her in the river. I don't know if there was any intermediary
stage, you know what I mean, torture or the like, although, given
the state they left her in, I'm very much afraid there was. There is
no doubt, though, that Señora de Otero had a pretty bad time of it
before leaving her apartment in Calle Riaño, and that by then she
was quite dead."

Campillo paused in order to put his glasses back on, having first
held them up to the light with an air of satisfaction.

"Quite dead," he repeated thoughtfully, trying to pick up the
thread of his thoughts. "In the bedroom we also found tufts of hair,
which, as we now learn, came from the dead woman. There was a
scrap of blue cloth too, possibly torn off in the struggle; that belongs
to the dress she was wearing when we found her in the river." The
policeman put two fingers into the upper pocket of his jacket and
brought out a small silver ring. "The corpse was wearing this on the
ring finger of her left hand. Have you ever seen it before?"

Jaime Astarloa's eyelids drooped and then opened again as if he
were waking from a long sleep. He turned slowly towards Campillo.
He was very pale; the last drop of blood seemed to have drained
from his face.

"I'm sorry?"

The policeman shifted in his seat; he had obviously hoped for
greater co-operation from Jaime Astarloa and was beginning to feel
irritated by his behaviour, which was very like that of a sleepwalker.
After the initial shock, the fencing master was now locked in a stubborn
silence, as if the tragedy were a matter of complete indifference to him.

"I asked if you had ever seen this ring before."

Don Jaime reached out his hand and took the slender silver ring between his fingers. The painful memory surfaced of that same ring glinting on brown skin. He placed it on the table.

"It belonged to Adela de Otero," he confirmed in a neutral voice.

Campillo made another attempt.

"What I can't understand, Señor Astarloa, is why they should treat her so mercilessly. Revenge perhaps? Maybe they wanted to drag a confession out of her."

"I've no idea."

"Did she have any enemies as far as you know?"

"I've no idea."

"It's terrible to do what they did to her. She must have been very beautiful."

Don Jaime thought of a bare, smooth-skinned neck beneath dark hair caught up at the nape with a mother-of-pearl comb. He remembered a half-open door and the rustle of petticoats, he remembered the warm, pulsating, languorous skin. "I don't exist," she had said to him once, on that night when everything was possible and when nothing had happened. Now it was true; she no longer existed. She was just dead meat rotting on a marble slab.

"Very beautiful," he replied after a while. "Adela de Otero was very beautiful."

The policeman judged that he had already wasted quite enough time on the fencing master. He put the ring away, threw his cigar into the spittoon and stood up.

"You're obviously very upset by the events of the day," he said, "I can understand that. If you like, we could talk again tomorrow morning, when you've rested and feel slightly restored. I'm convinced that the deaths of the Marquis and of this woman are directly linked, and you are one of the few people who can give me some clue to it all. Would ten o'clock in my office suit you?"

Jaime Astarloa looked at the policeman as if he were seeing him for the first time.

"Am I a suspect?" he asked.

Campillo winked one of his fish eyes.

"Who isn't nowadays?" he remarked in a frivolous tone, but Don Jaime did not appear satisfied with that reply.

"I'm serious. I want to know if I am under suspicion."

Campillo swayed back and forth on his feet, one hand in his trouser pocket.

"Not particularly, if that's any consolation," he replied after a few moments. "It's just that I can't afford to discount anyone and you are the only person I have to hand."

"I'm glad to be of use to you."

The policeman gave a conciliatory smile, as if asking for his understanding.

"Don't be offended, Señor Astarloa," he said. "After all, I'm sure you'll agree with me that there are a series of loose ends that insist on tying themselves into knots: two of your clients die; the common factor is fencing. One of them is killed with a fencing foil. Everything turns round the same thing, but what still escapes me is the point around which these events turn and what your role is in it all, if indeed you have a role."

"I see your problem, but I'm sorry to say that I can't help you."

"Not as sorry as me. You will understand, though, that, the way things are, I cannot rule you out as a possible accomplice. At my age, and with all I've seen during my years in this job, and given these circumstances, I wouldn't even rule out my own dear mother."

"To put it bluntly, then, I'm under surveillance."

Campillo pulled a face, as if such an expression when applied to the fencing master was excessive.

"Let's just say that I still require your esteemed collaboration, Señor Astarloa. The proof is that you have an appointment with me in my office tomorrow morning. And I ask you, with all due respect, not to leave the city and to remain contactable."

Don Jaime nodded silently, almost abstractedly, while he got to his feet and picked up his hat and cane.

"Have you interrogated the maid?" he asked.

"What maid?"

"The maid who worked in Doña Adela's house. I think her name was Lucía."

"Ah, yes, sorry, I didn't quite understand, yes, the maid, of course . . . Well, no, we haven't. I mean we haven't been able to locate her. According to the concierge's wife, she was dismissed about a week ago and hasn't been back. Needless to say, I'm moving heaven and earth to find her."

"And what else did the concierges in the building tell you?"

"They weren't much use either. Last night, what with the storm that broke over Madrid, they didn't hear a thing. As regards Señora de Otero, they know very little. And if they do know something, they're not saying, either out of caution or fear. It wasn't her apartment; she rented it three months ago through a third party, a commercial agent, whom we have also questioned but to no avail. She moved in with very little luggage. Nobody knows where she came from, although there are indications that she lived abroad for some time . . . I'll see you tomorrow, Señor Astarloa. Don't forget, we have an appointment."

Don Jaime looked at him coldly.

"I won't forget. Good night."

He stood for a long time in the middle of the street, leaning on his walking stick, looking up at the black sky; the blanket of clouds had parted to reveal a few stars. Anyone passing would doubtless have been surprised by the expression on his face, which was barely lit by the pale flame of the gas lights. His gaunt features seemed as if carved out of stone, like lava that had just solidified beneath a glacial blast of air. And it wasn't just his face. He felt his heart beating very slowly in his breast, calm and deliberate, like the pulse in his temples. He didn't know why, or rather he refused to go too deeply into it, but ever since he had seen the naked, mutilated body of Adela de Otero the confusion that had been tormenting him had vanished, as if by magic. It seemed that the icy air of the morgue had left a cold residue inside him. His mind was now clear; he could feel the perfect control he had over the smallest of the muscles in his body. It was as if the world about him had returned to its exact dimensions and he could once again study it with his old serenity, in his usual, rather distant manner.

What had happened inside him? He did not know. He felt only the certainty that, for some obscure reason, the death of Adela de Otero had liberated him, had put paid to the feeling of shame and humiliation which had tormented him to the point of madness during the last few weeks. He felt a kind of perverse satisfaction at learning that he had been deceived not by an executioner, but by a victim. This changed things. At last, he had the sad consolation of knowing that the plot had not been dreamed up by a woman, but meticulously carried out by someone completely without scruples, a cruel murderer, a callous swine, whose identity remained a mystery, but who might be waiting for him only a few steps away, thanks to the documents that Agapito Cárceles must by now have deciphered in Don Jaime's apartment in Calle Bordadores. It was time to turn the page. The puppet refused to play any more, he had broken free of the strings. Now he would act on his own initiative; that was why he had said nothing to the police. With the confusion gone, he was filled instead by a cold anger, by an immense, lucid, calm hatred.

Don Jaime took a deep breath of cool, night air, gripped his walking stick firmly and set off towards home. The moment to learn the truth had arrived, because the hour of vengeance was tolling.

He had to take a circuitous route. Although it was already eleven o'clock at night, the streets were full of people. Squads of soldiers and mounted policemen were patrolling everywhere, and on the corner of Calle Hileras he saw the remains of a barricade, which several local people were dismantling under the supervision of the police. Near the Plaza Mayor he heard the distant hubbub of a crowd, and a squad of halberdiers from the Civil Guard was patrolling outside the Teatro Real, with bayonets fixed. It looked like there would be trouble that night, but Jaime Astarloa barely noticed what was going on around him, so immersed was he in his own thoughts. He hurried up the steps and opened the door, expecting to find Cárceles there, but the apartment was empty.

He struck a match and lit the oil lamp, surprised by Cárceles's absence. Assailed by foreboding, he looked in the bedroom and in the fencing gallery, but no one was there. When he went back into the living room, he looked under the sofa and behind the books on the shelves, but he couldn't find the documents in either place. It was absurd, he said to himself. Agapito Cárceles could not simply go off without saying a word to him. Where would he have hidden the folder? He was forced to a frightening conclusion: could Cárceles have taken the papers with him?

He noticed a sheet of paper on his writing desk. Before leaving, Cárceles had written him a note:

Dear Don Jaime,
Everything is in hand, but I need to check a few facts. Trust me.

He had not even signed the note. Don Jaime held it in his hand for a moment before crumpling it up and throwing it on the floor. Cárceles had obviously taken the documents with him and that made Don Jaime feel suddenly angry. He immediately regretted having placed his faith in the journalist; he cursed himself out loud for his own stupidity. God knows where that man would be now with the documents, which had cost the lives of both Luis de Ayala and Adela de Otero.

It did not take him long to decide what to do and, without properly thinking it through, he found himself heading back down the stairs. He knew where Cárceles lived and he was prepared to go there, recover the documents and make him tell whatever he knew, even if he had to drag it out of him.

He stopped on the landing and forced himself to reflect on his actions. The whole story had taken a turn that was far from being a game. "Let's not lose our head again," he said to himself, trying to preserve the calm that was rapidly deserting him. There, in the darkness on the empty stairs, he leaned against the wall and thought about what he should do next. Of course he had to go to Cárceles's house, that much was clear. And then? There was only one reasonable course of action, the one that led him straight to Jenaro Campillo; his little game of hide-and-seek had gone on quite long enough. He thought bitterly about the precious time that he had wasted by his own dilatoriness, and he decided not to repeat that mistake. He would open his heart to the chief of police and hand Ayala's file to him, so that justice could at last take its conventional course. He smiled sadly to imagine Campillo's face when he saw Don Jaime appear the following morning with the documents under his arm.

He also considered the possibility of going to the police before visiting Cárceles, but that presented certain problems. It was one thing to arrive with the proof in his hand and quite another to tell a story that might or might not be believed; a story which, moreover, seriously contradicted what he had said in the two interviews he had had with Campillo during the day. Besides, he had no idea what Cárceles's intentions were; he might simply deny everything. He had not even signed the note and there was no reference to the matter preoccupying them. No, he would obviously have to look for his unfaithful friend first.

It was then and only then that he came to a realization that made an unpleasant shudder run through him. Whoever was responsible for what was happening had already killed twice and might be prepared, if necessary, to do so again. However, the idea that he, too, was in danger and could be murdered, along with the others, did not greatly perturb him. He thought about it for a few moments and discovered, to his surprise, that the possibility aroused in him more curiosity than fear. Seen from that point of view, things became simpler, they could be approached according to their individual merits. It was no longer a case of being involved in other people's tragedies despite oneself, in a state of enforced impotence; up until then, that and that alone had been the source of his feelings of torment and horror. However, if he was likely to be the next victim, then everything became much easier; he would no longer have to witness the bloody trail left by the murderers; they would come to him. To him. His blood beat steadily in his weary veins, ready for the fight. He had spent his life parrying all kinds of thrusts, and the thought of one more blow did not worry him, even if it came from behind. Perhaps Luis de Ayala or Adela de Otero had not remained sufficiently alert; Don Jaime would. As he used to say to his students, a thrust in tierce could not be carried out with the same ease as a thrust in quarte. And he was very good at parrying thrusts in tierce, and at dealing them out.

He had made his decision. He would go and recover Luis de Ayala's documents that very night. With this thought, he went upstairs again, opened the door, left his walking stick in the umbrella stand and picked up another, made of mahogany and with a silver handle, somewhat heavier than the other stick. He went downstairs carrying it in his hand, distractedly dragging it along the iron bars of the banister. Inside the stick was a foil made of the finest steel, as sharp as any razor.

He stopped in the doorway and glanced both ways before venturing out into the shadows engulfing the deserted street. He walked to the corner of Calle Arenal, and consulted his watch by the light of a street lamp, by the brick wall of the church of San Ginés. It was twenty minutes to midnight.

He walked on for a while. There was now hardly anyone about. Given the way events were shaping, people had resolved to shut themselves up in their houses and only the occasional nightbird braved the streets of Madrid, which, in the feeble light of the street lamps, had all the appearance of a ghost city. The soldiers on the corner of Calle Postas were wrapped in blankets, asleep on the pavement, next to their rifles stacked in a pyramid. A sentinel, his face lost in shadow beneath the peak of his cap, saluted in response to Don Jaime's greeting. Opposite the main post office, a few Civil Guards were watching the building with their hands on the hilts of their sabres and their rifles on their shoulders. At the far end of Carrera de San Jerónimo, a round, reddish moon was rising above the black silhouette of the rooftops.

He was in luck. A hired carriage passed him on the corner of Alcalá, just when he had despaired of finding one. The coachman was on his way home and accepted him as a passenger reluctantly. Don Jaime sat back in the seat and gave Agapito Cárceles's address, an old building near the Puerta de Toledo. It was only by chance that he knew the place, and he was glad of it. On one occasion, Cárceles had insisted on inviting everyone from the Café Progreso there in order to read them the first and second acts of a play he had written entitled: *All for One or*

The Sovereign People, a stormy drama in free verse, the first two pages of which, had they ever been performed on stage, would have been enough to consign the author to a good long spell in some prison in Africa, unless the fact that it had been blatantly plagiarized from Lope de Vega's *Fuenteovejuna* served as an extenuating circumstance.

The gloomy, deserted streets paraded past outside the carriage window; the horses' hooves and the occasional crack of the coachman's whip echoed down them. Don Jaime was thinking how best to behave when he found his friend. The journalist had doubtless discovered something scandalous in the documents and perhaps wanted to make some private use of them. Jaime Astarloa was not prepared to tolerate that, because, amongst other reasons, he was furious to have been the victim of such an abuse of confidence. Calming down a little, it occurred to him that Agapito Cárceles might not, in fact, have acted in bad faith by taking the folder; perhaps he had merely wanted to check something that appeared in the document against information that he had filed away at home. Don Jaime would soon find out. The carriage had stopped and the coachman was leaning down from the driving seat.

"Here it is, sir. Calle de la Taberna."

It was an ill-lit, narrow cul-de-sac, which smelled of grime and rancid wine. Don Jaime asked the coachman to wait for half an hour, but the coachman refused, saying it was too late. Don Jaime paid, and the carriage moved off. He walked down the cul-de-sac, trying to identify his friend's house.

It took him a while, but he found it, remembering that it was in an inner courtyard underneath an archway. Once there, he groped his way up the staircase to the top floor, leaning on the banister, conscious of the wooden stairs creaking beneath his feet. When he was in the inner gallery, which ran along the four walls of the courtyard, he took a box of matches out of his pocket and lit one. He hoped he had not got the wrong door, because then he would have to waste time in tiresome explanations; it was certainly not an hour to be waking up the neighbours. He knocked three times with the handle of his stick, then knocked again.

He waited in vain. He knocked once more and pressed his ear to the door, hoping to hear something. Inside, absolute silence reigned. Discouraged, he thought perhaps Cárceles wasn't there. Where would he be at that hour? He hesitated, uncertain what to do, then knocked more loudly, this time with his fist. Perhaps Cárceles was in a deep sleep. He listened again, to no avail.

He stepped back, leaning against the balustrade which ran round the gallery. That meant he could do nothing until the following day – hardly an encouraging thought. He had to see Cárceles at once, or at least rescue the documents. After a moment's hesitation, he decided to call them stolen documents. Because, whatever his motives, it was clear that what Cárceles had committed in his house was theft pure and simple. The thought infuriated Don Jaime.

An idea had been going round and round in his head for some time and he found himself struggling against his own scruples: should he break down the door? After all, why not? Cárceles had acted in a despicable manner by taking the documents. Jaime Astarloa's case was different. He only wanted to recover what, in the most tragic circumstances, had become his property.

He went back to the door and knocked again, with little hope. To hell with being considerate. This time, he did not wait for a reply. He felt for the knob, testing it. The door was locked. He struck another match and studied the lock. He could not break the door down, because that would wake the neighbours. On the other hand, the lock did not seem particularly strong. It was odd, but when he bent down and put his eye to the keyhole he thought he could see the end of the key, as if the door were locked from inside. He stood up, intrigued, wringing his hands with impatience. Perhaps Cárceles was in there after all. Perhaps, realizing who his visitor might be, he was refusing to open the door, hoping to make Don Jaime think that he wasn't at home. Don Jaime didn't like that and he felt his resolution growing by the minute. He would pay Cárceles for any damage caused, but he was determined to go in.

He looked about him in search of something to help him force the lock. He had no experience of that kind of thing, but he imagined that if he could find something to use as a lever the door would give way. He walked up and down the gallery, lighting his way with matches cupped in his hand; all in vain. He stopped where he was, almost ready to give up. He had only three matches left and had still found nothing that would serve as a lever.

Just when he had given everything up for lost, he saw a few rusty iron bars fixed in the wall, like steps. He looked up and saw a trapdoor in the ceiling of the gallery, which no doubt led to the roof. His heart beat faster when he remembered that Cárceles's house had a small terrace to one side; perhaps that was a more practicable way in than through the front door. He took off his hat and jacket, gripped his walking stick between his teeth and climbed up to the trapdoor. It opened easily and he emerged beneath the heavenly, star-filled vault. With great care he pulled the rest of his body up and out, feeling for broken tiles. It would be no joke to slip and go crashing down to the ground, three floors below. The constant practice of fencing kept him in reasonable shape for his age, but he was no longer a vigorous young man. He decided to move as carefully as he could, looking for solid holds and moving only one limb at a time, keeping the others fixed on some point of support. In the distance, a clock struck the four quarter hours, and then one. As he crouched on the roof, it occurred to him how utterly grotesque the situation was, and he was grateful for the cover of darkness so as not to be seen in that preposterous position.

He moved across the roof with infinite caution, careful not to make any noise that might alarm the neighbours. Miraculously, he avoided several loose tiles and found himself leaning over the eaves above the flat roof outside Agapito Cárceles's rooms. Holding onto the guttering, he lowered himself down. He waited there for a few moments, in waistcoat and shirtsleeves, his walking stick in his hand, whilst he recovered his breath. Then he lit another match and went over to the door. It was a glass door with a simple latch that could be worked from the outside. Before opening it, he looked through the glass; the place was in darkness.

He gritted his teeth and lifted the latch as quietly as he could. He found himself in a narrow kitchen, next to a stove and a sink. The moon filtered its feeble light through the window, allowing him to make out various pots on a table, next to what seemed to be the remains of a meal. He struck his penultimate match in search of something he could use to light his way; he found a candlestick on top of a cupboard. With a sigh of relief, he lit the candle. Cockroaches scuttled across the floor, fleeing from his feet.

He went from the kitchen into a short corridor, where the wall-paper was peeling off the walls in strips. He was about to draw a curtain that concealed a bedroom, when he thought he heard something behind a door to his left. He stopped, listening hard, but could hear only his own rapid breathing. His mouth was dry, his tongue was stuck to its roof, and his ears buzzed; he felt as if he were living through some completely unreal situation, a dream from which he could awake at any moment. Very slowly he pushed open the door.

It was Agapito Cárceles's bedroom and Cárceles was in there, but Don Jaime, who had several times imagined what he would say to him when he found him, was completely unprepared for the sight that met his eyes, which opened wide with terror. Cárceles was lying face up, completely naked, his hands and feet tied to the four corners of the bed. From chest to thighs, Cárceles's body was a bloody mass of cuts made by a cut-throat razor, which lay glinting in the candlelight; the mattress was drenched in blood. But Cárceles wasn't dead. When he saw the light he moved his head slightly, not recognizing the person in the room, and from his lips, swollen with suffering, came a hoarse cry of animal terror, a guttural, unintelligible plea for mercy.

Jaime Astarloa had lost the power of speech. Mechanically, as if the blood had curdled in his veins, he took two steps towards the bed, staring in astonishment at his friend's tortured body. Sensing him approach, Cárceles stirred feebly.

"No . . . I beg you," he murmured in a mere thread of a voice, whilst tears and blood ran down his cheeks. "For pity's sake . . . no more. That's all I know . . . I've told you everything. Merciful God, no . . . enough, for the love of God!"

His plea became a scream. His staring eyes were fixed on the candle flame and his chest fluttered as if he were taking his dying breath.

Reaching out a hand, Jaime Astarloa touched his forehead; it burned as if there were a fire blazing inside. His own voice was like a whisper, strangled by horror: "Who did this to you?"

Cárceles moved his eyes slowly in his direction, struggling to recognize the person speaking to him.

"The Devil," he said in a moan of infinite pain and distress. A yellowish scum bubbled in one corner of his mouth. "They are . . . the Devil."

"Where are the documents?"

Cárceles rolled his eyes and trembled, sobbing: "For pity's sake, take me away from here. Don't let them go on. Take me away from here, I beg you. I've told them everything. He's got them, him, Astarloa. I've got nothing to do with it all, I swear. Go and see him and he'll tell you. I only wanted . . . I don't know any more, for pity's sake, that's all I know."

Don Jaime started when he heard his name on the dying man's lips. He didn't know who Cárceles's executioners were, but it was clear that Agapito Cárceles had betrayed him. He felt the hair stand up on the back of his neck. There was no time to lose; he must . . .

Something moved behind him. Sensing an alien presence, Don Jaime half-turned, and the gesture possibly saved his life. A hard object brushed past his head and hit him on the neck. Stunned by the pain, he had enough presence of mind to jump to one side and he sensed a shadow bounding towards him just as the candle fell from his grasp, going out as it rolled across the floor.

He stepped back, bumping into furniture in the darkness, hearing his attacker's breathing immediately before him. With a kind of desperate energy he seized the walking stick, which he still had in his right hand, and held it out in the open space that his attacker would have to cross to reach him.

If he had had time to analyse his state of mind, he would have been surprised to find that he felt no fear at all, just an icy determination to give as good as he got. It was hatred that gave him the strength to fight, and the strength of his arm, tense as a spring, responded to the desire to harm, to kill the murderer. He thought of Luis de Ayala, of

Cárceles, of Adela de Otero. By God, they weren't going to slaughter him as they had the others.

At that moment, waiting steadfastly for the attack that would come from the shadows, Jaime Astarloa instinctively adopted the on-guard position, which he always took up when he fenced.

"To me!" he shouted defiantly into the darkness. Then he felt someone close at hand breathing hard and something touched the end of his walking stick. A hand grasped the end hard, trying to pull it from his hand, and Jaime Astarloa laughed silently when he heard the sound of the lower half of the walking stick slipping over the steel blade, which it served as a scabbard. That was exactly what he had expected; his attacker had just exposed the blade, at the same time involuntarily revealing approximately where he was and at what distance. Then the fencing master drew his arm back, pulling the blade completely free of the scabbard and, dropping three times onto his bent right leg, he lunged blindly three times into the shadows. Something solid interposed itself in the path of the third lunge and someone gave a cry of pain.

"To me!" Don Jaime shouted again, lunging in the direction of the door with his sword held out before him. He heard the noise of furniture being knocked over and an object flew past him, shattering as it hit the wall. The harmless lower half of the walking stick hit him rather feebly on the arm when he passed the place where his enemy must have been.

"Get him!" yelled a voice barely two feet from him. "He's heading for the door! He stuck a sword in me."

It seemed that the murderer had only been wounded. And, what was worse, he wasn't alone. Don Jaime hurled himself against the door and ran out into the passage, fencing wildly into the darkness.

"To me!"

The way out must be to the left, at the end of the corridor, on the other side of the curtain that he had seen when he came into the house. A dark shape stood in his way and something hit the wall next to his skull. Don Jaime lowered his head and walked forwards, his weapon in his hand. He heard the sound of someone panting and a hand grabbed him by his shirt collar; he smelled the sour odour of sweat close by, whilst two strong arms tried to hold him fast. The pincers closed ever more tightly round his chest. Suffocated by the pressure, unable to get far enough away to use the sword, Don Jaime managed to free his left hand and reach up; he touched an ill-shaven cheek. Then, mustering his waning strength, he grabbed his opponent by the hair and pulled the head forward as hard as he could, striking him with his own forehead. He felt a sharp pain between his eyebrows, and something crunched beneath the impact. A hot, viscous fluid ran down his face; he didn't know if it was his blood or if he had managed to break his attacker's nose, but at least he was free again. He pressed himself against the wall and slid along it, describing semi-circles with the tip of his blade. He knocked over something that fell to the floor with a crash.

"Here, you scum!"

Someone did, in fact, move towards him. He felt the man's presence even before he touched him, heard the scuff of feet on the floor, and lunged blindly, forcing whoever it was to step back. He leaned against the wall again, panting, trying to recover his breath. He was exhausted and didn't think he could go on for much longer; but in the dark he couldn't find the way out. On the other hand, even if he did find the door, he wouldn't have time to find the key and turn it in the lock before they were on him again. "This is as far you go, old friend," he said to himself, peering without much hope into the surrounding gloom. He didn't particularly mind dying there, in the dark; it only saddened him to have to go without learning the answer.

There was a noise to his right. He lunged in that direction, and the blade of his foil bent as it came in contact with something hard; one of the murderers was using a chair to protect himself as he advanced towards him. Don Jaime slid along the wall again to the left until his shoulder came up against a bit of furniture, possibly a wardrobe. He used the sword like a whip, enjoying the threatening whistle of the blade cutting the air; his enemies would hear it too, and the sound would warn them to be careful. For Don Jaime that might mean a few more seconds' life.

They were closing in again; he could sense them before he heard them move. He jumped forward, bumping into invisible furniture, knocking objects onto the floor, and reached another wall. There he stood still, holding his breath, because the noise of the air coming in and out of his mouth and nose prevented him from hearing the other noises in the room. To his left, very close, something crashed to the floor. Without hesitating for a moment, he put all his weight on his left leg and lunged again twice. He heard a furious moan: "He's stuck that thing in me again!"

The man was obviously an imbecile. Jaime Astarloa seized the opportunity to change position, this time without bumping into anything on the way. Smiling to himself, he thought that this was beginning to resemble a game of musical chairs. He wondered how much longer he could hold out. Not long, of course, but this wasn't, after all, such a bad way to die. Much better than, in a few years' time, fading away in some home for the infirm, with the nuns diddling him out of his last meagre savings stashed away under the bed, and with him cursing a God in whom he had never quite been able to believe.

"To me!"

This time, his now flagging call to arms rang out in vain. A shadow flitted by him, crunching over some broken shards, and suddenly a rectangle of light opened up in the wall. The shadow slipped rapidly through the open door, followed by another fleeting, lame silhouette. In the gallery he could hear the voices of neighbours who had been woken by the noise of the fight. There was the sound of footsteps, of shutters and doors opening, voices raised in alarm, the cries of old women. The fencing master staggered to the door and leaned, near to fainting, against the doorframe, gulping in lungfuls of cool night air. Beneath his clothes he felt his body drenched in sweat, and the hand holding the sword was trembling like a leaf. It took him a while to get used to the idea that he was going to go on living.

Gradually, various nightshirted neighbours crowded around, peering at him and lighting him with candles and oil lamps whilst they cast fearful glances into the apartment, which they did not dare to enter. A night watchman was coming up the stairs, bearing his lamp and pole;

the neighbours made way for this figure of authority, who looked suspiciously at the foil that Don Jaime still held in his hand.

"Did you catch them?" Don Jaime asked, without much hope.

The night watchman scratched the back of his head.

"Afraid not, sir. A neighbour and myself pursued two men who were running at full pelt down the street, but near the Puerta de Toledo they got into a carriage, which was waiting for them, and escaped. Has there been some trouble?"

Don Jaime nodded, pointing into the house.

"There's a man inside who's very badly wounded. See what you can do for him. You'd better call a doctor." All the energy that the fight had injected into his body was disappearing now, giving way to a great lassitude; he suddenly felt very old and tired. "You'd better send for the police too. It's vital that someone contact the chief of police, Don Jenaro Campillo."

The night watchman proved most obliging.

"Right away," he said, looking attentively at Don Jaime, and noticing with concern the blood on his face. "Are you wounded yourself, sir?"

Don Jaime touched his forehead with his fingers. His eyebrows seemed swollen, doubtless from the head butt he had dealt one of his opponents.

"It's not my blood," he said with a faint smile. "And if you need a description of the two men who were here, I'm afraid I can't be of much help. I can only say that one of them has probably got a broken nose and the other has two sword wounds somewhere on his body."

The fish eyes were looking at him coldly from behind their spectacles.

"Is that everything?"

Jaime Astarloa stared at the dregs of coffee in the cup he was holding. He was still feeling rather embarrassed.

"Yes, that's everything. Now I really have told you everything I know."

Campillo got up from his desk, took a few steps about the room and stood looking out of the window, his thumbs hooked in the armholes of his waistcoat. After a moment, he turned slowly and gave Don Jaime a disapproving look.

"Señor Astarloa, allow me to say that your behaviour throughout this whole affair has been that of a child."

Don Jaime blinked.

"I'm the first to admit that."

"Oh, so you admit it, well . . . But I ask myself what damn use it is to us now for you to admit it. Someone has been slicing away at this Cárceles fellow as if he were a side of beef, and all because you got it into your head to play Rocambole."

"I just wanted . . . "

"I know very well what you wanted. I prefer not to think about it too much, so as not to give in to the temptation to throw you in prison."

"My intention was to protect Doña Adela de Otero."

The chief of police gave a sarcastic little laugh.

"I might have known," he said, shaking his head, like a doctor diagnosing a hopeless case. "And we've seen how effective your protection turned out to be: one corpse, another on the way and you, by some miracle, still alive. And that's not even counting Luis de Ayala."

"I never wanted to get involved . . . "

"Just as well. If you had really put your oar in, all hell would have broken loose." Campillo took a handkerchief out of his pocket and started carefully polishing the lenses of his glasses. "I don't know if you realize the seriousness of the situation, Señor Astarloa."

"I do. And I'm prepared to take the consequences."

"You tried to protect a person who might have been implicated in the murder of the Marquis. Or, rather, who was implicated, because not even her death belies the fact that she was an accomplice in the intrigue. Indeed, that may have been precisely what cost her her life."

Campillo paused, put on his glasses and used the handkerchief to wipe the sweat from his brow.

"Just tell me one thing, Señor Astarloa. Why did you conceal from me the truth about that woman?"

A few moments passed. Then Don Jaime slowly raised his head and looked straight through the chief of police at some invisible point beyond him, in the distance. He half-closed his eyelids and the expression in his grey eyes grew steelier.

"I loved her."

Through the open window came the noise of carriages rattling along the street below. Campillo did not move or speak; it was clear that, for the first time, he was lost for words. He paced about the room; he cleared his throat, embarrassed, and went and sat down behind his desk again, not daring to look Don Jaime in the face.

"I'm sorry," he said after a while.

Jaime Astarloa nodded, without replying.

"I'm going to be quite honest with you," added the chief of police after a judicious pause, long enough for the echo of the last words they had exchanged to die away between them. "The more time passes, the more unlikely it is that we will resolve this matter, that we will ever nab the guilty parties. Your friend Cárceles, or what remains of him, is the only person alive who knows them; let's hope he lives long enough to tell us. Did you really not manage to identify either of the individuals who were torturing the poor wretch?"

"How could I? It all happened in the dark."

"You were very lucky last night. You could easily have ended up in a certain place with which you are already familiar, lying on a marble slab."

"I know."

For the first time that morning, the policeman smiled slightly.

"I understand that you proved a pretty hard nut to crack," he said, making a few two-handed gestures in the air. "At your age too . . . I mean it's pretty unusual. A man of your age taking on two professional murderers like that . . . "

Jaime Astarloa shrugged.

"I was fighting for my life, Señor Campillo."

The policeman raised a cigar to his mouth.

"That's a pretty weighty reason," he said, with an understanding look. "A very weighty reason indeed. Do you still not smoke, Señor Astarloa?"

"No, I still don't smoke."

"It's odd, sir," said Campillo, lighting a match and breathing in the first few mouthfuls of smoke with evident pleasure, "but, despite your rather foolish intervention in this affair, I can't help feeling a certain strange sympathy for you. I mean it. Will you allow me to place before you a rather daring simile? With all due respect, of course."

"Please do."

The watery eyes were looking at him hard.

"There's something . . . innocent about you, if you know what I mean. Your behaviour could be compared, although this may be going too far, with that of a cloistered monk who suddenly finds himself caught up in the maelstrom of the world. Do you follow? You float through this whole tragedy as if you were adrift in some private limbo, indifferent to the imperatives of logic and allowing yourself to be carried along by an extremely personal sense of reality, a sense which, of course, has nothing to do with what is actually real. And it is probably that very unawareness, if you'll forgive the term, which, by some strange paradox, has meant that we can have this interview in my office and not in the morgue. To sum up, I believe that at no time, perhaps not even now, have you fully realized the perilous nature of the situation you have got yourself into."

Jaime Astarloa put the coffee cup down on the table and looked at Campillo, frowning.

"I hope you're not implying that I'm a fool, Señor Campillo."

"No, no, of course not." The policeman raised his hands in the air, as if trying to fit his previous words into their proper place. "I see I haven't explained myself properly, Señor Astarloa, forgive my clumsiness. You see . . . when there are murderers about, especially murderers who behave in such a cold-blooded, professional manner, the matter should be dealt with by the competent authorities, who should be as professional as the murderers are, if not more so. Do you follow? That's why it's so unusual for someone as removed from this as yourself to become embroiled with murderers and victims and emerge without even a scratch. That's what I call being born under a lucky star, sir, a very lucky star. But luck, one day or another, has a habit of running out. Do you know the game of Russian roulette? They play it with those modern revolvers, I believe. Well, each time you try your luck, you have to bear in mind that there is always one bullet in the cylinder. And, if you go on squeezing the trigger, in the end the bullet comes out, and bang, end of story. Do you understand?"

Don Jaime nodded silently. Pleased with his own exposition, the policeman lounged back in his chair, the smoking cigar still between his fingers.

"My advice to you is that, in future, you avoid getting involved. To be doubly safe, it would be best if you temporarily vacated your home. Perhaps it would be a good idea to go on a little trip after all this excitement. Bear in mind that now the murderers know you had those documents and they will be very keen to silence you for good."

"I'll think about it."

Campillo held out his open hand, palm uppermost, as if to say that he had given Don Jaime all the reasonable advice he possibly could.

"I'd like to offer you some kind of official protection, but I can't. The country is in crisis. The rebel troops under Serrano and Prim are advancing on Madrid; they're preparing for a battle that could prove decisive, and it may well be that the royal family won't come back to Madrid but will remain in San Sebastián, ready to flee to France. As you can imagine, given my position here, I do have more important matters to attend to."

"Are you telling me that you're not going to catch these murderers?"

The policeman made an ambiguous gesture.

"In order to catch someone you have to know who he is, and I don't have that information. Almost no one has escaped unscathed: two corpses, a poor wretch tortured almost out of his wits who may not even live, and that's it. Perhaps a detailed reading of those mysterious documents would have helped us, but thanks to your, to put it kindly, absurd negligence, those papers have now disappeared, probably for ever. My one card now is your friend Cárceles; if he recovers, he might be able to tell us how the murderers knew that he had the folder in his possession, what was in it and, perhaps, the name we're looking for. Do you really remember nothing?"

Don Jaime shook his head, discouraged.

"I've told you everything I know," he muttered. "I only read the documents once, very quickly, and all I can remember are a lot of official notes and lists of names, amongst them various soldiers. Nothing that made any sense to me."

Campillo looked at him as one might look at an exotic curiosity.

"I assure you, Señor Astarloa, that you amaze me, word of honour. You really have no place in a country where the national pastime consists in firing a blunderbuss at the first person to appear around the corner, a country where two people having an argument will be immediately joined by two hundred more who just want to find out what the issue is and then take sides. I would like to know . . . "

Someone knocked at the door and a plain-clothes policeman came in. Campillo turned towards him, nodding, and the new arrival approached and whispered a few words in his ear. The chief of police frowned and shook his head gravely. When the other saluted and left, Campillo looked at Don Jaime.

"Our last hope has just disappeared," he said in a lugubrious tone. "Your friend Cárceles's suffering is over."

Jaime Astarloa dropped his hands to his knees and held his breath. His grey eyes, surrounded by deep lines, fixed on those of the policeman.

"I'm sorry?"

The policeman picked up a pencil from the table and broke it in two. Then he showed the two pieces to the fencing master, as if they had some meaning.

"Cárceles has just died in hospital. My agents were unable to get a word out of him, because he never recovered his reason: he died mad with horror." The policeman's fish eyes held Don Jaime's gaze. "You, Señor Astarloa, are now the last link in the chain."

Campillo paused and used a piece of the broken pencil to reach beneath the wig and scratch his scalp.

"If I were in your shoes," he added, coolly, ironically, "I wouldn't stray too far from that precious swordstick of yours."

VIII
With Bare Blades

*"In a fight with bare blades the same considerations do not apply,
and one should rule out nothing as a means of defence, as long
as it does not go against the laws of honour."*

It was almost four in the afternoon when he left the police station. The heat was suffocating and he remained for a moment beneath the awning of a nearby bookshop, distractedly watching the carriages travelling back and forth across the heart of Madrid. A few feet away, a pedlar selling *horchata* was crying his wares. Jaime Astarloa went over to him and asked for a glass of the milky liquid, which cooled his throat and offered some temporary relief. Beneath the sun, a gypsy with a barefoot child clinging to her black skirt was selling bunches of wilted carnations. The little boy suddenly ran off after a passing tram packed with sweating passengers; the conductor shooed him away with his whip, and the child returned, snivelling, to his mother's side.

The cobbles shimmered in the heat. Don Jaime removed his top hat to wipe the sweat from his brow. He stood for a while, not moving. He didn't know where to go.

He thought of going to the café, but he didn't want to have to answer any of the questions his colleagues would be sure to ask him about Cárceles. He realized that he had missed appointments with his students and this thought seemed to upset him more than anything else that had happened in recent days. He decided that the first thing he should do was write letters of apology.

Someone, amongst the knots of idle men chatting nearby, seemed to be watching him. It was a young man, modestly dressed, who looked like a workman. When Don Jaime turned to look at him, the young man averted his gaze and resumed the conversation he was having with four other men, who were standing on the corner of Carrera de San Jerónimo. Worried, Don Jaime examined the stranger distrustfully. Was he being watched? That initial fear gave way to a deep irritation with himself. The truth was, he saw everyone as a possible suspect; he saw a murderer in the face of every person he passed and who, for whatever reason, held his gaze for a moment.

Leave his home, leave Madrid. That had been Campillo's advice. Save himself. In a word, flee. He considered his options with growing unease. The only conclusion he was capable of reaching was this: to hell with them, to hell with the lot of them. He was too old to go scampering off into hiding like a rabbit. It was undignified even to think of it. His life had been long and eventful; he had stored up enough memories to justify having lived that long. Why, at the last minute, besmirch with the dishonour of flight the image he had managed to preserve of himself? Besides, he didn't even know from whom or what he was supposed to flee. He wasn't prepared to spend what remained of his life jumping at the slightest noise, running away from every unfamiliar face. And, he was too old to start a new life somewhere else.

From time to time, he felt again a sharp pang of sorrow when he remembered Adela de Otero's eyes, the Marqués de los Alumbres's frank laugh, Cárceles's fiery harangues. He decided to block all that out of his mind, for, if he did not, he risked being dragged down by melancholy and uncertainty and behind those feelings he could glimpse the fear which he refused, on principle, to acknowledge. He was neither the right age nor of the right character to feel afraid of anything, he told himself. Death was the worst thing that could happen to him and he was prepared for that. Indeed, he thought, with a sense of profound satisfaction, not only was he prepared, he had already faced it unabashed on the previous night whilst engaged in an apparently hopeless battle and the memory of how he had acquitted himself made him half-close his eyes, as if his pride had received a gentle caress. The solitary old wolf had shown that he still had a few teeth to bite with.

He wasn't going to run away. On the contrary, he would wait to see what happened. He remembered his old family motto, "To me", and that was precisely what he would do; he would wait for them to come to him. He smiled. He had always been of the opinion that every man should be given the opportunity to die standing up. Now, when the immediate future offered only old age, a decaying body, a slow decline in some home for the aged, or a despairing pistol shot, Jaime Astarloa, a fencing master of the Paris Academy of Arms, had the chance to play a trick on Fate by voluntarily embracing what anyone else in his place would recoil from in horror. He couldn't go and look for them because he didn't know who they were or where they were; but Campillo had said that, sooner or later, they would come to him, the last link in the chain. He remembered something that he had read a few days before in a French novel: "Even if the whole world turned against him, as long as his soul remained calm, he would feel not a moment's sadness." Those wretches would find out just what an old fencing master was capable of.

The direction his thoughts had taken made him feel better. He looked about him with the air of someone throwing down a challenge to the universe; he drew himself up and set off for home, swinging his walking stick. In fact, to those who passed him at that moment, Jaime Astarloa looked like any other scrawny, bad-tempered old man dressed in old-fashioned clothes, doubtless out for his daily constitutional to try to warm his weary bones. But had they stopped to look into his eyes they would have been surprised to discover there a grey glint of remarkable resolve, tempered like the steel of his foils.

He dined on a few cooked vegetables and put the coffee pot on to boil. While he was waiting, he took a book from the shelf and sat down on the battered sofa. It took him a little while to find a particular passage which he had carefully underlined in pencil ten or fifteen years before:

> Any moral character is closely bound up with scenes of
> autumn: those leaves that fall like our years, those flowers that

fade like our hours, those clouds that flee like our illusions, that light that grows ever feebler like our intelligence, that sun that grows colder like our loves, those rivers that freeze over like our life, all weave secret bonds with our fate . . .

He read those lines several times, silently moving his lips. Such a thought could easily serve as an epitaph, he said to himself. With an ironic gesture, which he imagined only he could appreciate, he left the book open at that page on the sofa. The smells coming from the kitchen told him that the coffee was ready; he went in and poured some. Then, cup in hand, he returned to the living room.

Night was falling. Venus shone all alone outside the window, in the infinite distance. He took a sip of coffee, standing beneath his father's portrait. "A handsome man," Adela de Otero had said. Then he went over to the framed insignia from his former regiment in the Royal Guard, which had symbolized both the beginning and the end of his brief military career. Beside it hung the diploma from the Paris Academy of Arms, now yellow with age; the parchment was stained with the mildew of many winters. He could remember, as if it were yesterday, the day he received it from the hands of a jury composed of the most respected fencing masters in all Europe. Old Lucien de Montespan, sitting on the other side of the table, had looked at his pupil with real pride. "The pupil outstrips the teacher," he would say to him later.

With his fingertips he stroked a small vase containing an open fan; it was the only thing that remained to him of the woman for whom he had one day long ago abandoned Paris. Where would she be now? She was probably a venerable grandmother, still sweet-natured and distinguished, who would be watching her grandchildren grow up whilst she busied her once-beautiful hands with some embroidery, silently caressing hidden, youthful memories. Or perhaps not even that; perhaps she had simply forgotten all about the fencing master.

A bit further along, on the wall, hung a wooden rosary, its beads worn and blackened with use. Amelia Bescós de Astarloa, the widow of a hero in the war against the French, had held that rosary in her hands until the day she died and a pious family member had later sent it to her son. Looking at it provoked a strange feeling in Jaime Astarloa: the memory of his mother's face had grow dim with the years; he could now no longer visualize it. He knew only that she was beautiful, and his memory preserved the touch of the fine, gentle hands that used to stroke his hair when he was a child, and the pulse in the warm throat, against which he would press his face when he believed himself unhappy. His memory also preserved a faded image, like an old painting: the foreshortened figure of a woman bending over to stir the embers in a great fireplace, which filled the walls of a dark, sombre living room with a flickering, reddish light.

Don Jaime finished his cup of coffee and turned his back on his memories. He remained for a long time without moving, with no other thought disturbing the peace that seemed to reign inside him. Then he put the cup down on the table, went over to the sideboard and opened a drawer, taking from it a long, flat case. He undid the clasps and removed a heavy object wrapped in a cloth. He unwrapped it to reveal a Lefaucheux revolver with a wooden handle and a capacity for five large-calibre cartridges. Although he had had the weapon, a present from a client, for five years, he had never wanted to use it. His code of honour was opposed in principle to the use of firearms, which he considered the resort of cowards who wanted to be able to kill from a safe distance. But, on this occasion, circumstances allowed him to set aside certain scruples.

He placed the revolver on the table and started loading it, inserting a cartridge into each chamber of the cylinder. Having done that, he weighed the weapon in the palm of his hand for a moment, then put it down again on the table. He looked around him, his hands on his hips, before moving an armchair so that it faced the door. He brought over a table and placed on it the oil lamp together with a box of matches. After another glance to see that everything was in place, he extinguished all the gas lights in the house one by one, apart from the light burning in the small hallway between the front door and the living room; that he merely turned down a little so it gave off only a pale, bluish light which left the hall in a kind of half-shadow and the living room in darkness. He unsheathed his swordstick, picked up the revolver and set both on the table opposite his chair. He stood there for a moment in the shadows, studying the effect, and seemed satisfied. Then he went to the hall and unbolted the door.

He was whistling to himself as he went into the kitchen to refill the pot with coffee and collect a clean cup. He took those over to the table and put them down next to the oil lamp, the matches, the revolver and the swordstick. Then he lit the oil lamp, with the wick turned down very low, filled a cup with coffee and, raising it to his lips, settled down to wait. He did not know how many of them there would be; but he was sure that, from now on, his nights were going to be very long.

His eyes were closing. His head nodded and he felt a sudden pain in his neck. He blinked, confused. In the dim light of the oil lamp, he reached for the coffee pot and poured a little more into his cup. He took his watch from his pocket; it was a quarter past two in the morning. The coffee was cold, but he drank it down in one, pulling a face. There was absolute silence around him, and he thought that perhaps, after all, they would not come. On the table, the revolver and the bare sword blade gleamed in the soft glow of the oil lamp.

The sound of a carriage passing reached him through the open window, and he listened attentively for a while. He held his breath, intent on the slightest noise that might indicate danger, and he remained like that until the noise had moved off down the street, fading into the distance. On another occasion, he seemed to hear a creak on the stairs and he sat for a long time with his eyes fixed on the bluish penumbra in the hallway, while his right hand stroked the butt of the gun.

A mouse came and went above him. He looked up at the ceiling, listening to the muted pattering as the little animal moved about the rafters. He had been trying to hunt it down for several days and had left a couple of traps in the kitchen, next to the hole near the fireplace from which the mouse usually emerged to make its nightly raids on the larder. It was obviously a very astute mouse because the cheese next to the spring was always gnawed, but the trap was never sprung. Clearly, he was up against a mouse of some talent, which made the difference between hunting and being hunted. And listening to the mouse scampering about in the roof space, the fencing master was glad that he had not yet been able to trap him. The minuscule company the creature afforded Don Jaime relieved the solitude of his long wait.

His mind, in that state of light, alert sleep, filled with strange images. Three times he thought he saw something moving in the hallway and sat up with a start, and three times he leaned back again in the chair, realizing that his senses were deceiving him. Nearby, the clock of San Ginés struck the quarter hours, and the bell tolled three times.

This time there was no doubt. There was a noise on the stairs, a quiet rustling. He leaned forwards very slowly, concentrating every ounce of his being on listening intently. Something was moving cautiously on the other side of the door. Holding his breath, his throat tight with tension, he put out the oil lamp. The only light now was the weak glow in the hallway. Without getting to his feet, he picked up the revolver in his right hand and cocked it, muffling the sound of the hammer between his legs. With his elbows resting on the table, he aimed it at the door. He was no marksman, but at that distance it would be difficult to miss. And there were five bullets in the chamber.

He was surprised to hear a gentle knocking at the door. It was odd, he thought, for a murderer to ask permission to enter his victim's house. He remained still and silent in the darkness, waiting. Perhaps they wanted to find out if he was asleep.

The knocking came again, a bit louder this time, although still far from energetic. It was clear that the mysterious visitor did not want to wake the neighbours. Jaime Astarloa was beginning to feel unsettled. He had expected them to force their way in, not come knocking at his door at three in the morning. Besides, he had left the door unbolted, and all they had to do was turn the handle to open it. He waited, holding the air in his lungs, the revolver firm in his hand, his index finger on the trigger. Whoever it was, they were bound to come in.

There was a metallic creak. Someone was turning the handle. He heard a slight squeak as the door swung on its hinges. Don Jaime gently expelled the air from his lungs, took another deep breath and again held it in. His index finger squeezed harder on the trigger. He would wait until the first figure was framed in the middle of the hallway and then he would shoot.

"Don Jaime?"

The voice came in an interrogative whisper. A glacial cold burst forth in the very centre of Don Jaime's heart and spread to his veins, freezing his limbs. He felt the grip of his fingers loosening; the revolver fell to the table. He raised a hand to his forehead as, stiff as a corpse, he got to his feet. For the slightly hoarse voice, with just a hint of a foreign accent, that came from the hall, reached him from the mists of the Beyond. It was none other than the voice of Adela de Otero.

A female silhouette appeared in the blue penumbra and stopped on the threshold to the living room. He heard a slight rustle of skirts and then the voice said again, "Don Jaime?"

He held out a hand, feeling for the matches. He struck one and the tiny flame created a sinister play of light and shadow on his tense features. His fingers were trembling as he lit the oil lamp and lifted it up to illumine the apparition that had just placed death in his soul.

Adela de Otero was standing at the door in a black dress, her hands folded. She was wearing a black straw hat with matching ribbons, and her hair was caught up, as usual, at the nape of her neck. She seemed shy and uncertain, like a disobedient child come to ask forgiveness for arriving home late.

"I think I owe you an explanation, Maestro."

Jaime Astarloa swallowed hard as he set the oil lamp on the table. Through his mind passed the image of a mutilated woman lying on a marble slab in the morgue, and it seemed to him that Adela de Otero owed him rather more than an explanation.

Twice he opened his mouth to speak, but the words refused to come. He remained there, leaning on the edge of the table, watching the young woman approach until the circle of light was breast high.

"I've come alone, Don Jaime. Will you hear what I have to say?"

Don Jaime's voice was a dull whisper.

"I will."

She moved softly and the light from the oil lamp reached her chin, her mouth and the small scar at the corner of her mouth.

"It's a long story."

"Who was the dead woman?"

There was a silence. The mouth and the chin withdrew from the circle of light.

"Be patient, Don Jaime. All in good time." She was speaking in a very soft, sweet voice with that slight hoarseness that once stirred such conflicting feelings in the fencing master. "We've got all the time in the world."

Jaime Astarloa swallowed again. He was afraid he might wake up from one moment to the next, close his eyes for an instant and, when he opened them again, find that Adela de Otero was not there. That she had never been there.

One of her hands moved slowly in the light, her fingers outstretched, as if to indicate that she had nothing to hide.

"In order for you to understand what I've come to tell you, Don Jaime, I must go back a long way – about ten years, more or less." Her voice was neutral now, distant. Don Jaime could not see her eyes, but he could imagine the absent look in them, fixed on some point in the infinite. Or perhaps, he thought later, she was watching, studying his face to see the reflection there of the feelings aroused by the memories she was recounting. "At that time, a certain young woman was living out a beautiful love story, a story of eternal love."

She fell silent for a moment, as if evaluating the words.

"Eternal love," she repeated. "To simplify matters, I won't go into details that you might consider to be in bad taste, I'll just say that the beautiful love story ended six months later in a foreign land, one winter evening, in tears and in the most complete solitude, on the banks of a river from which a mist was rising. Those grey waters fascinated the woman, you see. They fascinated her so much that she thought she might find in them what the poets call the sweet peace of oblivion. As you see, the first part of my story sounds like a rather vulgar novel."

Adela de Otero paused and gave a mirthless contralto laugh. Jaime Astarloa had not moved an inch and continued listening in silence.

"That was when it happened," she went on. "Just when the young woman was prepared to pass through her personal wall of mist, another man appeared in her life." She stopped for a moment; her voice had grown almost imperceptibly softer and that was the only time she tempered the coldness with which she told the story. "A man who – asking nothing in exchange and driven only by feelings of pity – took care of the woman lost on the banks of that grey river, healed her wounds and gave her back her smile. He became for her the father she had never known, the brother she had never had, the husband she never would have, a man who, stretching his nobility to the limits, never attempted to impose on her any of the rights which might have been due to him as a husband. Do you understand what I'm saying, Don Jaime?"

Don Jaime still could not see her eyes, but he knew that Adela de Otero was looking at him hard.

"I'm beginning to."

"I doubt that you can understand it completely," she said in such a low voice that Don Jaime guessed at rather than heard her words. There was a long silence, so long that he began to fear that she might not continue with her story, but after a moment, she spoke again. "For two years, that man devoted himself to creating a new woman, very different from the trembling young girl gazing into the river. And he still asked nothing in return."

"He was, it would seem, an altruist."

"Perhaps not, Don Jaime, perhaps not." She seemed to falter, as if thinking about the matter. "I imagine there was something more. In fact, his attitude was not entirely unselfish. It was possibly just a feeling of satisfaction at creating something of his own, the pride that came from a kind of possession that was never exercised, but that was there nonetheless. 'You are the most beautiful thing I have ever created,' he said once. Perhaps he was right, because he spared no effort in the task, no effort, no money, no patience. There were lovely clothes, dancing masters, riding, music . . . fencing. Yes, Don Jaime. By some strange quirk of nature, the young woman was very gifted at fencing. One day, because of his work, the man was obliged to return to his country. He took the young woman by the shoulders, led her to a mirror and made her look at herself for a long time. 'You're beautiful and you're free,' he said. 'Take a good look at yourself. That is my reward.' He was married, he had a family and obligations, but he was ready to continue watching over his creation, despite everything. Before leaving, he made her a present of a house where she could live in a suitable manner. And from a distance her benefactor continued to keep a careful watch, so that she should lack for nothing. And thus seven years passed."

She stopped talking for a moment and then repeated "seven years" in a low voice. When she did so, she moved slightly, and the circle of light rose up her body and reached her violet eyes, which glinted in the flickering light. The scar at the corner of her mouth still marked it with that indelible, enigmatic smile.

"You, Don Jaime, already know who that man was."

He blinked, surprised, and was about to express his confusion out loud. A sudden intuition counselled him, however, to refrain from making any comment, lest he cut the thread of her confidences. She looked at him, as if weighing his silence.

"On the day they said goodbye", she continued after a moment, "all the young woman could do was to express to her benefactor the immensity of the debt she owed him in these words: 'If you ever need me, call me, even if you want me to go down into hell itself.' I'm sure, Maestro, that if you had chanced to know that young woman's courage you would not have found such words out of place on a woman's lips."

"I would have been surprised if she had said anything else," said Don Jaime. She smiled again and nodded slightly, as if she had just been paid a compliment. Don Jaime touched his own forehead; it was cold as marble. The pieces were beginning slowly and painfully to fit together.

"And so the day came", he added, "when he asked you to go down into hell."

Adela de Otero looked at him, surprised by the aptness of his remark. She raised her hands and put them together again slowly, offering him silent applause.

"Well put, Don Jaime. Well put."

"I am merely repeating your words."

"It's still well put." Her voice was heavy with irony. "To go down into hell. That is precisely what he asked her to do."

"Was her debt so very great?"

"It was immense."

"Was the task to be undertaken so inevitable?"

"Yes. The man had given the young woman everything she possessed, and, more important, everything that she was. Nothing she might do for him could compare with what he had done for her. But allow me to continue. The man we are speaking of occupied a high post in a large, important company. For reasons that you can easily guess, he became embroiled in a particular political game, a very dangerous game, Don Jaime. His commercial interests led him to become involved with Prim, and he made the mistake of financing one of Prim's coups, which ended in the most complete disaster. Unfortunately for him, he was discovered. That would mean exile, ruin. However, his lofty position in society, along with certain other factors, enabled him to save himself." Adela de Otero paused; when she spoke again, there was a metallic edge to her voice, which became harder, more impersonal. "Then he decided to work with Narváez."

"And what did Prim do when he learned of this betrayal?"

She bit her lower lip, considering the word.

"Betrayal? Yes, I suppose you could call it that." She looked at him mischievously, like a child about to share a secret. "Prim never knew anything about it, of course. And he still doesn't."

This time the fencing master was truly shocked: "Are you telling me that you have done all this for a man capable of betraying his own friends?"

"You understand nothing of what I'm telling you." The violet eyes regarded him scornfully now. "You understand nothing at all. Do you still believe in good people and bad people, in just and unjust causes? What do I care about General Prim or anyone else? I came here tonight to tell you about the man to whom I owe everything I am. He was always good and loyal to me, wasn't he? He never betrayed me. Be so kind as to keep your namby-pamby scruples to yourself, sir. Who are you to judge?"

Jaime Astarloa let out a long breath. He was very tired, and he would gladly have lain down on the sofa. He longed to sleep, to remove himself, to reduce everything to a bad dream that would dissolve with the first light of dawn. He wasn't even now sure that he wanted to hear the rest of the story.

"And what would happen if he were found out?" he asked.

Adela de Otero made an indolent gesture.

"He never will be," she said. "He only had dealings with two people: the President of the Council of Ministers and the Minister of the Interior, with whom he was in direct communication. Luckily, both of them died . . . of natural causes. There were now no further obstacles to prevent him from remaining in contact with Prim, as if nothing had happened. In theory, there were now no troublesome witnesses."

"And now that Prim and his men are winning . . . "

She smiled.

"Yes, they are winning. And he is one of those financing the enterprise. Imagine the advantages that that could bring him."

Don Jaime narrowed his eyes and nodded silently. Now everything was clear.

"But there was one loose end," he murmured.

"Exactly," she said. "And Luis de Ayala was that loose end. During his brief passage through public life, the Marquis played an important role alongside his uncle, Vallespín, the Minister of the Interior, who had the understanding with my friend. When Vallespín died, Ayala was able to gain access to his private files, and there he came across a series of documents that contained a good part of the story."

"What I don't understand is what interest that could have had for the Marquis. He always said he kept well out of politics."

Adela de Otero raised her eyebrows. Don Jaime's remark seemed to amuse her greatly.

"Ayala was bankrupt. His debts were mounting and most of his property was heavily mortgaged. Gambling and women," at that point Adela de Otero's voice took on a note of infinite disdain, "were his two weaknesses, and both cost him a lot of money."

That was too much for Jaime Astarloa.

"Are you insinuating that the Marquis was intent on blackmail?" She smiled mockingly.

"I'm not just insinuating, I'm saying that he was. Luis de Ayala threatened to make those documents public, even to send them directly to Prim, if certain non-recoverable loans were not paid off. Our dear Marquis demanded a high price for his silence."

"I can't believe it."

"I really don't care whether you believe it or not. The fact is that Ayala's demands made the whole situation very delicate. My friend had no choice: he had to neutralize the danger, silence the Marquis and recover the documents. But Ayala was a cautious man . . . "

Don Jaime rested his hands on the edge of the table and hung his head.

"He was a cautious man," he repeated in a dull voice, "but he liked women."

Adela de Otero gave him an indulgent smile.

"And fencing, Don Jaime. That was where you and I came in."

"Oh, my God."

"Don't take it like that. You had no way of knowing . . . "

"Oh, my God."

She reached out a hand as if to touch his arm, but stopped. Jaime

Astarloa had drawn back as if he had just seen a serpent.

"My friend brought me over from Italy," she explained after a moment. "And you were the means for me to reach Ayala without arousing his suspicions. We never imagined that you would become part of the problem. How were we to know that Ayala would give you the documents for safe keeping?"

"So his death was in vain."

She looked at him with genuine surprise.

"In vain? Not at all. Ayala had to die, with or without the documents. He was too dangerous, too intelligent. Latterly, his attitude towards me had changed, as if he were beginning to grow suspicious. We had to settle the matter once and for all."

"Did you do it yourself?"

Her eyes fixed him like a steel blade.

"Of course." There was something so natural, so calm about her voice, that Don Jaime felt terrified.

"Who else if not me? Things happened very quickly, and there wasn't much time. That night we dined in the salon as usual. Alone. I remember that Ayala was being much too nice; he was clearly suspicious of me. That didn't worry me too much because I knew this would be the last time we would see each other. While he was uncorking a bottle of champagne, pretending a happiness that neither of us felt, I found him particularly handsome, with his thick mane of hair and those perfect white teeth, always smiling. I even regretted what Fate had in store for him."

She shrugged, making Fate responsible for everything. After a pause, she added: "My earlier attempts to get the secret out of him proved unsucccessful; I only succeeded in provoking his distrust. It didn't matter by then, so I decided to ask him straight out. I told him exactly what I wanted, making him the offer I had been authorized to make: a large sum of money in return for the documents."

"But he didn't accept," said Jaime Astarloa.

She looked at him oddly.

"No, he didn't. In fact, the offer was a trick to gain time, but Ayala had no way of knowing that. He laughed in my face. He said that the papers were in a safe place and that my friend would have to go on paying for them for the rest of his life if he didn't want to end up in Prim's hands. Oh, and he called me a whore."

Adela de Otero stopped speaking and her last words hung in the air. She had said them quite objectively, flatly, and Don Jaime knew then that she would have behaved in exactly that way in the Marquis's palace: no tantrums, no temperamental scenes, but with all the calculated coolness of someone who places efficiency above passion – that she had been as lucid and cold as when she was fencing.

"But that wasn't why you killed him."

The young woman looked intently at Don Jaime.

"No, you're right, that wasn't why I killed him. I killed him because it had already been decided that he must die. I went to the gallery and calmly chose a foil without a button on the tip; he seemed to treat it as a joke. He was very sure of himself, looking at me with his arms folded, as if waiting to see where it would all lead. 'I'm going to kill you, Luis,' I said very calmly. 'You may wish to defend yourself.' He laughed, accepting what seemed to him an exciting game, and he chose another foil. I imagine that afterwards he intended to take me to his bedroom and make love to me. He came towards me wearing that brilliant, cynical smile of his; he looked handsome in his shirtsleeves, a fine figure of a man, and he crossed his sword with mine, at the same time blowing me a kiss with his left hand. Then I looked him in the eyes, made a feint and stuck the foil in his throat, just like that: a short thrust and a flick of the wrist. Even the greatest purist among fencing masters could have raised no objection, nor did Ayala. He looked at me in astonishment and he was dead before he hit the floor."

Adela de Otero faced Don Jaime defiantly, as brazenly as if she had just reported a mere piece of mischief. He couldn't take his eyes off hers, fascinated by her expression; there was no hatred in it, no remorse, no passion at all, just blind loyalty to an idea, to a man. There was something simultaneously hypnotic and terrifying about her awful beauty, as though she were the embodiment of the Angel of Death. As if she had guessed his thoughts, the young woman withdrew from the circle of light projected by the oil lamp.

"Then I searched the place thoroughly, although without much hope of finding anything." Her faceless voice emerged once more from the shadows and Don Jaime could not decide which was more disquieting, her voice or her facelessness. "I found nothing, although I stayed there until nearly dawn. Besides, the revolt in Cádiz meant that Ayala had to die anyway, whether we had the documents or not. There was no other solution. All I could do was get out of there quickly and hope that, if the papers really were that well hidden, then no one else would find them either. Having done what I could, I left. The next step was to vanish without trace from Madrid." She seemed to hesitate, looking for the right words. "I had to return to the obscurity out of which I came. Adela de Otero was leaving the scene for good. That too was part of the plan."

Jaime Astarloa could no longer remain standing. He felt his legs give way beneath him and his heart was beating feebly. He let himself drop slowly into his chair, fearing that he might faint. When he spoke, his voice was a fearful whisper, because he knew what the terrible reply would be: "What happened to Lucía, your maid?" He looked up at the shadow standing before him. "She was the same height, more or less the same age as you, and with the same colour hair. What happened to her?"

This time there was a long silence. Finally, Adela de Otero said in a neutral, unemotional voice: "You don't understand, Don Jaime."

Don Jaime raised a tremulous hand and pointed at the shadow. A blind doll floating in a pond; that is what had happened.

"You're wrong," he said. This time he felt the hatred in his voice and he knew that she felt it too, with perfect clarity. "I understand everything. Too late, it's true, but I understand it all very well. That is precisely why you chose her, isn't it? Because she looked like you. Everything, down to the last horrible detail, was planned from the first moment."

"I see we were wrong to underestimate you." There was a touch of irritation in her voice. "You are a perceptive man, after all."

He smiled a bitter smile.

"Did you take care of her as well?" he asked, spitting out the words with infinite scorn.

"No, we contracted two men to do it, who know almost nothing of the story. A couple of common thugs. The same ones you met in your friend's house."

"The swine!"

"Perhaps they went a bit far."

"I doubt it. I'm sure they were merely scrupulously carrying out the worthy instructions given them by you and your companion."

"If it's any consolation to you, I should tell you that the girl was dead when they did all that to her. She didn't suffer much."

Jaime Astarloa looked at her open-mouthed, as if he could not believe what he was hearing.

"That was most considerate of you, Adela de Otero. Always assuming that is your real name. Most considerate. You tell me that the poor woman didn't suffer much. That, doubtless, does honour to your feminine instincts."

"I'm glad to see you've recovered your sense of irony, Maestro."

"Don't call me 'Maestro', please. You may have noticed that I am not calling you 'Señora' either."

This time she laughed out loud.

"Touché, Don Jaime, touché. Do you want me to go on, or do you already know the rest and would prefer me to stop?"

"I would like to know how you found out about poor Cárceles."

"It was very simple. We had given up the documents for lost. Naturally, we never even thought of you. He turned up at my friend's house out of the blue, asking to talk to him urgently about a serious matter. He was received, and he told us what he wanted: certain documents had come into his possession, and, knowing that my friend was comfortably off, Cárceles asked for a certain sum of money in exchange for the papers and his silence."

Jaime Astarloa drew a hand across his forehead, stunned by the sound of his world crashing about him.

"Cárceles too?" The words escaped from him like a lament.

"And why not?" she asked. "Your friend was ambitious and poor,

195

just like anyone else. I imagine he was expecting that the deal would help him escape from his grimy little life."

"He seemed honest," protested Don Jaime. "He was so radical, so intransigent. I trusted him."

"I'm afraid that, for a man your age, you have trusted far too many people."

"You're right. I even trusted you."

"Oh, come on." She seemed irritated. "Sarcasm will get us nowhere. Do you want to know the rest?"

"I do. Go on."

"He said goodbye to Cárceles in the nicest possible way and an hour later our two men arrived at his house to recover the file. Duly persuaded, your friend ended up telling them everything he knew, including your name. Then you arrived, and I have to say that you put us all in a tight spot. I was waiting outside, in a carriage, and I saw them come running out as if the Devil himself were after them. You know, if the situation hadn't been so awkward, I would have found it most amusing. Considering you're not a young man any more, you certainly gave them a hard time: you broke the nose of one and the other you hit twice with your sword, in the arm and in the groin. They said you fought like Lucifer himself."

Adela de Otero fell silent for a moment and then said, intrigued: "Now it's my turn to ask you a question. Why did you get that poor wretch involved in all this?"

"I didn't. I mean I did so unwittingly. I read the documents, but I couldn't make head or tail of them."

"Are you serious?" The young woman seemed genuinely surprised. "Didn't you just say that you read the documents?"

He nodded, confused.

"Yes, I did, but I didn't understand what it was all about. The names, the letters and all the rest meant nothing to me. I've never taken any interest in such matters. When I read what was in the folder, all I could make out was that someone was betraying someone else, and that there was some matter of state involved. I went to Cárceles precisely because I couldn't work out who the traitor was.

He obviously succeeded, perhaps because he knew about the events being referred to."

Adela de Otero leaned forward a little, and the light again fell on her face. There was a small worried line between her eyebrows.

"I'm afraid there's some misunderstanding here, Don Jaime. Do you mean to say that you don't know the name of my friend, the man we've been talking about all this time?"

Jaime Astarloa shrugged, and his frank grey eyes held her gaze unblinkingly.

"That is correct."

The young woman put her head to one side and looked at him, absorbed. Her mind seemed to be working very fast.

"But you must have read the letter, since you took it out of the folder."

"What letter?"

"The main one, the one from Vallespín to Narváez. The one in which they mention the name of . . . Didn't you hand it over to the police? You still have it?"

"I don't know what wretched letter you're talking about."

This time Adela de Otero was the one to sit down, tense and fearful. The scar on her mouth no longer seemed to smile; instead, her face bore a look of confusion. It was the first time he had seen her like that.

"Let's get this quite clear, Don Jaime. I came here tonight for one reason only. Amongst Luis de Ayala's documents there was a letter, written by the Minister of the Interior, in which he gave detailed facts about the agent who was passing them information about Prim's conspiracies. That letter, of which Luis de Ayala himself made a copy for my friend when he first started to blackmail him, was not in the folder that we recovered from Cárceles's house. Therefore you must have it."

"I've never seen that letter. If I'd read it, I would have gone straight to the house of the criminal responsible for organizing all this and put a sword through his heart. And poor Cárceles would still be alive. I hoped that he would be able to deduce something from all those documents."

Adela de Otero made a gesture to indicate that at that moment she didn't give a damn about Cárceles.

"He did," she said. "Even without that letter, anyone who had kept abreast of the political ups and downs of the last few years would have seen it. The documents mention the matter of the silver mines in Cartagena, which pointed directly to my friend. There was also a list of suspects for the police to watch, people high up in society, and his name was amongst them; however, his name didn't appear afterwards in the list of people detained. In short, there was a whole series of clues which, if you put them together, would have allowed you to discover the identity of Vallespín's and Narváez's confidant without too much difficulty. If you didn't live with your back turned to the world, you would have found that out as easily as anyone else."

The young woman got up and paced the room, deep in thought. Despite the awfulness of the situation, Jaime Astarloa could not but admire her sang-froid. She had been involved in the murder of three people, she had come to his house, thus risking falling into the hands of the police, she had told him the whole horrific story quite calmly, and now she was pacing about the room, taking no notice of the revolver and sword on the table, concerned only with the whereabouts of a mere letter. What was this woman, who called herself Adela de Otero, made of?

It was absurd, but the fencing master found that he too was thinking about where the mysterious letter could have got to. What had happened? Had Luis de Ayala not trusted him enough? Of one thing Don Jaime was sure, he had not read it.

He sat very still, barely breathing, his mouth half-open, trying to hold onto a fragment of something that had just flashed through his mind. He grasped it, his face contorted with the effort. Adela de Otero turned to look at him, surprised. It couldn't be. It was ridiculous even to imagine that such a thing could have happened. It was absurd, and yet . . .

"What's wrong, Don Jaime?"

Without answering, he got very slowly to his feet, picked up the oil lamp and stood for a few moments motionless, looking around him as if waking from a deep sleep. Now he remembered.

"Are you all right?"

The young woman's voice seemed to come from a very long way off as his mind worked at top speed. After Ayala's death, after opening the folder and before starting to read it, he had tried to put it in some kind of order. It had fallen from his hands, and the papers had scattered on the floor. That had happened in one corner of the room, next to the walnut sideboard. Borne along by a sudden inspiration, he walked past Adela de Otero and crouched down by the heavy piece of furniture, slipped one hand between the legs and felt the floor underneath. When he got up, he was holding a piece of paper. He stared at it.

"Here it is," he murmured, waving the piece of paper in the air. "It's been here all this time. How could I have been so stupid?"

Adela de Otero went over to him, looking at the letter incredulously.

"Are you telling me that it was there the whole time, that it fell underneath?"

Don Jaime had turned pale.

"Good God," he murmured in a low voice. "Poor Cárceles. However much they tortured him, he couldn't tell them about something whose existence he didn't even know about. That's why they were so merciless with him."

He left the oil lamp on the sideboard and held the letter to the light. Adela de Otero was by his side, looking at the piece of paper, fascinated.

"Please, Don Jaime, don't read it." There was a strange mixture of command and supplication in her dark voice. "Just give it to me without reading it, please. My friend thought that you would have to be killed too, but I persuaded him to let me come here alone. Now I'm glad that I did. Perhaps we're still in time . . . "

Don Jaime looked at her hard.

"In time for what? In time to bring the dead back to life? In time to make me believe in your virginal innocence or in your benefactor's kindly feelings? Go to hell."

He screwed up his eyes while he read in the smoking light of the oil lamp. This was, in effect, the key to everything.

To: Don Ramón María Narváez, President of the Council of Ministers

Dear General,
The matter we spoke about privately the other day has taken an unexpected turn, in my view a very promising one. Bruno Cazorla Longo, manager of the Bank of Italy in Madrid, is involved in the Prim affair. Doubtless you are familiar with the name because he was an associate of Salamanca's in the Northern Railways deal. I have proof that Cazorla Longo has been providing generous loans to Prim, with whom he remains in close contact from his luxurious office in the Plaza de Santa Ana. For some while I have kept him under discreet surveillance and I think the time is now ripe for us to strike. We have in our possession enough information to uncover a scandal that would ruin him; we could even have him spend a good few years pondering the error of his ways in some delightful place in the Philippines or Fernando Po, which, for a man as accustomed to luxury as he is, would doubtless prove an unforgettable experience.

However, with regard to what we were discussing the other day about the need for more information on Prim's plotting, it occurred to me that we could make better use of this gentleman. So, I obtained an interview with him and put the situation to him as subtly as possible. He is a very intelligent man, and since his liberal beliefs are not as strong as his commercial ones, he has declared his resolve to provide us with certain services. After all, he knows what he stands to lose if we were to take firm action against his revolutionary dabblings, and, like any good banker, he is terrified of the word "bankruptcy". So he is prepared to co-operate with us, as long as it is done discreetly. He will inform us of any movements by Prim or his agents and continue supplying them with funds, but, from now on, we will know exactly to whom and for what.

Of course, he places certain conditions on this agreement. The first is that no word of this matter should go beyond you and me. The other condition is of a remunerative nature. A man like him won't be satisfied with the usual thirty pieces of silver, so he's asking for the concession for the Murcia silver mines, which is to be decided on at the end of the month, a deal in which both he and his bank are extremely interested.

In my view, this would suit both the government and the Crown, for our man has the best possible relationship with Prim and his top brass, and the Liberal Union considers him one of the pillars of the Party in Madrid.

The matter has a great many other ramifications, but there is no need to put it all down in writing. I would add only that, in my judgement, Cazorla Longo is intelligent and ambitious. For a very reasonable price, we could have an agent at the very heart of the conspiracy.

As I do not judge it prudent to mention the subject during the Council of Ministers tomorrow, it would, therefore, be useful if you and I could discuss the matter in private.
Respectfully,

Joaquín Vallespín Andreu
Madrid, 4 November
(Only copy)

Jaime Astarloa finished reading and stood in silence, slowly shaking his head.

"So that was the secret," he muttered at last, in a barely audible voice.

Adela de Otero was looking at him, not moving, watching his reaction with furrowed brow.

"Yes, that was the secret," she said with a sigh, as if regretting the fact that the fencing master had gained access to the final corner of the mystery. "I hope you're satisfied."

He gave the young woman a strange look, as if surprised to see her still there.

"Satisfied?" he seemed to savour the word, only to find that he did not like the taste of it. "What satisfaction could I find in all this?" He held the letter between thumb and forefinger and shook it gently. "I suppose now you're going to ask me to give you this bit of paper. Or am I wrong?"

The young woman's eyes glinted in the light. She held out her hand.

"Please."

Jaime Astarloa looked at her long and hard, again amazed at her courage. She was standing there before him in the gloom, coolly demanding that he hand over written proof of the identity of the person responsible for the whole tragedy.

"Perhaps you're thinking of killing me too, if I don't give in to your demand?"

A mocking smile appeared on her lips. She watched him like a snake trying to fascinate its prey.

"I didn't come to kill you, Don Jaime, but to reach some agreement. No one thinks it necessary for you to die."

He raised an eyebrow, as if her words disappointed him.

"You're not going to kill me?" He seemed to be giving the matter serious consideration. "I must say, Doña Adela, that's very considerate of you."

Another smile appeared on her lips, more mischievous than malign. Don Jaime realized she was choosing her words carefully.

"I need that letter, Maestro."

"Please don't call me 'Maestro'."

"I need it. I've come too far for it, as well you know."

"Yes, I do. I think I can safely say that I can testify to that."

"I beg you. We still have time."

He regarded her ironically.

"That's twice you've said that, but time for what?" He considered the bit of paper in his hand. "The man this letter refers to is an utter wretch, a knave and a murderer. I hope you're not asking me to co-operate in covering up his crimes; I'm not used to people insulting me, far less at this time of night. Do you know something?"

"No. Tell me."

"At first, before I knew what had happened, when I saw your . . . that body on the marble slab, I resolved to avenge the death of Adela de Otero. That's why I didn't say anything to the police at the time."

She looked at him thoughtfully. Her smile seemed to soften.

"Thank you." There was a distant echo of sincerity in her voice. "But, as you see, no vengeance was necessary."

"Do you really think so?" This time it was Don Jaime's turn to smile. "Well, you're wrong. There are still people to avenge. Luis de Ayala, for example."

"He was nothing but a bon viveur and a blackmailer."

"Agapito Cárceles."

"A poor wretch killed by his own greed."

His grey eyes fixed on the woman with infinite coldness.

"That girl Lucía," he said slowly. "Did she deserve to die as well?"

For the first time, Adela de Otero could not hold his gaze. And when she spoke, she did so with great caution.

"Please, believe me, what happened to Lucía was unavoidable."

"Of course. Your word is quite enough for me."

"I'm serious."

"Naturally. It would be an unforgivable crime to doubt you."

An oppressive silence grew between them. She had bent her head and seemed to be immersed in contemplation of her hands, folded on her lap. The two black ribbons from her hat fell across her bare neck. Despite himself, Don Jaime thought that, even if she were the Devil incarnate, Adela de Otero was still maddeningly beautiful.

After a few moments, she looked up.

"What do you intend to do with the letter?"

He shrugged.

"I'm not sure," he replied simply. "I don't know whether to go straight to the police or to go first to the house of your benefactor and put a few inches of steel through his throat. Don't tell me you have a better idea."

The hem of her black silk dress rustled softly as she moved across the carpet towards him. He could smell, very close, the scent of rosewater.

"I do have a better idea, as it happens." She was looking into his eyes, her chin lifted defiantly. "An offer you can't refuse."

"You're mistaken."

"No, I'm not." Her voice was now as warm and soft as the purring of some beautiful feline. "I'm not mistaken. There's always something hidden somewhere. Every man has his price. And I can pay yours."

Before Don Jaime's astonished eyes, Adela de Otero raised her hands and undid the first button of her dress. His throat went suddenly dry as he stared, fascinated, at the violet eyes fixed on him. She undid the second button. Her perfect white teeth gleamed softly in the darkness.

He tried to move away, but those eyes held him hypnotized. At last he managed to look away, but instead he saw her bare throat, the delicate suggestion of a collarbone beneath the skin, the voluptuous pulse of smooth skin that formed a soft triangle between the young woman's breasts.

The voice came again in an intimate whisper: "I know you love me. I've always known it, right from the start. Perhaps everything would have been different if . . . "

The words died away. Jaime Astarloa held his breath, feeling as if he were floating far above reality. He felt her breath on his lips, her mouth half-opening like a bleeding wound full of promises. Now she was unlacing her bodice, the ribbon unravelling between her fingers. Then, incapable of resisting the seduction of the moment, he felt her hands seeking one of his hands; her touch seemed to burn his skin. Slowly, she guided his hand to one of her bare breasts. Her pulsating flesh was warm and young, and Don Jaime trembled to feel again an almost forgotten sensation, one he thought he had renounced for ever.

He moaned and half-closed his eyes, abandoning himself to the sweet languor filling him. She smiled quietly, with unusual tenderness, and, releasing his hand, she lifted her arms to remove her hat. As she did so, she raised her chest slightly, and Don Jaime slowly brought his lips closer until he felt the soft warmth of those beautiful, bare breasts.

The world was somewhere very far from there; it was just a confused, distant tide, beating weakly on the shore of a desert island, the sound dimmed by distance. There was nothing, only a vast, bright, luminous plain, a complete absence of reality, of remorse, even of sensation . . . An absence even of passion, for there was none. The only note, monotonous and continuous, was that moan of abandonment, a lonely murmur long held in, that the contact with her skin brought to his lips.

Suddenly, some part of his sleeping conscience seemed to cry out from the remote region where it still remained alert. The signal took a few moments to find its way to the springs of his will, and just when he heard that danger signal, Jaime Astarloa looked up into the young woman's face. He shuddered as if he had received an electric charge. Her hands were occupied in removing her hat, but her eyes glowed like burning coals. Her mouth was fixed in a tense rictus, which the scar at the corner transformed into a diabolical grimace. Her features were stamped with a look of extraordinary concentration which was engraved in fire on his memory: it was the face Adela de Otero wore when she was ready to lunge forward and deal a decisive blow.

Don Jaime leapt back with a cry of fear. She had dropped the hat and was holding the hatpin in her right hand, ready to plunge it into the neck of the man who, only seconds before, had been kneeling before her. He staggered away, bumping into the furniture, feeling the blood freezing in his veins. Then, paralysed with horror, he saw her throw back her head and let out a sinister laugh, like the funereal tolling of a bell.

"Poor Maestro." The words emerged slowly, as dully as if she were referring to some third party whose fate were a matter of utter indifference to her. There was neither hatred nor scorn in her words, only a sincere but chilly kind of commiseration. "Ingenuous and credulous to the last, isn't that right? My poor old friend!"

She laughed again and looked curiously at Don Jaime. She seemed interested to observe in detail the look of horror on his face.

"Of all the people in this drama, Señor Astarloa, you have been the most credulous, the most likeable and the most worthy of pity." Her words seemed to drip slowly out into the silence. "Everyone, both the living and the dead, has been making a complete fool of you. You're like a character out of some feeble farce, with your outmoded ethics and your vanquished temptations, playing the role of the cuckolded husband, the last to find out. Look at yourself, if you can. Find a mirror and tell me what good all your pride and your composure and your fatuous smugness are now. What the hell did you think you were playing at? Well, it's all been very touching, of course. You may, if you like, allow yourself one last round of applause because the time has come to lower the curtain. You deserve a good, long rest."

Still talking, without hurrying her movements at all, Adela de Otero had turned towards the table on which lay the revolver and the swordstick; she took hold of the sword having discarded the now useless hatpin.

"For all your ingenuousness, though, you're a sensible man," she said, looking appreciatively at the sharp steel blade, as if weighing up its qualities. "That's why I'm sure you will understand the situation. In this whole story, all I have done is play the role assigned to me by Fate. I can assure you that I have put into that role not one jot of malice more than was strictly necessary, but, then, that's life. The life that you always tried to stand aloof from and which now, tonight, is slipping unbidden into your home to call you to account for crimes you never even committed. Do you see the irony of the situation?"

She had been coming closer, talking all the time, like a siren using her voice to charm the sailors while their boat is hurled onto the rocks. She was holding the oil lamp in one hand and the sword in the other; she was standing opposite him, as still as a statue carved out of ice, smiling, as if, instead of threatening him she were extending a pleasant invitation to peace and oblivion.

"It's time to say goodbye, Maestro. No hard feelings."

When she took a step forwards, ready to plunge the sword into him, Jaime Astarloa again saw death in her eyes. Only then, emerging from his stupor, did he have sufficient presence of mind to jump back and flee to the nearest door. He found himself in the dark fencing gallery. She was right behind him, and the oil lamp lit up the room. Don Jaime glanced about him, searching desperately for a weapon with which to confront his pursuer; he saw only the rack of foils he used in classes, all with a button on the tip. He picked one up – after all, it was better than nothing – but when his hand closed about the hilt, he felt little comfort. Adela de Otero was already at the door of the gallery, and the mirrors multiplied the light from the oil lamp as she stooped to place it on the floor.

"A most appropriate place to settle our business, Maestro," she said in a low voice, relieved to see that the foil in Don Jaime's hand was harmless. "Now you can find out just how good a student I am." With icy calm, unconcerned that her breasts were exposed beneath her unbuttoned bodice, she took two steps towards him and assumed the fighting position. "Luis de Ayala experienced for himself your excellent two hundred escudo thrust. Now it is the turn of the creator of that thrust. I'm sure you will agree that the situation is not without its humorous side."

She had barely finished speaking when, with astonishing speed, she thrust the hilt forward. Don Jaime stepped back, covering himself in quarte, opposing her sharp blade with his blunt-pointed weapon. The old, familiar movements of fencing were gradually restoring his lost aplomb, wrenching him out of the state of horrified stupor into which he had been plunged only moments before. He realized at once that he could not make any effective thrusts with his foil. He would have to limit himself to parrying all the attacks he could, keeping himself always on the defensive. He remembered that at the other end of the gallery was a closed cupboard containing half a dozen fighting foils and duelling sabres, but his opponent would never let him get that far. Besides, he wouldn't have time to turn round, open the cupboard and pick one up. Or perhaps he would. He decided to make his way, still fighting, towards that part of the room, awaiting his opportunity.

Adela de Otero seemed to guess his intention and closed on him, pushing him towards the corner of the room occupied by two mirrors. Don Jaime understood her intention. With nowhere to go, with no possible escape, he would be helplessly skewered.

She was fighting hard, frowning, her mouth reduced to a thin line, clearly intent on gaining control of his foible, forcing him to defend himself with the part of the blade nearest the hilt, which greatly limited his movements. Don Jaime was about three yards from the wall and unwilling to go back any further, when she made a half thrust inside the arm that put him in serious difficulty. He parried, conscious of his inability to respond as he would have had he been using a fighting foil, and then, with extraordinary nimbleness, Adela de Otero effected the movement known as *vuelta de puño*, changing the direction of the tip of her blade when the two blades touched and making an angulated attack. Something cold tore his shirt, penetrating his right side, between his skin and his ribs. He jumped back at that very moment, teeth gritted to suppress a strangled cry of panic. It would be too absurd to die like this, in his own home, at the hands of a woman. He put himself on guard again, feeling the warm blood soaking his shirt beneath his armpit.

Adela de Otero lowered her sword slightly, and paused to take a deep breath and give him a malevolent smile.

"Not bad, eh?" she asked with a look of amusement in her eyes. "Now, if you don't mind, it's time for the two hundred escudo thrust. On guard!"

Their blades clashed. He knew that it was impossible to parry the thrust without a point on his sword with which to threaten his opponent. On the other hand, if he concentrated on always keeping the upper part of his body covered against that particular attack, Adela de Otero could take advantage of this and attack with another, lower thrust, with equally fatal results. He was helpless and he could sense the wall at his back, very close now; out of the corner of his eye, to his left, he could see the mirror. He decided that his only chance was to try and disarm the young woman, or to aim for her face, where even the blunted weapon he was using could do some harm.

He opted for the first possibility, which was easier to achieve, by leaving his arm loosely bent and putting his weight on his left thigh. He waited for her to engage in quarte, then parried, turned his hand into pronation, beat his foil hard against the enemy blade, only to find to his dismay that she held firm. Then, somewhat desperately, he lunged in quarte over the arm, threatening her face. The lunge fell somewhat short and the button on his blade came only within inches of her face, but it was enough to force her to take a step back.

"Now, now," said the young woman with a mischievous smile. "Is the gentleman trying to disfigure me? We'd better bring things to a swift end, then."

She frowned, and her lips contracted into a look of savage joy whilst, steadying herself on her feet, she made a false thrust that forced him to lower his foil to quinte. He realized his mistake half-way through the manoeuvre, just before she shifted the hilt to go for the decisive thrust, and all he could do was hold up his left hand to the enemy blade, which was by then aimed at his chest. He pushed the blade away with his unarmed hand, then executed a flanconnade as he felt the sharp blade slice across the palm of his hand. She immediately withdrew her weapon, for fear that he might grasp it and snatch it from her, and Don Jaime looked for a moment at his bloody fingers, before putting himself on guard again to stop another attack.

Suddenly, he saw a glimmer of hope. He had made another thrust, again threatening her face, obliging her to parry weakly in quarte. While he put himself on guard again, Jaime Astarloa's instinct whispered to him with the speed of a lightning flash that, for a brief moment, there had been an opening, in which her face was uncovered; and it was his intuition, not his eyes, that told him of this weak point. In the seconds that followed, his trained professional reflexes functioned almost automatically, with the cold precision of clockwork. Forgetting the imminence of the danger, absolutely lucid after that moment of insight, conscious that he had neither the time nor the resources to confirm it, he decided to stake his life on his years as a veteran fencer. And while he initiated the movement for the second and last time, he was still calm enough to understand that, if he was wrong, he would never have a chance to regret his mistake.

He took a deep breath, then repeated the thrust in the same way he had before, and Adela de Otero, more confidently this time, opposed a parry in quarte in a rather forced position. Then, instead of immediately going back on guard, as might have been expected, Don Jaime only pretended to do so, instead cutting over and then attacking over the young woman's arm, throwing his own head and shoulders back and driving the blunt point upwards. The blade slipped through unopposed, and the metallic button on the tip of his foil entered Adela de Otero's right eye, penetrating straight to the brain.

Quarte. Parry in quarte. Doublé in quarte over the arm. Lunge.

It was growing light. The first rays of sun were filtering through the cracks in the closed shutters and the line of light was multiplied to infinity in the mirrors in the gallery.

Tierce. Parry in tierce. Thrust in tierce over the arm.

On the walls there were displays of old weapons in which rusty steel blades, condemned to silence, slept an eternal sleep. The soft golden light filling the room could no longer wrest a single gleam from those old dust-covered guards darkened by time, the metal marked by old scars.

Low quarte. Semi-circular parry. Thrust in quarte.

A few yellowing diplomas were hanging on one wall, their frames warped. The ink in which they were written had faded; the passing of the years had transformed them into pale signs, barely legible on the parchment. They bore the signatures of men who had died long ago and they were dated in Rome, Paris, Vienna, St Petersburg.

Quarte. Head and shoulders back. Low quarte.

There was a sword abandoned on the floor, with a highly polished silver handle, worn smooth by use, the hilt of which was decorated with slender, snaking arabesques and an exquisitely engraved motto: "To me."

Quarte over the arm. Parry in prime. Lunge in seconde.

On a faded carpet stood an oil lamp, burning without a flame now, the spent wick spluttering and smoking. Next to it lay the body of a once-beautiful woman. She was wearing a black silk dress, and beneath her motionless neck, next to her hair caught up with a mother-of-pearl comb in the form of an eagle, there was a pool of blood soaking the carpet. It gleamed red in the slender ray of light falling directly upon it.

Quarte inside. Parry of quarte. Thrust in prime.

In a dark corner of the room, on an old walnut pedestal table, gleamed a slender, chased glass vase, in which stood a faded rose. Its dry petals, crumpled and pathetic, were scattered on the surface of the table, presenting a miniature picture of decadent melancholy.

Seconde outside the arm. Your opponent parries in octave. Thrust in tierce.

From the street came a distant rumble, like the sound of a raging storm when the foam breaks furiously against the rocks. Through the shutters you could hear the dim clamour of voices joyfully celebrating the new day that brought with it their freedom. An attentive listener would have heard what those voices were saying; they spoke of a Queen going into exile and of just men coming from afar, their battered suitcases laden with hope.

Seconde outside. Parry of octave. Thrust in quarte over the arm.

Indifferent to everything, in that gallery in which time had stopped, an old man was standing before a large mirror, as still and immutable as the objects contained in the silence. He was a slender, utterly serene figure; he had a slightly aquiline nose, an unlined brow, white hair and a grey moustache. He was in shirtsleeves and seemed unconcerned by the large brownish stain of dried blood on his side. He looked dignified and proud; in his right hand, with graceful ease, he held a foil with an Italian hilt. His knees were slightly bent, and he raised his left arm until it was at right angles with his shoulder, allowing his hand to fall forward in the refined style of the old fencers, paying no heed to the deep cut in the palm of this hand. He was measuring himself against his reflection, concentrating on the movements he was performing, whilst his pale lips seemed silently to enumerate them, tirelessly repeating the sequences over and over with methodical exactness. Absorbed in himself, he was trying to remember, fixing in his mind – uninterested in anything else that the universe might contain around him – all the phases which, linked with absolute precision, with mathematical certainty, would lead – he was sure of this now – to the most perfect thrust ever conceived by the human mind.

La Navata, July 1985

The translator would like to thank Annella McDermott, Antonio Martín and Ben Sherriff for all their help and advice and, in particular, E. D. Morton for his invaluable advice on fencing terminology.